THE

CIRCUS

Bob Joswick

The Circus

Bob Joswick

Publisher's Note:
This is a work of fiction. All names, characters, places, and
events are the work of the author's imagination.
Any resemblance to real persons, places, or events is
coincidental.

Solstice Publishing - www.solsticepublishing.com

Introduction

This story is fiction, as are the characters. Some of the locations exist and have been altered by the writer, others are only located in the writer's imagination. What is true are the two presidential acts referred to in this book, The Gold Confiscation Act of 1933, and The Japanese American Internment Act of 1942.

Below are brief summaries:

The Gold Confiscation Act of 1933

Executive order 6102 prohibited the owning and hoarding of gold coin, bullion, and certificates within the continental United States by individuals, partnerships, associations, and corporations.

President Franklin Roosevelt declared, due to the ongoing national banking emergency, all persons owning more than one hundred dollars of gold were required to deliver it to a Federal Reserve Bank within twenty-three days of its signing, and be compensated in paper money. Failing to do to so would result in a fine up to $10,000 ($167,700 in 2010 dollars) and, or ten years in prison.

This action increased the gold assets of the United States and stabilized the monetary system. Immediately after confiscation gold prices rose nearly forty percent, benefiting those citizens who hid or transferred their gold in countries such as Switzerland.

In 1974 President Gerald Ford repealed the act, once again allowing United States citizens to own gold.

The Japanese American Internment Act of 1942

Executive order 9066 forced the Internment of nearly 110,000 Japanese Americans, including American citizens of Japanese descent following Imperial Japan's bombing of Pearl Harbor, Hawaii in 1942.

Fearing the large population of Japanese Americans on the West Coast might commit acts of espionage or sabotage, President Franklin Roosevelt signed the order, establishing military control over all people of Japanese ancestry. No one was exempt: women, children, including Japanese men who had fought for and defended the United States in its wars.

All Japanese Americans were ordered to secure or sell their houses and possessions. Families were registered, tagged and taken to busses and trains to be delivered to isolated prison camps to live behind barbed wire while guarded by armed soldiers for the duration of the war.

Housing meant a horse stall in an unused fairgrounds or hastily built barracks in a barren, isolated area. Privacy and sanitary facilities were nonexistent for many.

The United States Government built sixteen temporary assembly centers and ten fulltime internment camps scattered throughout the remote areas of the United States. These remained open until March, 1946.

It was not until February, 1976 that President Gerald Ford, celebrating our Bicentennial, officially terminated the original proclamation.

Years later Presidents, Ronald Reagan, and then George H.W. Bush signed legislation, which apologized for the internment and guaranteeing funds for reparation to the survivors. It stated the actions were based on: "race prejudice, war hysteria, and failure of political leadership". About 1.6 billion dollars was paid to the surviving internees and their heirs as reparations.

During her World War Two internment, the noted Japanese artist, Mine Okubo, posted a notice on the stable she lived, "Quarantined—Do not enter", claiming to have "hoof and mouth disease". She exclaimed, "Humor, is the only thing that mellows life, and shows life as the circus that it is."

Chapter One

1957

Mid-October brought two surprises to Western Pennsylvania. Unseasonably mild and balmy weather settled in the region. Also, out of season, a circus arrived when the others headed south to their winter homes in Florida.

No advance man, only a few handbills pasted over past summers' posters and ratsheets promoted the unexpected spectacle. Missing were the zany clowns, elephants, giraffes, and shiny suited stilt walkers jaunting in a grand parade down Uniontown's Main Street. The biggest surprise came from the sky prior to opening day. Two large, red and gray striped, hot air balloons floated over the area dropping free tickets, like confetti, to its one and only performance.

Jumbo's Big Top Circus, unlike the other traveling shows, pitched their tents far outside of town, on an abandoned military air base. Two enormous gray and red striped tents flanked a slightly smaller white tent resembling the Taj Mahal.

Sam Simon, in his overalls, along with his life-long friend, Doc Martin, still in his tweed suit, walked along the abandoned airport runway toward the cluster of tents. Lacking parking attendants, cars sped helter-skelter, their drivers searching for the few remaining open spots.

Mothers and fathers yanked their children's arms, prodding them along. Doc held up his tickets, waving them close to Sam's face. "Let 'em hurry for the cheap seats," he shouted. "I got tickets in the reserved section. Star seats. Did I tell you?"

Sam stooped down looking at short, plump friend. "Bad enough you drag me to this. I don't need to hear your bragging."

6

Doc smiled. "Somebody dropped them off at my office."

"One of your patients?"

"Nope, my nurse would have known 'em. Just left them, no name." Together they shrugged and kept walking.

Something was wrong. Sam looked at the former military base not able to place what was missing.

Reaching the straw and sawdust covered grounds a scattering of badly missed notes came from horns while drums and symbols clashed out of sequence, forcing Sam and Doc to cover their ears. Simultaneously the stench from the animal pens greeted them.

"Elephant crap," Doc said covering his nose and mouth, stepping over a steaming pile.

Several loud crashes slashed the air from behind them. Both turned. An elephant was tossing empty oil drums into a gilly wagon. Turning back they were taken by surprise, coming face to face with a sad, oversized red and black-faced clown. He positioned himself so close, Sam was able to see his beard stubble and tiny gaps make-up failed to overlap. A scent of fresh bourbon came with his words. The clown held up a black box. "Wanna see the monkey in my box?" He inched closer.

"What monkey?" Sam asked.

"The monkey in this box." The clown shoved it at him.

"Why not? Show me," Doc answered.

The clown forced the box to Doc's face. There was no monkey, only a mirror. After slamming the lid shut the clown leaned in close. "Enjoy the show. You rubes got the star backs, best seats in the house." He dragged out the word house, making it sound like a hiss.

At first they said nothing. Then Doc, refusing to back away, finally spoke, "Yeah, we will."

They expected the large clown to move-on as the crowd grew. Instead, he stood in their path. His sad face contorted, pulling the red outline of his curled mouth downward into the shape of an inverted "U". The large diamond pattern of his harlequin costume seemed to swell, billowing in the wind, growing larger the longer he stood blocking their path. Finally, Sam and Doc stepped back and circled around him.

"How'd he know where we're sitting?" Sam asked

"Must have seen the tickets in my pocket," Doc answered, looking back over his shoulder.

They hurried past a sideshow pitchman, calling attention to a painted canvas banner, **"Nature's forgotten freaks—Live inside."** Doc paused, motioning to Sam. "Let's take a look, my treat."

After sliding two quarters under the glass window of the ticket booth they entered the small, cramped tent.

"Look at this," Doc said, pulling Sam along.

The cracked and washed-out canvas sign in front of them read, **Bat Boy, Drinks human blood to live.** A bald dwarf with a puffy round face slumped on a stool wearing a tight black and brown body suit. Long upper and lower incisors curved over bloody lips.

Sam gripped Doc's arm, pulling him away to the shows entrance. "Shows starting."

"Welcome to Jumbo's Big Top Circus," shouted the ringmaster.

A calliope played while the center ring filled with prancing, dapple-gray horses. Next came four pairs of galloping white stallions. The riders wore sequined chaps and stood, straddling a pair of horses, circling the ring in opposite directions of the dapple-grays. In an adjacent ring a troupe of clowns ran in circles, mimicking the horses, while throwing buckets of confetti into the crowd. A spotlight swung from the ringmaster, centering on the clowns, while he announced the shows star attraction— "Snookey, the Prince of Chaos". He entered the ring standing atop two mules riding and waving to the cheering crowd.

Sam and Doc leaned forward in their rickety seats. Despite the specks of shredded bark, which flew from trotting horses and sprinkled their faces, they recognized the red and black faced clown.

Doc nudged Sam. "He knew we had these seats."

"Something about that clown, Snookey, bothers me," Sam said, although there was much more he kept from his friend.

Doc remained quiet, watching the horses exit as the high wire act took center ring. The clowns stood in the entrance, holding a safety net. The crowd watched Alberto, nearly sixty feet in the air, juggling burning torches while balancing on his unicycle.

Sam and Doc kept their eyes on Snookey.

Outside, loose hay and small debris blew across the grounds. A curling mass of storm clouds had grown rapidly since crossing the Canadian border earlier that day. In less than thirty minutes, they'd descend on Jumbos Big Top Circus.

The acrobatics and juggling acts failed to hold Sam and Doc's attention until they caught the last of the ringmaster's introduction. ".... Now let's bring out the big cats." The ringmaster stood in the spotlight, and as he finished, Snookey crept up behind him and without warning pulled down the ringmaster's pants to howls of laughter. He chased the clown, while struggling to pull up his pants. Snookey ran wildly, arms flailing, into the round cage housing two large lions and three orange stripped tigers. He came to a panicked stop, realizing he was standing in the middle of five large cats perched on elevated platforms. He did a slow exaggerated backward step, retreating to the open cage door. The ringmaster quickly appeared, slamming the door shut on Snookey.

Sam leaned close to Doc. "I'm root'n for the cats."

Outside, heavy wind gusts battered the big top. Its towering center and quarter poles quivered. Large expanses of the red and gray canvas raised and lowered like rolling ocean waves. Inside, lights flickered but remained on. The circus band went silent, as did the overflow audience.

During this time, Snookey had acquired a bullwhip and held a chair in front of him. Cracking the whip, he shouted rapid-fire commands to a tiger that leaped from its perch to sit obediently next to him. The others stood and roared. He cracked the whip a few more times, quieting them. Snookey slowly pried the big cat's mouth open, sticking his face within inches of its large teeth. Waving his arms over his head, he slowly placed his head into its mouth, and then just as slowly, pulled back. While he panned to the hushed crowd, he shook his head while tapping a finger to his temple. Then, to their surprise he placed his arm deep into the tiger's mouth.

Unexpectedly, a lion jumped from its perch, startling the clown. At the same time the tiger turned his head, biting down, ripping the clown's arm off at the elbow. The audience was stunned. Screams and cries followed from everyone except Sam and Doc. The panicked clown ran after the large cat, attempting to retrieve his severed arm, which dangled from the cat's mouth. Everyone stood in panic, screaming. Snookey hopped up to an empty animal stand, producing his real arm that was hidden inside his costume. Weak laughter and applause came from the exiting crowd that filed from the wooden bleachers.

Sam and Doc remained seated until the audience exited. They looked in all directions, hoping to avoid Snookey who disappeared in the rush.

Stepping outside into the gale force wind, they shook their heads, watching the tent's heavy canvas sway and billow. The heavy wood pegs, surrounding its parameter, strained, threatening to pull free.

Only a few feet apart, Sam shouted to Doc. "Long way to the car. Can you make it?"

10

Doc nodded. "Don't wait on me." He pulled his lapels tightly together and began walking, splashing through mud and straw.

Sam hesitated. He couldn't help wondering what was behind the offbeat gathering of performers. In a hurry, he took one last look back, hoping not to see Snookey, and ran from the tent, leaving Doc behind.

Within the last few hours, the day's mild temperature dropped twenty degrees. The once charming afternoon ripped off its disguise, revealing its sinister alter ego.

Unable to find his truck in the maze of exiting cars, Sam stopped to get his bearings. Luckily, nearly fifty feet ahead, a car's headlights flashed on his battered Ford pick-up. Now, he'd find Doc in the downpour and get away. From what, he wasn't sure. He stumbled several times in the rutted field, finally falling into one of the remaining parked cars. Rain hit like stinging pellets on his exposed arms and neck. When he reached his truck, frozen balls of ice plunked the roof and hood.

In the headlights, Doc stood in the distance, holding a jacket over his head, staggering toward him.

Doc climbed into the truck, still catching his breath. He forced out, "One hell of a final act."

"What?"

"Said the circus had one hell of a final act."

Sam cut his eyes to him, "I got a bad feeling about this place."

"Doesn't matter, they'll be leaving town after the show."

"Where'd they come from?" Sam asked.

"That was bizarre," Doc said.

Once on the main road, Sam looked into the rear-view mirror. "Notice anything missing from the airport?"

Doc gave him a puzzled look.

"The Quonset hut, near the control tower. It's missing."

11

Chapter Two

Exhausted, Sam returned to his narrow two-story home that night. From habit, he checked the locks and windows. As usual, he started with his garage and laboratory near his house. Sticking his head inside the lab, everything seemed in order, but until the over-sized clown left town he planned to be more cautious.

He thought of his dog, Pal, buried in the garden, and how he had slept under the lab tables.

Cold rain continued its steady rhythm on the corrugated tin roof.

"Shit," he muttered as a few drops tapped on the tile floor next to him.

The blue northerner struck quickly, erasing a calm Indian summer. The forecast called for heavy rain through the night, changing to frigid near arctic conditions the next few days. Sam, still wet and muddy, debated waiting out the rain in his lab, but then with a quick shrug, jogged across the coal ash driveway to his kitchen porch.

Inside the house, he took a towel from a laundry shelf and stood on it. He peeled off his soggy clothes, rummaged through a pile of dirty laundry and dressed himself. After a check of the windows and doors, Sam plopped into a chair at the kitchen table. Sitting with his arms crossed on the table, he remained nearly motionless, resisting the urge. Eventually, his weary eyes followed a path of cracked linoleum to the sink, then up to a set of shelves covered by a drab set of curtains. Tonight he needed it. He pushed back from the table. His hands shook—a single shot... maybe two.

While sipping Jim Beam whiskey from a chipped water glass, the deep voice of a news commentator, on the continually playing radio, grabbed his attention. The reporter lamented over the Russian satellite, Sputnik, which circled overhead, threatening America. Just as the irate

12

journalist began to berate congress, Sam yanked the plug. Not needing more bad news, he would listen to his deceased wife's old, 'rainy night albums', as Emma had loved to call them. Standing there holding the plug to the radio, he recalled a night three years ago.

He was alone with Emma in her hospital room. SHE'D suffered so long and pleaded for him to end her unbearable pain. He kissed her with a deep passion and tenderness that only comes after a lifetime of love. She smiled. They both knew it would be the last. He saw her bright eyes glisten. He squeezed her hand gently. With the other, he eased the plug from the outlet above her bed. The equipment surrounding her became mute and dark. She smiled and slowly her grip released. She was free.

Sam threw the radio's plug against the wall, denting the plaster. Now, he stood alone in the kitchen, staring down at her battered cedar chest containing her old phonograph albums.

Settling into his worn chair, he let the soothing melody of Bennie Goodman and warm whiskey relax him.

* * * *

Sam awoke the next morning. Easing up from the chair, he kicked over the empty bottle of Jim Beam, which spun across the kitchen, stopping at the door. Hunched over and barefoot, he tiptoed across the kitchen floor and pushed open the curtain to a battleship gray sky.

While coffee perked, he sliced crusty bread, placing it in the oven to toast. The heavy door stuck, he slammed it several times, and grimaced with the clash of metal on metal, before it remained closed. Spotting the newspaper lying on the grass, he balanced on one leg to pull on his house shoes. The light drizzle and chill helped little to clear his head from the jolts of pain shooting between his temples.

13

Catching his reflection in the kitchen window, he watched himself, looking for evidence of who he once was. The tall, thin man, his eyes followed, walked with a slight stoop and limp. The creased and wrinkled face bore slight resemblance to the young man who often rushed into the kitchen to swarm his wife with warm kisses.

Taking a few deep breaths, he convinced himself he'd feel better after breakfast. He hoped his memory of the aggressive clown, Snookey, would swiftly fade. He pushed open the kitchen door. The phone was ringing.

"Hello," he answered.

"Sam, the Caddy's back!" Doc shouted.

"Say that again."

"My Cadillac, the one I pushed off the cliff."

Doc stopped to take several deep breaths, then began again. "It's parked in front of my house."

They both fell silent.

Sam finally spoke. "Sure it's the same one?"

"It's my car. I should know. Yeah, I'm damn sure."

"Hold on." Sam reached to the oven, pulling out the black crusted toast. "I'm back. That was over two years ago you dumped it in the river, can't be."

"It's covered in mud and rust. It's beat to hell…it's mine."

"How in hell did…"

Doc cut him off. "Vince, gotta be him. He knows what we did."

"He left years ago," Sam said, raising his voice. "Don't panic. We'll figure this out. I'll call the police."

He was about to hang up.

"No!" Doc shouted. "There's something else."

A thought flashed across Sam's mind. "Was it a coincidence the circus had located itself at the shut-down military airport where Vince committed his crimes?"

"Come again," Sam said, putting the phone back to his ear.

14

"I said that's not all."

"What else, Doc?"

"There's a body in the trunk."

Sam lowered the phone, nearly dropping it. Trembling, he propped himself against the wall. At the same time a taste of bile rose to the back of his throat.

He knew this was a warning from Vince, stronger than several years ago. He'd found his dog wrapped in a burlap sack, a bolt from a crossbow stuck in his chest. Following that, he and Doc had nearly been killed after discovering Vince's involvement in several crimes.

Sam had been certain they wouldn't return after escaping with hundreds of thousands of dollars worth of stolen artifacts.

He put the phone back to his ear. "You open it?"

"Hell no."

Sam squeezed the phone in his hand, forcing himself to remain calm. "How do you know?"

"Smelled it."

"Call the cops."

"Can't," Doc stammered. "You gotta come over right away."

"On my way." Sam put the phone into the cradle. His hand still rested on it when it rang again.

"Bring your shotgun," Doc said.

* * * *

Sam steered his truck, driving slowly, dodging displaced rails, which littered the abandoned railroad tracks. As always, he asked himself why his friend liked the desolate location. Ahead, appearing suspended in early morning fog and haze, he spotted Doc's home perched on a concrete platform next to the unused tracks. Surrounding it, like medieval sentinels, cast iron lampposts loomed over the converted train station. After yesterday, he would not have been surprised to see the coal black, cylindrical body of a locomotive burst from the shadowy, murky gloom and roar by.

Doc's rotund frame nearly filled the terminal's double doors as he rushed out to the platform. He wore a scowl and the same rumpled tweed suit from the day before. With both hands jammed on his broad hips, he silently watched Sam walk up the loading ramp.

"Took long enough," Doc said, turning away, rushing to the far side of the platform. "Car's back here."

"Call the cops," Sam said, striding behind.

"No cops, what are they gonna think when my car shows up two years later with a dead body in it? What do I tell 'em?"

"The truth."

"Never told anyone what really happened," Doc said, waving his arms, hurrying Sam.

"You saved my life."

"If I told 'em I pushed it over the cliff, my insurance wouldn't have paid. The adjustor assumed it was stolen. I never told him different. That's fraud, no police, yet."

"When do you plan to?"

"Let's see who's inside. That might tell us who dredged it from the Monongahela River."

"We both know who did this," said Sam. "Questions why?"

Sam whistled and stepped back after seeing the battered and mud-crusted Cadillac, knowing he would not have survived that night two years ago.

Trapped on the doors of the river lock, and too exhausted to escape, Doc sacrificed his new car, pushing it over a rocky cliff near the lock. Vince was aboard the tugboat that headed into the lock's chamber, bearing directly down on him. The diversion worked, allowing Doc to reach him, rescuing him from probable death from

16

Vince's crossbow. He'd never forget looking up and seeing Doc's out-stretched hand.

"What do you want me to do?" Sam asked.

"Tow it into one of the freight stations." Doc pointed to a long row of aged storage buildings near the railroad terminal. "Then help me open the trunk."

Sam wrapped chains around the Cadillac's rusted and smashed front bumper. He backed his Ford pick-up within a few feet of the battered car. Doc hooked the chains to the truck and stepped aside, waving Sam forward.

Sam revved the engine several times, took a quick look back over his shoulder and slipped the clutch pedal out. The chain tightened, trying to pull itself apart, while the tires spun in the soggy ground, nothing moved.

After several attempts Sam shut the engine off and climbed from the cab. "Not work'n, Doc. Any more ideas?"

"Might be in gear," Doc said, holding his handkerchief over his nose and mouth. "Put it in neutral."

Sam looked at Doc, and walked around the car nodding at it. He grabbed the handle to the driver's door, yanking it several times. It remained shut.

"Try the other side," Doc said, not making a move to help.

After a few hard tugs, the door flung open, releasing a flow of muddy water on to Sam's shoes. River silt, the color of rat fur and greenish strands of scum covered the Caddy's white leather interior. Sam stepped back, forcing his nose and mouth against the shoulder of his denim coat. He fought, swallowing several times, to keep his stomach from turning itself inside out.

Sam took another deep breath, his nose and mouth still tucked into the shoulder of his coat. He dropped into the sludge covered leather seat, leaned over and grabbed the gearshift, yanking it to neutral. "Should move now."

"We got company," Doc said in a low voice.

A police cruiser appeared, inching along the road leading to the railroad terminal. As it did, the early morning drizzle fell harder while low ground fog rapidly enveloped the terminal area. Visibility was near zero. The patrol car's roof lights flashed on, looking like the menacing red eyes of a giant predator.

Sam and Doc approached the police car as it crept along the weed-lined road. Only when they were within a few yards of the car did they notice it and stopped.

The officer stood near his car. Slowly, he unclasped his holster. "Who's there? That you, Doc?"

"Rizzo, yeah, it's me."

"Who's with you?"

"Friend of mine, Sam Simon."

Rizzo dropped his hand from his service revolver. "Bad stuff, fogs been moving along the river all morning." He nodded back towards downtown. "It'll move out of here in no time, always does."

Sam glanced back in the direction of the terminal. The Cadillac remained unseen, enveloped in the fog.

"What brings you here?" Doc asked.

"Circus is in town. Keep your eyes open. Ya know how carnies and circus people are."

Sam and Doc nodded, hoping a faint wind wouldn't break up the fog bank.

"That was a surprise, wasn't it?" Rizzo asked.

"What?" Doc asked.

"Strange, huh?" Rizzo said. "A circus this time of the year."

Doc shook his head, agreeing.

"Get in the car," Rizzo said, opening the back door.

"Why?" Doc said, immediately knowing, he asked too quickly.

"Drive you back, it's raining."

The Cadillac, along with Sam's truck remained hidden, but the fog would lift any moment.

18

"Thanks...we're walking-off breakfast. Doc patted his ample gut. "Besides, we need the fresh air, doctor's orders." Doc forced a laugh.

Rizzo leaned forward, over the open car door, squinting into the dense fog. 'Without a smile, he stood erect and still looking off into the distance, eased the door closed. "Understood. Call the station if ya spot anything unusual."

The patrol car swung around and faded into the fog bank. Sam and Doc stared into the dense layer of clouds. It was only after hearing the cruiser clank over the short bridge near the main road that they returned to Doc's car. By that time the fog thinned and lifted.

Doc kicked the side of the car. "Let's get her out of sight before the mayor shows up."

Sam climbed into his pick up. "Spot me. Let's get this inside."

Inching the truck forward, the chain tighten between his bumper and the Cadillac. After giving a slight touch to the gas pedal they moved. With a waddle, the Caddy rolled, its flattened tires fought to pull themselves from the rims.

Doc stood in the doors of the storage building waving his arms, giving directions. Inside, Sam rolled to a stop. Doc hurried to shut both doors and turn on a long string of hooded lights suspended along the tall center beam of the building.

Inside, the stench strengthened, forcing Sam and Doc to back away from the Caddy.

Sam walked to a set of windows. What little saliva he had, turned bitter. "This is too much," he said, rolling open a casement window, taking in a long breath. "I can't deal with a dead body."

Both scrutinized the recently exhumed Cadillac as if it were a denizen of another world. Garlands of river slime draped the steering wheel. A frosting of reddish silt coated its leather seats, dashboard and floors. The once regal grill, with its distinctive bullet bumpers were crushed and driven back into the frame. The small, rudder-like tailfins remained, surviving the crushing plunge down the rocky and stump covered cliff.

Was it sulking, expecting its ravaged body to be restored?

Doc snapped his fingers. "Surgical masks...I'll get surgical masks. Sprinkle 'em with Old Spice, we won't smell a thing."

Before Sam argued, Doc walked toward his house.

Sam stuffed his hands deep into his coat pockets, feeling the sudden chill of a draft. Instinct told him to follow Doc and call the police. Instead, he stood frozen, inhaling the rotting odor of the decomposing body sitting a few feet from him, curious who it was.

Rain pelted the storage building's tin roof, breaking the dead quiet. His eyes remained fixed on the Cadillac. Its deformed face seemed to stare at him just as Snookey, the circus clown, had the day before. Despite knowing it had to be his imagination, he also thought the car moved slightly.

Doc returned in minutes, tromping through the door, carrying an umbrella and medical bag. After tossing the umbrella aside, he splashed Old Spice on a surgical mask, handing it to Sam. Doc tugged another over his mouth and nose. He pulled a flashlight from his jacket pocket. "Let's see what we have in the trunk." His high pitched voice now muffled.

Outside, torrential rain, reinforced by a bitter north wind, pounded the storage building. Several strips of thin metal fell from the roof, glancing off the car.

"Let's get it over with," Doc said. "The trunk was open when it went in the river. I saw it. Whoever's in there was put in after it was pulled from the water. My guess, that's only been a few days."

From a storage bin Doc removed a sledgehammer for himself while handing Sam a long, steel pry bar.

"Call the police." Sam said. "They can't blame you. You got two witnesses that saw what happened." Sam counted them off on his fingers. "Nick, your friend the bar owner, he drove the tug boat. He saw everything."

Doc shook his head. "Sold his place. Moved away once he got out of the hospital."

"Afraid Vince would come back?" Sam asked.

Doc nodded.

"The lock operator, Herkey, was there. He must have seen it go in the river."

"Herkey was in the control room. I saw him run in," Doc said.

"Maybe he saw something. Worth asking."

Doc brought the sledge to his shoulder. "I'm ready to open her up. You with me?"

"The cops should be doing this and…" Sam quickly jumped away from the car, as Doc stumbled, swinging the sledge, striking the area near the trunk's latch. The trunk lid remained shut. After several more whacks, Doc was splattered with reddish, slimy mud, the lid remained shut.

While Doc rested, Sam hefted the pry bar, sliding its tip into the narrow opening between the trunk and the car's body. As he did he noticed something. "Look at these marks."

Sam used the pry bar as a pointer. "Somebody jammed the latch to keep it shut. This proves somebody put the body in here after they pulled it from the river." Sam stepped back, dropping the bar. "We should leave it closed."

"No." Doc said. "I want to know who's in there. Besides, the body will tell us when it died. Once we figure out what's going on, we go to the cops."

They stood a few feet back from the trunk. The surgical masks puffed in and out with their heavy breathing. Despite that, they both heard it from deep within the car's fractured body, a dull, hollow wheezing. The

21

Cadillac gave a long, low primal groan. As the echoes faded in the rafters, the car's rear-end collapsed, slamming onto the flattened tires. For a moment the wind and rain paused. The cavernous storage building ceased swaying and rocking. Then, like an ancient crypt, the trunk eased itself open.

Chapter Three

Waves crashed over a rocky shoreline on the hot and sticky day. Two men stood on their patio drinking beer, watching a distant cargo ship crest the horizon. Vince Pergalsky angled his fedora, shading his face against an intense Mexican sun. He stood watch, hoping his prey would glide closer to the nearby cliffs. He had not taken a shot all day.

His friend, Stumpy, hobbled to a deck chair. "They should have our message by now," he said, easing into the green padded canvas chair.

Vince exhaled, held his breath and sighted in his prey as it floated effortlessly in the updraft of the coastal hillside. Leading it slightly, he gently squeezed the trigger of the crossbow. In an instant, the bolt pierced the egret's chest. Pleased with himself, he turned to Stumpy. "I'd like to see their faces."

Stumpy, giving a short laugh held up his beer can. "To revenge."

Vince noticed the rare laugh. His scarred, misshapen face and torso disguised a cunning mind. Their villa's housekeeping staff had grown accustomed to his appearance but occasionally stared at his distorted roving eye.

Vince looked over the wall down to the rocky shore. The dead bird's body had washed up into the jagged rocks. He put another bolt into it and laughed.

Stumpy shouted, "Save those for Sam Simon and Doc Martin."

Vince dropped his large frame into the lounge chair next to Stumpy and reclined back. "Got plenty, don't worry. I got something better. They're gonna want to die."

The housekeeper delivered a frosted pitcher of cold beer, placing it on the table next to Vince. With one hand, he grabbed it and began chugging, nearly pouring it down his throat, spilling large amounts down his chest.

Stumpy took his empty Dos Equis can, crushing it. "Thought the plan was to kill Simon and Doc at the circus." His deformed eye blinked several times, then stared at Vince. "Hell, I gave 'em tickets. That was the plan, wasn't it?"

"Storm came in. Snookey couldn't get to 'em." Vince shrugged taking the last sip of his lager. "We're gonna have some fun, scare 'em a little, then feed 'em to the cats."

"Cops were supposed to find three bodies in Doc's car," Stumpy said.

"We're gonna give 'em one more surprise, then…" Vince grinned, and ran two fingers across his throat. "Traps set. Those two are gonna walk right in, then the cage springs shut."

Stumpy smiled.

"You wait here. When I get back, we'll have our gold and revenge," Vince said, turning to grab another cerveza.

Chapter Four

The Cadillac's trunk stood open. Water, the color of rusty mud, dripped from its lid. Now stronger, the stench forced Sam and Doc to back away, despite heavy doses of Old Spice sprinkled on their face masks. They stood at a distance, unable to see inside the dark trunk.

"Let's have a look," Sam finally said, adding more cologne. Walking toward the trunk, he fought off gagging and held his breath. The body had not decomposed and was positioned with its back to them, partially hidden in shadow. He wore only boxer shorts and one badly scuffed, muddy brown shoe with no socks.

Doc poked the body with a fountain pen. "If he drowned, he wasn't in the water long."

"Why's that?" Sam asked his eyes fixed on the pasty white body.

Pointing to the shoulder area, Doc explained, "Skin would be waxy, yellowish and wrinkled, like a washer woman's hands." He tapped the corpse again, hard enough to leave indentations. "My guess he's been dead two…maybe four days, tops."

"Somebody dumped him in here after the car was pulled from the river," Sam said.

Doc nodded. "Now, what killed him?" He pulled on rubber household gloves, stretching them tight over his short stubby fingers. "Let's see what we have." He nudged Sam. "Give me a hand. Pick up the pipe and wedge it behind the body, then roll it over."

Kneeling in the well of the trunk floor, Doc tugged at the rigid shoulders while Sam pried the pipe against the body's chest. The corpse was stiff, lying in an angled, near fetal position. As it turned, Doc immediately recognized the scars. They were from surgeries he preformed.

"It's Herkey…Herkey Dixon," Doc said, barely above a whisper.

Sam's eyes widened. "Who?"

"Herkey Dixon, the lock operator, from the river."

Sam recalled that night. Doc distracted Herkey in the operations office. This allowed him to crawl to the middle of the giant lock's doors. It had taken every ounce of strength and energy he could muster to wrap chain between the two steel doors. Their plan was to trap the tug and barge, loaded with stolen artifacts and waste chemicals, inside the lock.

Doc grabbed the rigid shoulder, pulling the body toward him. "Here he comes."

Sam held the flashlight on the body. Herkey's face was frozen in permanent terror. His gaping mouth and wide-open eyes fixed aimlessly. Crusted, brownish blood covered his chest.

Doc ran his gloved hand over the area, stopping at a spot between the shoulder and sternum. "Here we are." He pointed at two small stubs protruding from the chest. "He didn't drown."

"Nocks," said Sam. His hand shook slightly. "They killed him with a crossbow."

Doc gripped one of the stubs, sliding it out easily. Holding it up to the light, he examined the nine-inch bolt. "Judging by the angle, this one hit the heart." The second one came out just as easily. "One of these wasn't necessary,"

"Huh?"

"He only needed one. Herkey was dead after the first one. Both of 'em hit his heart. Amazing, they missed the ribs,"

"Shot up close?"

"Had to be," Doc said. "The shooter had the right angle to miss the sternum and hit his heart." Doc tossed the bolts into the trunk. "You know who did this?"

"Why would he?" Sam said.

As Doc pulled himself from the trunk, he stopped and pointed to something packed between the sole and heel of Herkey's only shoe. Doc pulled a tongue depressor from his jacket pocket and scrapped a sample, wrapping it in a spare rubber glove. With deliberate slowness, he closed the trunk, careful not to lock it.

"Vince is back," Sam said.

As if in a duel of nerves, both faced Herkey's battered tomb, sweat prickled their foreheads. Sam felt suddenly touched by ice. The wrecked Cadillac appeared to enlarge, swelling abnormally, filling the terminal.

Challenging them.

They backed away.

"What's it been, two years since he went missing?" Doc said. "What does Vince want?"

"Us, he tried to kill us before."

"Guess so."

"Gonna leave the car here?"

"Yeah…no, there's a drive-in freezer the railroad used. Still works." Doc pointed to the end of the large building. "I'll turn it on. For now, we'll put it in there."

Once the car was inside the freezer, Doc took a last look and slammed the heavy steel doors together, padlocking them. The large compressor was at work, vibrating overhead.

"We have to call the cops. Let 'em figure this out," said Sam.

"Not yet. Herkey and the car are gonna tell us what happened."

The compressor sputtered several times, threatening to quit. They eyed each other. Neither said anything. Then it began to run smoothly.

Sam used a roll of black tape and placed small strips on both sets of doors entering the building.

"By morning he'll be frozen stiff," Doc said, slipping the heavy padlock into place on the terminal's door. He turned to Sam. "There's more you need to know."

Chapter Five

For the last twenty years, the abandoned railroad terminal had been Doc Martin's home. The brick and wood frame exterior remained as it was since the last train pulled away twenty-five years ago. Wood benches were pushed against weathered walls while baggage carts sat as if awaiting the next arrival. From the roof's patchwork shingles, stove pipes pushed up seemingly at random. Washed-out signs also poked up at both ends of its long roof, welcoming weary travelers to Uniontown, Pennsylvania.

Doc and Sam rushed through the heavy doors, just ahead of the monsoon-like rain. Ornate steel lampposts, that once surrounded the exterior, illuminated the long narrow room. Couches, bookcases and Persian rugs divided the open floor plan. Ceiling fans hung from exposed joists of a sloping roof, which rose to a glassed-in raised summit.

Doc headed to the sparse kitchen to brew strong coffee.

"Splash 'a whiskey would take the chill outta my bones," Sam shouted to Doc as he eased himself onto his favorite armchair in front of a hot potbelly stove. Another half dozen antique, wood and coal burning stoves were scattered about the terminal.

Staring at the squat stove in front of him, then at the nearby tall cylindrical stove, Sam chuckled, as he always did. He often wondered if the two were cleverly intended to portray him and Doc, giving him another reason to feel at home.

His thoughts tugged at him, returning to the gruesome sight of Herkey's pallid, dead body. Images played over like echoing flashes across a black sky, buzzing in his mind.

"There's something else I didn't tell ya Sam," Doc said, sliding a mug of coffee next to him.

For a moment, Sam savored the warmth and the soothing aroma of the steaming coffee. He blew into it, avoiding Doc's eyes. "Hell, I don't want to know. Let's just drink this."

"I committed a crime. The cops and the insurance company think Vince stole the Cadillac."

"Why would they think that?"

"When he and Stumpy disappeared, I told the police Vince stole it," Doc said. "Insurance wouldn't have paid-off. By the way, I pushed it over the cliff to save your life. Remember?"

"Now you got it back. We're even."

"What we gonna do?" Doc asked, sniffing the air. He paused. "Just a minute, I can't get rid of this smell. It's following me."

"Check your pockets."

He pulled out the forgotten rubber glove containing the tongue depressor and held it at arm's length. "From Herkey's shoe."

"So, he stepped in cow shit," Sam said, rubbing his hands together in front of the stoves open door. "He has a farm in Smock."

"Gonna run some tests on this." Doc squinted at the specimen. "It's got something mixed with it."

Sam raised his voice. "Forget the test. What are we going to do with the body?"

"Nothing," Doc said. "Not 'til we figure out how Vince and Stumpy did this." He rewrapped the tongue depressor back into the rubber glove, then in wax paper. "I'll put this in the icebox and take it to the office in the morning."

Walking from window to window Sam carried his rifle, checking locks, closing shutters. Darkness came early as the steady downpour continued.

After supper, they had a few more drinks and turned in. Sam held up his rifle and offered to be first to stand guard.

Doc waved his pistol in the air. "I'm keeping this close."

Throwing a blanket over his shoulder Sam waved to Doc. "I'll be in the ticket office watching the storage building. Relieve me at two."

As usual, Doc retreated to a small corner of his library and his prized cello. Within minutes Sam relaxed, listening to the peaceful, low pitched tones of a sonata, filling the station.

* * * *

Morning sunshine poured through windows from the roof's high peak. Sam jumped awake, nearly kicking over a small table holding a thermos of coffee. A new fire burned in the nickel and cast iron box stove warming him. From one open eye, he watched the minute hand of the large wall clock grind its way toward the Roman numeral twelve. When it finally sprung into place with a few quivers, it clanked to a stop. The venerable timepiece announced seven a.m.

Last night's supper, a baloney sandwich with thick slices of raw onion and spicy dark mustard grumbled in his stomach. Despite how he felt, his thoughts went back to the Cadillac. Easing out of the oversized sofa, he noticed he had somehow managed to keep hold of his rifle while he slept.

Biting cold air greeted him when he stepped outside, wearing only shoes, bib overhauls and a white long sleeve shirt. Frost glistened, covering frozen ground. Sam hurried to the storage building, checking for tape he had hidden on both the door and double doors of the freezer. Both were in place. No one entered the building. Before returning to the house, he noticed several footprints frozen in mud near the storage building's windows. By their shape and size, Sam guessed the intruder wore rubber boots. Looking closer, he spotted something unusual, the right heel had a long slash running across it.

The boot tracks ended at the pea gravel covered parking lot. At its far end there were a frozen set of tire tracks leading to the end of Doc's property, fading away on the main road. Sam wrapped both arms around his chest, suddenly feeling the cold air boring through him. He hurried back to the house but not before glancing around, hoping not to see Vince and Stumpy appear.

Once inside, he looked into the library, expecting Doc to be asleep in his wingback chair, embracing his prized cello. Instead, he saw only the valuable Derazey cello leaning against a music stand. No sign of Doc.

Sam rushed back to the small area of the ticket office for his shotgun. It lay on the table next to the metal thermos he had nearly knocked over earlier. This time he noticed the folded, typed note beneath the thermos.

I could not sleep. Went to my office to examine the feces from Herkey's shoe. I took your truck. Hope you don't mind. The cabs weren't running yet. Meet me at The Town Talk I'll buy breakfast. Take the jitney. I left a number near the phone.
Doc

Sam hurried to the far corner of the terminal. He looked out, the truck was gone.

Within ten minutes a pale green 1950 Plymouth stood outside. The driver honked the horn several times. Sam looked around the area then rushed out, still pulling on his denim miner's jacket.

The jitney driver leaned across the car's seat, opening the door. "Doc said you'd call. I'm Woodrow."

"That so," Sam muttered, as he bent over, getting into the front seat.

"Got one more pick-up, then I'll deliver you to The Town-Talk," Woodrow said, pulling away from the terminal.

For the next five miles they rode in silence. The driver finally spoke, "Call me Woody. I drive Doc everywhere since they stole his car."

A short time later, they stopped in front of a large Victorian home. Rushing from a side door, under a portico, a lady ran, gathering up her long evening gown in front of her. She crossed the expansive lawn, hurrying to the Plymouth.

She was shivering by the time she reached the car. Sam tilted his seat forward allowing her to climb into the back. A shout came from the house as someone stepped out of the door. Seeing the Plymouth, they quickly retreated. They wore an apron and held both hands over their face crying. The screen door slowly closed as the cab pulled from the curb. Looking over his shoulder, Sam read the street sign, Ben Lomond Avenue.

Sam caught a glimpse of the passenger when she lifted her face to look back at the house. She was strikingly beautiful. Her teeth chattered and her bare shoulders trembled. Without hesitating, he tugged his coat off, passing it to her over the seat.

She didn't speak, nor did Woodrow ask for a destination. Sam watched the driver. His face had a sympathetic look while his eyes continually shifted into the rear-view mirror, inspecting her more than admiring her.

Chapter Six

Sam took a last look at the lady in the Plymouth's back seat as he paid Woodrow his fifty-cent fare. Except for her hazel eyes, her face was hidden by the turned-up collar of his coat. She appeared to be in her early twenties and deeply distressed. Before he asked for his jacket, the car sped away.

While Sam stood in the street watching the jitney, someone shouted.

"Where in hell have you been?" Doc held open the door to The Town Talk Diner. "Where's your coat?"

"Where's my truck?" Sam asked, squeezing past Doc into the crowded restaurant.

As usual, the Saturday morning crowd was huddled in the cramped vestibule waiting for tables. Doc pointed to the back of the diner. "Got my usual spot."

Weaving past closely spaced tables they stepped around rushing, white-aproned servers, carrying steaming platters of breakfast foods.

Their booth was nearly hidden in a small niche not far from the clatter and shouts that drifted from the cramped, hectic kitchen. A coffee pot and sturdy mugs waited on the checkered tablecloth.

Sam quickly got to the point. "What did you find out about the…"

Tilley cleared her throat, interrupting. "If you sit here you're gonna need to order something." She smiled, then sat and poured herself a cup. "You know, Doc, if you sold me your place I could open one heck of a large diner." She winked and took out an order pad.

After ordering, Doc leaned over the table, resting on his elbows. "The feces on Herkey's shoes wasn't human."

"He has a farm, remember. Probably cow."

"Didn't match the samples I took." Nodding his head, Doc smiled. "I went to his barn and checked. That's why I borrowed your truck."

"Anybody see you?" Sam's voice rose quickly.

"Nope." Doc waved off more questions. "Nothing matched the stuff on his shoe."

"Then, what is it?"

"Don't know. I called a friend. She's a vet at the zoo in Pittsburgh."

Sam blew on his coffee and took a slow sip. Leaning back in the booth, he looked around at the dozens of eaters grazing over their plates. No one appeared to be paying attention to them. He spoke quietly anyway, "Somebody might have seen us with Herkey's body yesterday."

"Couldn't have," Doc said.

"I found footprints near the storage building."

"When?"

"Close to seven, when I woke up." Sam looked around again. "I might be able to learn who our spy is and about when he was there."

"How? Are you Sherlock Holmes?"

"The freeze last night kept the boot print solid. I'll recognize it if I see it again. I'll need to call the radio station to find out when the rain quit and when the freeze hit."

Doc's brow furrowed as he scratched his chin. He snapped his fingers. "Yeah, our visitor had to be there after the rain quit, but before the freeze."

Sam pointed at his friend, "Bingo. Otherwise, no frozen prints in the mud, Doctor Watson."

Before Sam could say anything more, plates of sausage, eggs and toast were slid in front of them.

From habit, Doc unwrapped his silverware and rubbed his fork against his rumpled and coffee stained necktie. "The vet's expecting us this afternoon."

35

* * * *

Woody's Plymouth rose over a small crest, an outline of red tiled roofs appeared against a backdrop of pines and firs at Summit Mountain. White smoke climbed in a straight line into the cold and bitter morning air from chimneys of Mission-style buildings.

During the last twenty minutes, the woman in the jitney's back seat yanked the evening gown off, stuffing it into a large carpetbag along with her shoes and jewelry. Her little make-up had been wiped away and her long black hair had been twisted into a bun, bobby-pinned under a simple veil. She wore a long black, rough woolen habit with a heavy black leather belt. Over her chest was the unique badge of her order, a large heart, the size of a man's fist, with a cross rising from its top. To her, the emblem was a constant reminder she'd failed her vows.

Heading to a concealed, rear entry gate, the jitney sped past the main entrance. The car slowed, and before it came to a stop, she kissed her hand and pressed it against the driver's cheek. Without a word, she tilted the front passenger seat forward and swung open its door. After tossing her bag to the ground, she slipped effortlessly out of the car. She gave the driver a quick glance then she disappeared into the garden, hidden behind an ivy covered rock wall.

Sam's coat lay in the seat.

The tower bell tolled, for a moment, interrupting the oppressive silence of the monastery. The mid-morning prayers were about to end and the sisters would return to their daily chores. The expansive halls of the Gothic arched passageways were empty except for the marble statues of the Catholic Church's sainted men and women. The soft sounds of sandals approached. She slipped into her room, unseen, returning to the silent isolation. Her life here was to be a saintly woman of God, spending her days in

36

meditation, prayer and manual labor. Her vows, poverty, chastity, obedience, and her order, the Passionist Nuns, added the vow of enclosure, forbidding personal contact with anyone outside the walls of the monastery. It was a life of solitary confinement until her death.

Her room was furnished with a small table and a crucifix, hanging over a cot-sized bed. She was nearly able to reach her arms out to touch both sides of the windowless room. After shoving her carpetbag under the bed, she stepped out into the terra cotta hallway. It was cold under her bare feet. Sandals were a privilege she had not earned. She bowed her head in prayer, walking to the monastery's kitchen to prepare lunch. As always, the sisters would assume her previous day's absence was due to her remaining in her room, praying and fasting, a weekly requirement.

Chapter Seven

As they approached Pittsburgh, the cold gray day grew more dismal, matching Sam's mood. He steered his truck, dodging potholes that had appeared with the early freeze.

An oily sheen of blue and crimson floated on rain soaked streets causing the pavement to glisten in the passing headlights. The road snaked along the broad Monongahela River, where seemingly endless rows of shadowy steel mills lined its banks like medieval fortresses. Giant smoke stacks disappeared into the charcoal sky.

"Liberty Tubes coming up. What do we do?" Sam asked.

"Where are we?" Doc asked, jerking awake. With the sleeve of his jacket, he rubbed frost from the window. "Through the tunnels, stay to the left."

With a quick jerk of the wheel, they crossed several lanes, bumping over rows of trolley tracks embedded in the roadway. Doc tilted his head back into the corner of the truck and nodded off.

"This is crazy. We should turn around, go home and call the cops," Sam said.

Exiting the long tunnel, they veered left, melding into stop and go traffic of Carson Avenue, gaining a glimpse of the city's somber skyline.

Doc sat up. "Follow this 'til the Mount Washington sign."

After several miles, they spotted Mount Washington, exiting the busy highway to an unmarked road. In a short time, they drove along a quiet street. Dead leaves covered curbs and most of the sidewalks.

Doc sat at the edge of the seat, craning his neck, looking at the thick cloudbank clinging to the top of a ridge. "Our vet lives up there."

The single lane brick street twisted up a short grade. Sam slammed the brakes, stalling. Just ahead, a flow of brownish mud covered the road. A 'ROAD CLOSED' sign leaned against a yellow and black saw horse.

Doc studied the washed-out hillside for a moment. "The incline, it'll go to Grand Avenue. We can walk to Perkin's house from there."

Following Doc's directions, Sam drove through a maze of streets, backtracking toward the Ohio River. They parked next to a bright red painted terminal sitting at the base of the hillside. Behind it, twin cars, the size of a small bus, operated in pairs, attached to opposite ends of a hidden cable. One climbed to a matching upper terminal, while the other, simultaneously, came down the nearly forty degree grade.

Holding their tickets, Sam and Doc waited with housewives carrying shopping bags and groceries in the long line to pass through the single turnstile. After entering the incline car through a side door they found two wood seats facing each other.

Doc inhaled and spoke under his breath. "Stale tobacco and garlic sausage, I'm gonna like this."

A bell clanged three times. The doors shut like an elevator. With a jerk, the wheels began to roll up the four hundred foot-long track. The view below, of three joined rivers, faded as they ascended.

At the upper terminal the incline stopped with a lurch, as if someone suddenly yanked the attached cable. Passenger heads bobbed in unison. Those standing staggered forward, regaining their balance.

"We're here," said Doc, stepping to the curb. "I love the view. On a clear day you'd see the whole river valley, all three rivers." He stepped onto Grand Avenue pointing, "This way to Perkin's house."

The two-story, brown, rock house sat at the highest point of Mount Washington. Rain dripped from contorted, beaked faces of gargoyles perched on its steep, black slate roof.

The main door was open a crack.

Doc clanged the doorknocker several times shouting, "Lenora Perkins, you home? Hello." Doc leaned close to Sam. "The house scared me at first, but now only she does." From somewhere in the house they heard a yell.

"Doors' open. Come in."

She strode toward them, shoulders pulled back, wearing jodhpurs and riding jacket. Her black hair, pulled in a ponytail, lay over the front of her right shoulder. "Miserable day, I couldn't take my horses over a single jump, knocked down more poles than we cleared." In a quick movement she extended her hand and smiled to Sam. "I'm Lenora Perkins." She pointed to the kitchen. "Hot chocolate?" Her tone made it sound like an order.

Soon, oversized, steaming mugs were slid in front of them without a sound.

"Sit, relax. I'll make us something. I'm starving."

Sam and Doc sat, hardly speaking, almost like strangers, each stirring hot chocolate. She moved about the kitchen like a master chef. Onions and red peppers were quickly chopped as thick bacon sizzled on an over-sized griddle.

"Hope you like lots a cheese on your omelet," Lenora shouted from across the kitchen while she forced a long knife through a block of cheddar.

She continued a non-stop monologue of her morning jumping session as she worked, enjoying their company.

Dim light filtered through the windows, flattering her perfectly formed face, discreetly veiling the slight imperfections of her sixty-year old complexion. Doc looked at her, knowing their past history, thinking he shouldn't involve her in Herkey's death.

Everything came together. She flipped omelets onto plain white dishes. Toast and chilled orange juice sat on the granite-topped table. Silverware sat in a tray at one end.

Nothing fancy.

They ate without speaking. Occasionally, a hurried fork scraped against a plate. Finally, Lenora leaned back in her chair, unbuttoning her riding jacket. "Now," She sniffed. "Remind me what brought you here."

Doc raised one finger, swallowing the last of his eggs. "This may not be the best subject to discuss in the kitchen."

A big smile came to her face as she waved him off. "Come on, I'm a zoo vet." She flung both her arms out. "Try me."

From his jacket pocket, Doc pulled a rubber glove wrapped in wax paper and unfolded it. Inside were the feces, still on the tongue depressor, he'd scraped from Herkey's shoe. He placed it in front of her. "What kind of animal is it from?"

Without hesitating, she reached for a wall switch and flicked it on. Several more lights and a large ceiling exhaust fan kicked to life. Holding it close, she examined it as if it were a rare jewel. Sniffing the sample resembled the act of a wine taster checking its bouquet. "Why do you wanna know?" she finally asked.

Doc hesitated, not wanting to involve her more than he had to.

She asked again, "Well, why do you? It's a simple question." She held her stare on him.

"It's a complicated answer."

"Apparently," she said.

"Better if you don't know."

"For you or me?"

"All of us." Doc motioned to Sam.

"You sound like my ex."

"First or second?"

"The one who buys the horses. Who else?" She laughed.

"And who bought you the indoor riding arena." Doc gave a slight laugh, leaning into her shoulder.

41

"Hamilton Jaminson is generous with money he never earned," she answered, now standing to clear the table. "It must be important. You drove here in this storm. You can trust me."

Again, Doc looked straight at her, knowing he was dealing with a woman who was use to getting her way. "Can't tell you now. We haven't broken the law . . . but the cops may not think so."

"I have friends in high places. I'll help. Just ask…okay."

Doc nodded.

"When you need this?"

"Sooner the better."

"Tomorrow's Sunday, I'll take it to the zoo, run some tests…call you when I know." She re-wrapped the sample, placing it in a large walk in refrigerator.

She then spun around to face them. "Now, I have a personal need. Which one of you will it be?" She grinned at Sam, making a come here sign with her finger. "You're big and strong. I choose you." Lenora plopped herself into a padded bench below a large lancet window. Stretching out her long legs, she lifted them a few feet off the ground. "Help me out of these."

Sam straddled her leg with his back to her and lifted her riding boot. He pulled the boot while she pushed the other into his backside. She groaned, as the boot slid off. Sam held a wooden foot, which had been connected, to her ankle.

"Lost it riding years ago. I fell and my damn foot stuck in the stirrup." She said, as Sam strained pulling the other boot off. With a few well practiced hops, she crossed the kitchen and arrived at a small desk. She pulled a newspaper from a drawer. "Says Herkey Dixon is missing. Wasn't he the lock operator you had a run-in with a few years ago?"

* * * *

Doc strained, climbing into the truck at the incline's lower terminal. Sam grabbed his arm, pulling him in. The rain turned to sleet, striking the truck with sharp pinging sounds. Waiting for the engine to warm and defroster to clear the windshield, Sam pumped the gas pedal several times. "What are we gonna do with Herkey's frozen body? His family has to be told."

"Wait and see what Lenora finds out. Then we decide, okay?"

"Only because I owe you. I swear. This is it." Sam said steering away from the curb, revving the engine more than needed.

* * * *

Late that night, approaching Doc's home, they were forced to a sudden stop as a police car blocked the road ahead of them. Another patrol car came up on them and passed. Sam immediately shut off the headlights. Clusters of red flashing lights surrounded the railroad station. Spotlights shone on the terminal's last remaining wall, while jagged flames shot from the roof. A bullhorn trumpeted over shouts of firefighters, warning everyone to back away. The last wall collapsed, as Sam and Doc watched, laying over in slow motion, surrendering to the inferno.

Doc sat in quiet disbelief his home was gone. Shadows moved in and out of the glaring spotlights. On the far side, a large pumper sprayed water on what remained. In the background, the long storage building containing the Cadillac and Herkey's frozen body remained untouched.

Sam and Doc raced away, unsure where they were headed.

Chapter Eight

Sam woke from a fitful sleep, still dressed in his white shirt and overalls, staring at the canopy of a four-poster bed, surrounded by fluffy pillows and silk sheets. Lethargic, he remembered they spent the night at Lenora's home and hoped this and yesterday's events had been a dream. Over the past few years, he endured the slow, painful death of his wife, which led to his binge drinking, and attempted suicide. Had his mind given way, stripping him of his sanity? The answer came quickly with a rapid knock.

Doc entered, waving a newspaper. Flecks of pastry clung to the curled lapels of his rumpled jacket. He dropped onto the bed, holding the paper to Sam's face. "That's my home. It's gone along with my cello."

Still groggy, Sam raised up, squinting. The photo and everything in the room was blurred. "We gotta do something," said Doc.

Sam gradually rolled out of the overstuffed bed. "Why?"

"The power was shut off, freezer isn't running."

"Shit," Sam said under his breath. "First, what about us? Where we gonna stay? My place isn't safe."

"Lenora has a place we can use." Doc cleared his throat. "Told Lenora everything last night. She'll help us."

After hooking his glasses over his ears, Sam spread out the paper. "Says here they found gas cans and suspect arson. We're go'n to the cops. Somebody burned down your house."

"How do we explain the body in the freezer?" Doc said, looking out the window. "Herkey's gonna thaw out, we gotta move."

"And do what?"

"We know who killed him. Knowing where the feces came from will help us prove it."

44

"This is a mistake," Sam grumbled, pulling on his shoes.

"We need to meet her at the zoo."

* * * *

They passed through Highland Park and turned onto Baker Street. Dazzling sunshine camouflaged the day's twenty-five degree temperature. Ahead, Sam and Doc spotted, 'Pittsburgh Zoo' lettered from large, white painted boulders set against a hillside of green grass. Driving past the main entrance, they spotted the employee parking area. After passing through its rock archway, they followed animal shaped signs leading them to the zoo's administrative offices. The last one, shaped as a giraffe, read, 'Zoo Veterinarian'.

Leafless ginkgo and maple trees crowded next to a gray cobblestone building. Lenora stood at the large doors waving as Sam pulled on the hand brake. Screams and cries of birds and wild animals surrounded them.

"Have a look, boys," she said, smiling, and led them to the lab.

Two Zeiss microscopes and several mounted slides sat on a laboratory table.

"I collected stool samples from our small animals," she said. "Then I thought, why not the big ones?" Lenora mounted the glass slides on each of the microscopes. "Nothing matched for the small animals, but look at this, it can't be right."

Doc squinted into the eyepiece. "What is this?"

Sliding close to him, adjusting the focus, she let her long hair brush against his face. She frowned. "This came from a Proboscidea, an elephant. I must have mislabeled it."

Doc dropped onto a lab stool. Sam looked at her as if she had just announced Eisenhower was a communist.

She went on, "Your sample had to come from a zoo."

"Not the zoo," Sam said, quickly. "Herkey stepped in elephant dung at the circus."

"Not him. He wouldn't go," Doc said.

"Somebody forced him," Sam said.

"Has to be," Doc said, as he stood. "His other shoe and clothes may still be there. We have to go back to the circus."

Lenora led them to the door and stopped. "Almost forgot." She held out a key. "To the apartment in Smock. It's inside the riding arena. Everything you'll need is there." She winked at Sam.

Leaving, Sam noticed a row of mud-covered, rubber boots lined against the building. He inspected them for a match to the frozen print he had found at Doc's home; none had the slash across the heel.

* * * *

Tired and hungry, Sam and Doc returned home, driving through the Schenley Park area of Pittsburgh. Doc recognized the grimy soot-covered brick building near Forbes Field, home to the Pirates and the Steelers. The Moose lodge and bar was a private club, exempt from the states strict Sunday blue laws.

"Pull in," Doc said. "Lunch time and I need to make a call."

A handful of customers sat hunched over a long bar, nursing drinks. No one bothered to look up when they entered. Squares of light hit the dusty wood floor from a row of high windows.

At the bar, Sam pushed aside an overflowing ashtray, then ordered two cheese on rye with mustard and bottled Iron City beer. He vowed only to have one drink.

Doc checked his answering service, from a payphone. Six calls waited from the fire department and two from the fire investigator, all urgent. He took the names and numbers, scribbling them on a matchbook he found on the floor near a beat-up cigarette machine. He dug out a worn business card from his over-stuffed wallet. Looking over the top of his glasses, he placed a call to the home of his insurance agent. "It's Doc. I had a..."

"What took you so long?" his agent shouted.

"For what?"

"To call me. That's what."

"When can we meet?"

"Now! I'll meet you at your house."

"Give me two hours."

Doc hung up and tugged the gold chain hanging near his waist. The pocket watch popped from a small slit in his vest. Looking at it, he shouted to Sam, "We gotta go."

They cleared the tab. Both grabbed the beers and cold sandwiches while heading to the door. Sam flipped a nickel to the bartender, grabbing a pickled egg from a jar at the corner of the bar. He stopped at the door, looking back at the cheerless men sitting in near blackness, recalling how the whiskey became tasteless, drinking it only to numb his memory and pain. Nights and days melted together, sometimes misplaced and forgotten into his Nothingness Place. From there, he had watched his soul evaporating. He swore to himself he'd not return.

"Shut the damn door," the bartender shouted. "You're lettin' the heat out."

* * * *

The smell of charcoal was heavy in the frigid, still air when the insurance agent climbed from his car shaking his head. Posted warning signs circled the foundation and rubble that had once been Doc's home.

Doc fixed his attention on his potbelly stoves. Like the last remaining soldiers of a bloody battle, they stood defiantly in the ruins. For a moment, he didn't speak. When he did, his voice shook. "What do you think, Ottley?

"Nothing left."

"Can you believe this?"

"You should have carried more coverage."

"I know, I know. Next time." Doc kicked a charred piece of metal. It slid, and disappeared into the ashes of the wreckage.

Ottley walked off, taking photographs of the jumbled and blackened wood heaped in front of them.

Doc stood, quietly, pushing his foot through the ruins of where the ticket office once was. "I don't see the clock."

"Clock?" asked Sam.

"It was wide across as your arm." Doc held his hands apart.

"Melted in the fire."

"The case was set in marble. My old man was the stationmaster. He loved that clock."

Sam kicked away more debris. "The case should be here."

They searched, giving up after a few minutes.

Sam noticed it first. His mouth was suddenly dry. He nudged Doc's arm and tilted his head to the storage building.

"What in hell?" said Doc. "Was it like that yesterday?"

"Don't know."

Ottley dropped his Brownie camera into the pocket of his heavy overcoat. "I'll call the fire inspector for a report," he shouted. "Come by the office tomorrow. We'll go over the paper work."

After Ottley drove away, Sam and Doc hurried to the storage building.

The large sliding doors stood wide open. Their thoughts were identical. Was Herkey still in the car?

Chapter Nine

The doors to the storage building were wide open. Its flat iron padlock lay on the frozen ground.

"Somebody cut it," Sam said, picking the lock up by the shackle.

Doc stepped inside the dark warehouse, switching on the main breaker. Nothing happened. He pulled the metal lever several times, nothing.

"Power's still off at the pole," Sam said.

After several more yanks, Doc gave up and flipped open his Zippo lighter, bringing a small flame to life. "Stay put, I got a flashlight out here." Doc's voice boomed in the long, cavern-like building.

Within a minute a larger light glared into Sam's face. Doc waved a flashlight, bouncing the shaft of light off walls and rafters. A lone bat flapped its silent wings, gliding to another dark rafter.

Outside, murky, stone gray clouds slid across bright sunshine, shutting out the little warmth there had been. A bitter freezing day got colder.

"Let's get this over with," Doc said, shuffling to the end of the long building. The light beam was focused on the large freezer, skipping and leaping in cadence with Doc's awkward pace.

Like a solitary tomb, the freezer sat in front of them. Within the cone of light, they saw the shut door. The padlock, however, lay on the concrete floor in several pieces that were bent and twisted.

"Car's gone. I know it," Doc said in a whisper, fighting off panic.

"Maybe not. Help me slide these doors open."

The Cadillac sat coated in frost crystals, exactly as they left it, captured in a state of suspended animation, as if waiting to be restored in a future life. Its trunk still closed, requiring it to be pried open. Herkey's frozen body remained in the fetal position, as they had left him. Doc held the light on the body, finding something he'd missed yesterday. Using his Zippo, he thawed the frost near Herkey's temple. He carefully dabbed at a red and black smudge with his white handkerchief.

"I'll examine it later." Doc aimed the light on the freezer door. "We're letting out the cold air. Let's close it up."

After pushing the freezer doors shut, they heard tires crunching outside, near the building. "There another way out?" Sam asked.

"Only one door," Doc said, turning off the light. From his jacket, he pulled a thin profiled 9mm Luger. They forced their backs against the building's cold cinder block wall, staring at the opened doors. Sweat ran down Doc's hand as he squeezed his palm around the gun's wood grip, believing he and Sam had walked into a deadly trap.

No one appeared in the door.

"They might drive off," Sam whispered.

An engine idled. The sudden slam of a car door caused them to jerk back, pressing harder against the wall. In a moment, footsteps paced around the building. "There's only one," whispered Doc. "He's gonna come inside sooner or later."

"When he goes around back, we'll get outta here," Sam said, as he moved toward the door.

Doc grabbed his arm. "Somebody could be in the car watching."

A darkened figure appeared at the door holding a compact, twelve gauge, short barrel shotgun across his chest.

"Doc, you in here?" He shouted.

In the cold stillness, the quick action of the pump slid forward and back along the magazine, making it ready to fire. At the same time Doc stepped forward. Sam shoved him back, putting a hand across his chest.

50

A thin light flashed on, scanning the inside of the building, running up and down the walls and roofline. Again he called, "Anybody here?" This time the tone was stern and annoyed.

Sam and Doc inched their way back to the freezer, planning to hide inside. The heavy handle of the breaker switch clanked several times, to no avail. Footsteps echoed, on the concrete floor, following the beam of light, heading toward them. There was no chance of reaching the freezer before being found. Doc aimed the Luger at the sweeping light. His hands shook, waiting for a shot. This would be his only chance. What happened to Herkey Dixon would happen to them if he missed.

The intruder stopped. Shouting again, "Police. It's me Rizzo."

Outside, another car pulled near the storage building. A car door slammed and someone approached the open doors. "Doc, you in there? It's Ottley. There's a cop car out here."

Doc and Sam remained silent.

Ottley stood at the door and called again. "Just saw the power company. The lineman is up on the pole, you should have..."

At that moment, lights flashed on, illuminating the entire building in dingy gray light. In the briefest of moments it took the light to fill the room, Rizzo had dropped to the floor in a shooting position. Doc still pointed the Luger, but at no one.

"What's going on?" Ottley asked, walking into the building.

Rizzo snapped to his feet, clicking on the oversized safety of his one handed shotgun. "Saw the door open, just checking. You know, with the circus in town." He brushed dirt from his trousers that were tucked into his boots, as he strode to his patrol car.

51

Ottley held up two new padlocks. "Came back to tell you the fire department cut the locks off. I brought you these."

Once the patrol car pulled away, Ottley walked to the open doors, watching the cruiser exit the parking lot. "What was that about?"

Doc and Sam remained silent for a moment, not moving, remaining braced against the block wall. Short spurts of vapor rose from their noses and mouths. Doc slid the Luger into his jacket pocket, keeping it from Ottley's view.

"Don't know for sure," Doc answered, tasting the bitterness of adrenalin that coated his mouth.

"How do I get in touch?" Ottley asked.

They moved to the open door, near Ottley. Doc fumbled for a prescription pad, finally pulling it from his breast pocket. He circled his office address, handing it to Ottley. "Send the paperwork to this address. For the time being, that's where I'll be."

* * * *

After leaving the burned-out remains of Doc's home, Sam purchased several bags of sand. Cold temperatures had not allowed the icy roads to thaw.

He loaded them into the bed of his truck for extra weight, hopefully, preventing them from sliding into a ditch, while driving the narrow road to Lenora's stables in the remote village of Smock. "Tomorrow we pay a visit to the circus," said Doc.

Sam glanced into the rear view mirror, watching for a patrol car.

52

Chapter Ten

The following morning a ringing telephone, in Lenora's riding stable, jarred Sam and Doc awake. They rushed from bedrooms into the large common area of the suite. Doc picked up the black wall phone.

"It's Lenora," he told Sam.

Sam relaxed, looking over the vast indoor riding arena stretched out below them.

"Found the place fine," Doc answered. "You're sure it's no trouble?" He nodded several times. "That so? Interesting." He gently placed the handset back in its metal hook. "She's gonna stick her nose into this. I know it," Doc said under his breath.

Sam bent into the refrigerator, rummaging for breakfast when Doc dropped into a yellow, vinyl and chrome chair in the kitchen.

"You're not gonna believe it," Doc said.

"Try me," Sam said, balancing an arm full of plates while closing the door with his foot.

"Lenora called a booking agent for carnivals and circuses."

"For what?"

"She told him, she needed to examine the animals."

"She can do that?" Sam asked.

"She's a vet. You bet she can and she did." Doc held up his hand, stopping more questions. "There's no record of Jumbo's Big Top Circus anywhere. They shouldn't be here. They don't exist."

"Snookey was a dream?" Sam said. "Now, tell me we didn't go to a circus and see a midget dressed like a bat. While you're at it, tell me we're not going back."

"We have to. I'm curious why a circus shows up in the middle of October?" Doc said.

"Let the cops do it."

"After yesterday, you trust Rizzo?"

"I'm not sure," Sam said, shaking his head.

"Lenora's got a friend at the county. They'll check on the permit."

Sam stopped breaking eggs. "Enlighten me."

"Permits, whoever owns the circus needs permits from the state and county," Doc said, while he moved to the large window, watching horses entering the riding arena below. "Said it may take a few days, but we'll know who Snookey works for."

After breakfast, they rode the elevator to the ground floor. Stepping outside, they were met by bitter cold temperatures and an armed security guard who stepped into their path.

"Bone chilling day, wouldn't you say?" the guard asked, patting his holster.

"Yeah, too cold to snow," Sam countered.

"I'll keep an eye on you while you're a guest here of Mrs. Jaminson's."

Driving away, Sam asked, "How'd he know we're here?"

"Security cameras saw 'em last night." Doc slapped Sam on the back, giving him an extra shove. "They're for protection and to watch the horses, not us."

Sam remained quiet, keeping his eyes fixed on the road. Barren farmland glistened from the morning frost. Plumes of smoke and steam, as if measured on a plumb line, rose from distant hillsides. A few remaining brown leaves drooped from gaunt trees along the winding road. Nearby, long rows of coke ovens, like giant beehives stacked on hillsides, burst flames and smoke, painting the morning sky hazy red, baking raw coal into coke vital to steel making. The sound of the truck's engine and humming tires on gray asphalt lulled Sam's mind back to discarded memories.

Layers of newspapers covered windows and doors of his home once shared with Emma. Her favorite albums,

Kay Star, Les Brown and Rosemary Clooney played over and over. A solitary candle flickered from the center of the kitchen table. His hands hovered over the open flame, not withdrawing, until he smelled flesh burning, wanting pain.

Sam jerked, suddenly smelling sulfur from the burning coke ovens, which looked like giant beehives in the distance. He had no idea what they would find at the circus. The sudden reappearance of Doc's Cadillac, with Herkey's body, pointed to a plan, but for what? He hoped to find something that would persuade Doc to go to the police.

In the distance, the gray and red-striped tent stood alone. Triangular pennants flapped from the peaks of its steel masts.

An abandoned Dairy Queen sat near the edge of the narrow road. Sam pulled off, coasting to a stop near it.

"Other tents are gone," Sam said, pulling the emergency brake tight.

"Let's see what's going on," said Doc, opening the truck door.

Sam leaned close to him. "Keep your voice down, sound travels farther in the cold."

Rubbing his hands together for warmth, Sam noticed several of the smaller tents and wagons were missing from the circus grounds. He hoped it was a sign they were moving from town.

Walking behind an over-grown hedgerow, dry, yellow, frost-bound grass crunched under their feet. Doc led the way, waving to Sam to catch up. Sam's heart was pounding against his chest. Instinct told him to turn back.

Nearing the remaining tent, they passed black and white "NO TRESPASSING" signs, which had replaced the colorful banners of a few days ago. Resting near the airports aged control tower, Doc pointed to the far off tent. "That's where the Quonset hut was."

"That's not the same tent we saw the show in," Sam said. "The other one was bigger."

Only a few battered cars and trucks, splattered in brownish mud, sat near the remaining tent. The dozens of travel trailers and wagons that once crowded the lot were gone.

"Hear that?" Sam said.

"Yeah, just started, sounds like machinery."

Sam stamped his feet and pulled his stocking cap over his ears. "It's coming from the tent."

"Hope it's warm," Doc said. "Let's take a look."

Approaching the tent, the low rumble grew louder. Within moments they walked alongside the tent's exterior wall. Doc stopped frequently, turning to look behind.

"What are you doin'?" Sam asked.

"Watching for Snookey."

Sam kicked the sides of the gray and red canvas. "I'm lookn' for a place to crawl under."

Sam finally spotted what he looked for, a missing tent peg. On their knees, they poked their heads under the heavy canvas, finding a mound of dirt in their path.

Giving several grunts, Doc lifted the tenting and crawled under. Sam followed, finding Doc with his chest heaving, sitting on a crumbled sheet of corrugated metal. Stacks of dirt and rubble blocked their view of the interior. Wedging themselves between the sides of the tent and mountains of dirt, they tramped through ankle-high drifts. Overhead, a belt conveyor, angled out over the piles, suddenly hummed to life, flinging out debris, bringing an avalanche of rock. Doc and Sam dodged what tumbled at them, fighting their way to an open area.

"I'll be go to hell," said Doc, shaking dirt from his cuffs. "Looks like we found what's left of the Quonset hut."

Only the top half of a massive yellow excavator was visible as it spewed black exhaust while ripping out chunks of earth where the hut once stood. Dozens of heavy-duty fans rattled near the dig site, pulling exhaust fumes from the tent.

Sam and Doc slipped behind a semi-trailer when two men, dressed in coveralls, exited a storage building near the dig site. With their appearance, the digging equipment stopped, and the driver climbed down, half-jogging toward them.

From the distance, there was something familiar about the equipment operator, he stood very near the two men, too close, inches separated their faces.

"Doc...that big guy, is he the damn clown?"

"Don't know."

"Think it is."

Doc took a careful look. "The jerk with the monkey box, Snookey?" he said.

"Think that's him," Sam said, moving back further behind the trailer. "Take another look. He's wearing rubber boots. Remember the prints at your place? Might be them."

Doc stepped closer, squinting. As he did, he stumbled, kicking an empty fuel can. Sam and Doc stood, unmoving, holding their breath. The three glanced in their direction, then returned to the blueprints they stood over.

"That was close." Sam said as they stepped back between two tractor trailers. "What are they digging for?"

Doc shrugged. "No clue."

The equipment operator vanished. The digger stood idle. The other men remained, studying the plans. "Where did he go?" said Sam.

A voice boomed from behind. "You rubes came back. Must' a liked the show, huh?"

They both jerked around, staring at the familiar figure.

"You're the clown," Doc shouted. "You're Snookey. You killed Herkey."

"Never heard of him."

Doc pointed a finger at him, shouting, "Like hell. I found your makeup on him. You put him in my car."

57

Snookey gave them a smile. He reached behind his back, returning with a gun.

Even without his clowns face paint, they saw his sneering red and black face from the circus.

"You're on private property, but hey so what, I'm glad you're here." Snookey waved the gun at the trailer. "Up the steps, door's open at the top."

The two climbed the rickety steps, stopping at the steel door.

"Take off your shoes and belts," Snookey said calmly.

Looking back at him, they hesitated.

"Toss 'em down, now," he shouted.

Leaning against the trailer, they yanked off their shoes and belts.

"Open it. Get in." Snookey shook his gun at the door, then lifted his revolver high in the air, shoving it into the back of Doc's knee. "Who wants it first?" The hammer clicked. "Inside, now."

Using his shoulder, Sam forced the heavy, steel door open. A rush of stale air carried the smell of rotting meat, nearly gagging them. Snookey came to the top of the steps, slamming the butt end of the revolver into the top of Doc's shoulder, collapsing him into Sam, sending them both to the floor inside the trailer.

They sat in the pitch black trailer, expecting to be shot. Instead the door banged shut, a lock clicked. Outside, rapid footsteps thumped down the stairs. Moments later, the heavy machinery started up.

Sam's eyes adjusted slightly, seeing shades of gray and brown. Across the room he made out a steel wall with a locked metal door in the center. With his palms, he felt the straw covered floor of the empty trailer.

Both beat the walls and shouted for help until exhaustion took the force from their arms and shoulders.

They sat in darkness, their fists bleeding.

Low rumbling roars came from the other side of the wall, like waves building to a tsunami far out at sea. Fierce raging roars of tigers rocketed through the room, thundering off walls, rumbling, shaking the trailer.

The terror built in Sam, and he couldn't hide it.

"Oh, shit," he yelled, "Remember the big cats at the circus?"

"Can't be."

"Afraid it is," said Sam. "We woke 'em up."

For a moment it was quiet, then furious scratching began on the adjoining door. A deep, hollow roar came, sounding more agitated. The first assault was a light jab, a tap, testing the defense, followed by a combination of battering rams, rattling the wall, denting the door.

"Holy hell, the cats know we're here. They're trying to get to us," Doc said.

"They smell us," Sam said, running his hands around the doorframe. "It opens in. We gotta brace it."

Without hesitation, Doc scooted in front of the door, blocking it. "How many in there, ya think?"

"Not many. We got to keep the doors shut," Sam shouted over the noise.

Another series of blows rattled the wall and door. Something shook loose, and clanked to the floor. On hands and knees, Sam padded the floor until his fingers nudged it. He put it in his pocket, knowing immediately what it was and didn't want to frighten Doc more than he was.

"Push with all you got, Doc," he shouted, leaning against the door alongside him. "Put all you got into…"

A caged light flashed on inside the trailer. Briefly blinded, they shielded their eyes. The outside door had unexpectedly swung open. An image materialized in the shadowy darkness, as though an illusion.

"Hurry, we gotta get outta here." The voice came from a bald Japanese dwarf, standing in the doorway.

Stumbling several times, Sam and Doc hurried to the door. Bits of straw and sawdust clung to their clothes. Sam turned back, slamming and locking the outside door as they followed the dwarf down the steps. He swiftly ushered them behind a mound of debris where a small tent flap opened to the outside. He pointed to his 1949 VW minibus running near an unused backhoe.

Once safely inside, the dwarf drove off the property, to the main road. He sat, raised-up, on a thick, yellowed, foam pad held in place with layers of electrical tape. The three pedals were modified with extensions made of blocks of wood. Sam and Doc sat on dingy carpet in a space, which had been turned into a kitchen and bedroom. Heavy, gray velvet curtains covered the surrounding windows. Dirty clothes, piled in a frayed wicker basket, sat on the passenger seat.

Doc cleared his throat, then spoke, "Thank you, but who in blazes are you?"

"Jake Ozaki, I work at the...."

Doc cut him off. "You're the Bat Boy. Saw you in the sideshow."

"Yeah." Jake turned, giving a full smile, exposing his teeth. "No fangs like before."

"You're Japanese," said Sam.

"I'm Nisei, second generation, Japanese-American."

Sam lifted an edge of the curtain, looking back, seeing if anyone followed.

"No one saw us," Jake said. "We got away clean." With a quick glance, he checked his rearview mirror. "Lucky, I spotted you getting in the tiger cage."

"Yeah, damn lucky," Sam said.

"Snookey is a crazy man," Jake said, giving another look back. "Those tigers aren't trained, and they're in a frenzy to eat. Snookey planned to put them in the cage with you, bad stuff."

60

Jake pulled off the road after seeing their truck parked near the vacant building. "Get out. I have to get back before they miss me. For your own good, don't come back, keep out of this."

Climbing from the minibus, Doc asked, "Why did he take our shoes and belts?"

"Young tigers are valuable," Jake answered. "Snookey doesn't want the cats choking on 'em."

The battered minibus churned its wheels through pea-sized gravel, bouncing onto the black top road. Sam and Doc stood shoeless in the parking lot, watching it speed off.

Holding his injured shoulder and arm close to his body, Doc grimaced climbing into Sam's truck. "What just happened?" he asked.

"Don't know, but we were just saved by a midget from California."

"California?"

"That's what the license plate said," Sam answered and turned away, using the steering wheel to pull himself into the cab.

Looking back at the tent, Doc asked, "Why dig up the old army air base and why do it under a tent?"

Sam leaned forward, looking Doc directly in the eye. "The bigger question, why was Snookey going to feed us to the tigers and who in hell was the midget? Why did he save us?"

"I'm afraid we're gonna find out soon enough," Doc said.

"I did answer one question."

"That is?"

Snookey's boots match the prints I found outside your storage building."

"That so?"

"Spotted the prints before we got in the trailer."

"What else you know?"

Sam pulled a twisted door hinge from his pocket, laying it on the seat. "This is what fell off the door. We didn't have a lot of time."

Chapter Eleven

Riders and horses glided, in stride, over manicured ivy walls and white painted rail fences.

Sam and Doc leaned back in matching chairs watching from the lofty penthouse of the arena. Hot cocoa blended with Kahlua rested in their still trembling hands. A rapid knock on the door quickly brought their heads off the cushions.

In the far end of the suite, elevator doors sat open and Lenora stuck her head into the room. "You two decent?" She walked in carrying sacks from several department stores. "Got both of you shoes and for Doc, some of my ex's clothes. Hamilton won't miss 'em."

She tossed her riding jacket and gloves on the sofa, then dropped into it herself. "County treasurer called about the old airport," she said, struggling to pull off her boots.

"So...who owns it?" Sam asked.

"The good old U.S. Government," Lenora said, with a gasp, as her boot slid off. She rubbed the joint near her artificial foot. "Here's the surprise." Her voice rose slightly. "Eisenhower leased the land to a private company. Hold on." She pulled a yellow paper from her purse. "Here it is. It was leased to Jumbo's Big Top Circus. Papers filed in Delaware, about a year ago. Listed Vince Pergalsky as president of the corporation." She leaned back, laughing, waving the paper in the air.

"Anything else?" Doc asked.

"Hold on, you'll love the name on the lease . . . Snookey. That's all just Snookey. Is that keen?"

"You sure?" asked Sam.

Lenora nodded, showing them the carbon copy.

Sam dropped his head, looking at the name. "Afraid it would be. Somehow I knew."

"That's not all," she said, "They have a permit to operate a mine on that property." She looked at the lease again. "That must be a mistake."

Sam and Doc exchanged looks. "Could be," Doc said. "They were digging. I guess they call that mining. And by the way, we met Snookey."

Lenora let her smile drop. "What's he like?" she asked, while she hopped to the bar across the room. The sock covered, prosthetic foot remained next to her boots on the floor. She pulled a beer from a refrigerator under the bar and hoisted herself she hoisted herself up into a barstool.

"We had an unusual day," Doc began.

"No, wait. Tell me about today and this Snookey while we eat. I ordered take-out. Like deer stew? It'll be here soon. Wash your hands."

In minutes, an aproned, middle-aged lady, absent a waist, marched from the elevator. In her husky arms she carried a large metal pot while a basket of hot crusty breads swung from a forearm. Moving smartly from pantry to drawers she gathered utensils and bowls, fussing over them until the table was set. She laid the bill on the table, as if it were a final garnishment, then departed.

As soon as the door slid shut, they rushed the table. Doc sloshed his heavily buttered rye into his stew then quickly popped it into his mouth. Swallowing, he pointed his spoon to Sam. "Tell Lenora about Snookey's cats and the midget."

She listened as they recounted their near disaster. When Sam finished, she asked. "Now, why would this Japanese midget, Jake, help you?"

"No clue," said Sam.

Doc yawned. "Yeah, he came into the room and got us out of there. That simple."

"You've told me everything?" she said, taking a sip of beer.

They both nodded, like schoolchildren.

Lenora raised her bottle. "I'll be in California a few days buying horses. Go with me."

"Can't," Doc said. We're close to solving this. Then we'll go to the police." Below them, rows of overhead lights gradually went out. They sat, staring into the arena's shadows.

"You know," Lenora said, breaking the silence, "This apartment's sound proof and odor proof. Notice you can't smell the horses?"

"That so?" said Doc.

"It is, but I can smell bullshit up here." She finished peeling the label from the bottle and flicked it at Doc. "You have a dead body in your car, your house is burned down, and a clown named Snookey tries to feed you to tigers. And you think you are close to figuring this out, bull. I'm leaving town, you need to go with me and stay away from that circus."

"We're gonna follow the midget," Doc said. "See where that takes us. Then the cops. Promise."

* * * *

Inside the circus tent, Snookey leaned against the excavator, looking into the pit of dirt, rock and rusted sheets of tin roofing where the Quonset hut once stood. Vince's map was checked again. There was no sign of the vaults, after three days of digging. He'd dig one more day, then call Vince with the bad news. It was unavoidable.

Smiling to himself, Snookey headed to the tiger cages, remembering his big cats would be hungry for dinner. It had been earlier in the day that he put Sam and Doc in the trailer. Approaching, he noticed the heavy padlock, hanging open in the hasp. A pry bar lay near the base of the stairs. Entering the empty room, he saw the steel door had been destroyed, hanging by a single hinge. Slamming the door several times, he awakened the sleeping tigers.

65

Jake was at the far side of the tent, about to fall asleep, in the rear of his mini-bus, when he heard the rage of a tiger's roar. Not opening his eyes, he reached under the mattress, gripping his pistol.

He was no closer now than he was nearly a year ago.

Chapter Twelve

Morning arrived, attired in thin gray clouds.

Inside the brightly lit arena, Lenora and other riders took their horses over low fences, warming up. Others stood chatting in the judging area while stable boys finished grooming their mounts.

Sam and Doc watched from the suite. "Her warning to stay away from the circus is good advice," Sam said.

"Just look around," Doc said. "See what Jake is up to."

"Then the cops."

They quickly dressed in their newly donated clothes and shoes, escaping, before Lenora returned.

Sam eased the clutch in and out while gently pumping the gas pedal, keeping the cold engine alive. Lines of trucks passed them towing horse trailers, into stalls beneath the arena.

"This a good idea . . . spying on Jake?" Sam asked.

"Was last night."

"We had a little to drink last night. Is it still a good idea?"

Doc ran his hand over his mouth. "I'm not sure of anything anymore. Just want to get this over with."

"As long as we stay out of Snookey's way," Sam said.

"We're not going in the tent, and…." Doc patted his jacket pocket. "This time I brought a gun."

"The fire at your house…I'm sure Snookey and Vince did it."

"I'd bet on it," said Doc, looking at another horse trailer that passed. "Vince got away with a lot of artifacts. Now he's back with Snookey for revenge."

"He used the money to buy the circus. Why?" Sam asked. "Got to be something else. What's he gonna bury under that Quonset hut?"

"Or dig up," Doc said.

Sam recalled how Vince, many years ago, had used an abandoned mine shaft to methodically stash away stolen, ancient relics that were illegally shipped into the country. His disappearance with the artifacts had not been solved.

When Sam and Doc arrived at the remote circus, hard gusts of wind began to rock the multi-spired tent. Its massive top billowed and rolled like an ocean storm.

Sam parked in the same spot as the previous day. He dreaded the day ahead, but knew it was the only way to satisfy Doc's curiosity.

To begin their vigil, Sam arranged blankets and a Thermos of coffee between them. Sam eyed his truck's clock. "Say we give it four hours, get lunch and back for another four?"

Doc agreed.

They waited throughout the morning, planning to follow Jake should he leave. No one entered nor left the red and gray big top. The only sign of life, within the tent, came from the persistent drone of earthmovers. The minute and hour hands became anchored, unmoving on the truck's clock. The ticks echoed in slow motion, like tolling bells, rehearsing the same moment again and again.

Sam changed positions every few minutes, looking for a spot behind the steering wheel, which didn't hurt his already aching back. Next to him, Doc sprawled, asleep, his mouth hung open. Occasionally, Sam ran the engine, warming the cab. At noon, overcome with hunger pains and boredom, they abandoned their watch and headed to the A & P market for chipped ham and a loaf of bread. Within thirty minutes they returned to their post

The afternoon offered a slight change, frequent visits of freezing rain left a thin coating of ice on the truck. Wrapped in wool blankets, they drank warm coffee and silently stared into the dull winter day.

Moaning, Doc arched his back, sliding a pocket watch from his vest. "Almost two, I won't last. "

Sam rested his head on the steering wheel. "I'm ready to call it a day."

"What in blazes?" Doc wiped the frost from his window with his jacket's sleeve. He was the first to spot the green Plymouth creeping toward them. Its tires crunched on the gravel parking lot.

"What the hell," Sam said, watching the car stop next to them. He recognized Woodrow at the wheel.

"Don't trust anyone," Doc said, as he gripped the gun in his pocket.

"You left this in the car the other day," Woodrow shouted, pulling something from his car's front seat. He climbed from the car, holding up a denim jacket.

Sam and Doc sat rigid, watching him approach. Suddenly, Woodrow pushed his face within inches of the truck's window.

Doc nearly pulled the trigger.

"Thought that might be you." Woodrow said, holding the coat up to the window. "Lucky I spotted you."

"Glad you did," Sam said, taking the coat.

Woodrow returned to his car, but stopped and glanced back over his shoulder, as if to speak, then pulled the door open and got in.

Doc stared at Sam. "What was Woodrow doing out here?"

Sam shook his head. "Better yet, why didn't he ask us the same question?"

"Maybe he knew?" Doc said, sliding his handgun back into his pocket.

"Don't know. Where did he come from?"

The Plymouth soon climbed to the edge of the road and sped away. Its trailing exhaust quickly vanished around a long sweeping turn of the highway.

Sam held his coat in his lap looking at it. After a moment, he pulled it close to his face, inhaling. He then reached across and held it to Doc's face. "Smell anything?" he asked.

Doc pushed it away. "No, should I?"

"Didn't either. That's my point. I left it with a lady wearing an evening dress in Woodrow's backseat. She wore my coat."

Doc gave him a blank stare.

"When you took my truck, I took Woody's jitney to meet you for breakfast."

"Now, I remember?" Doc said.

"She wore an evening gown, but no perfume. My Emma would've worn perfume with a dress like that."

Doc grabbed the coat, inhaling deeply into it, "Pity, no scent of a woman."

"Till now, I didn't think about it," Sam said. "What kind of a woman doesn't wear perfume?"

"Some don't, maybe an allergy."

"Yeah, probably," said Sam. "Seems unusual to me, anyway."

Doc slumped back into the seat, "Wake me if you spot our midget." Neither spoke, as the day drug on, both comfortable in silence.

* * * *

In the late evening, a glimmer of thin winter sunlight parted the murky sky. Soon afterward a large moon, reddened by the glow of flaming coke ovens, sat on the horizon.

The drone of heavy machinery stopped, waking Doc. "Any sign of Jake?" he asked.

"No, but its gettin' dark," Sam said, reaching behind the driver's seat. He pulled out a hand drill, giving the handle a quick turn, spinning the drill bit. Sam got out of the truck and slammed the door before Doc argued.

Relying on light from a nearly full moon, Sam bent low, carefully stepping through hard, bare, rutted soil. Against a stand of full-grown eastern pines, he disappeared into their shadows. Ahead of him, the solitary tent stood, like a canvas citadel. He followed a thin hazy light that escaped between its seams, outlining its oval shape.

Inside, spotlights flickered and seemed to jump as the digging equipment rushed back to work. Between their rumblings, angry growls raged from the tiger cage, touching a raw nerve in Sam. He became colder, trembling more than he had been, denying he was frightened. It was the cold night, he thought to himself. Ahead, he saw what he'd been looking for.

* * * *

Doc pulled himself up, shifting to a new position on the worn out truck seat, hoping to relieve his stiff, throbbing back. Glancing toward the distant tent, under the shine of a utility light, he recognized the tall lean figure of Sam kneeling behind Jake's mini-bus. The backlit profile of Sam stood and was gone again.

Upset he lost site of Sam, Doc leaned against the passenger door, resting his head against the cold window, staring into the darkness. He patted the 9mm in his jacket pocket, hoping it wouldn't be needed.

A pounding on the glass jolted him upright.

"Open it," Sam said, yanking on the handle.

"What in hell were you doing?"

"Made it easier to follow Jake," Sam said, climbing into the truck.

"Good, but I'm done." Doc looked back at the tent, worried Sam may have been followed. "Its dinner time. Start her up."

The starter slowly grinded, and reluctantly the cold engine kicked over.

"Gonna need a battery pretty soon," Sam said, pulling away from the parking area.

Nearing a heavily traveled crossroads, Sam sped by a tall, slender sign shaped like a giant arrow. Within it, outlined in red neon, THE NICKEL INN flickered in deep blue letters.

Doc twisted in his seat, staring at the sign. "Why didn't you stop?"

"Don't like 'em getting in my pockets."

"There's nothing else out here."

Sam slowed, making a quick U-turn, backtracking, until he steered into the parking lot toward a long unpainted, cinder block building. In its large picture window a solitary red sign flashed EAT. Nearly a dozen trucks and cars sat nosed-in, snuggling close to the low slung building. They pulled next to an idling flatbed, loaded with toilets.

Inside, a twangy guitar blared from a jukebox near a compact dance floor. Aromas of spicy chili brought a slight grin to Sam's mouth. From the darkened bar, a waitress pushed away a beaded curtain that separated the bar from the dining area. Smiling she put a tooth pick in her mouth and stepped between them.

"Just routine," she said and patted Sam's pockets. Hearing the jingle of change, she stepped behind him, and reached deep into his pocket, returning with a handful of coins. "Good," she said, separating the nickels. "Glue one to the bar. Get a beer on the house." She winked and pranced away shaking her long ponytail, not looking back.

Doc was stopped by the sight. Silver buffalo nickels blanketed nearly every surface of the oval bar. He was quickly distracted by links of Polish sausage smothered in sauerkraut riding by atop a serving platter, carried by the same friendly waitress. Candle flames, inside amber globes, danced at every table. From an unseen room, occasional

72

sharp cracks of an ivory cue ball smashed into clustered billiard balls.

Sam and Doc hunched over the bar, shoveling down soupspoons of chili and crackers, chased with Iron City beer. Neither spoke until Doc pushed the bowl away while brushing away cracker crumbs from his vest. "What now?" he asked.

"Come back tomorrow," Sam said, pointing toward a Jumbo's Big Top Circus poster tacked to the wall near a pay phone. "Maybe Jake eats here?"

"Maybe Snookey does," Doc said, turning to scan the dark dining room.

Doc gripped the bar for balance, and dropped from the stool. After he slapped a crumbled five dollar bill across the bar, they headed to the door.

Sam was about to slide the key into the truck's lock when he spotted the battered VW mini-bus drive into the parking lot. Its headlights flashed across them. "There he is," Sam said.

"Who?" Doc shouted.

"Jake, the midget. He's pulling in here."

The VW accelerated, throwing gravel from under its wheels, as it pulled away and raced across the lot to the highway.

"He saw us, Sam said.

"Follow him." Doc shouted.

Sam swung his truck around in a tight turn, fishtailing onto the main road. In a panic, he slammed on the brakes, skidding to a sideways stop at the intersection's flashing red four way signal.

"You lost 'em," Doc said. "It's too dark to follow him."

"Maybe not." Sam's hands gripped the wheel with white knuckles as he gunned across the intersection, speeding to where he last saw the VW.

The two-lane road they followed for several miles, wound through man- made mountains of smoldering slate dumps, veined with a blue fire deep within their cores that had burned for decades.

After crossing several intersections of merging cars they were now trapped behind a Mack truck hauling a load of coal.

"Still got my sights on him," Sam said as he inched over the double line, checking the string of distant taillights.

Doc gripped on the dashboard as they approached the five corners junction at the edge of downtown. Several cars waited, the drivers watched the multiple sets of traffic lights, which hung over the intersections five crossing streets.

"You lost him, admit it," said Doc.

"No, still got him."

Sam yanked the wheel, making a sudden turn, driving through a corner gas station, bypassing the intersection. After making another sharp left onto Morgantown Road, they were able to see the far off taillights of two cars.

"Which one is it?" asked Doc, after the two distant cars turned, going different directions.

"Still got him." Sam pointed to his nose. "Part blood hound."

Not taking his eyes from the road, he reached under his seat, handing Doc the small hand-drill.

Doc looked at it, puzzled.

"Put a small hole in his brake light." Sam pointed to a bright dot of white light coming from a car in the distance.

"Clever. Now where's he going?" Doc said. "He's not from around here."

They looped around downtown until reaching North Main. Passing Fayette Tire Company, they slowed, making a sharp turn on Ben Lomond Street.

"I was on this street the other day," Sam said.

74

"For what? This is old money over here," Doc said, then paused. "And from what I hear, some of it's crooked."

"Your jitney driver, Woodrow, stopped here. Remember the girl I loaned my coat to?"

"Yeah."

"He picked her up here."

Ahead, the VW stopped. Its lights flashed out.

Remaining in the distance, Sam pulled to the curb near a brick archway guarding a private driveway.

"He's getting out," Doc said, slumping down.

In the porch light, they saw Jake's diminutive shape approaching the side door of a large Victorian home.

"That's the same house the girl ran from," Sam whispered.

Chapter Thirteen

Breathing out clouds of steam, Jake Ozaki knocked on the servant entry door. He adjusted his tie then ran his hands down the sides of his wool jacket as the door swung open. He immediately stepped inside, greeted by a nervous Taki and Grace Sasaki.

He bowed, then asked, "Where can we speak privately?"

"Captain Semans and his family are away. You can speak freely," Taki answered.

Taki and Jake took seats in a small sitting area near the kitchen while Grace boiled water for tea.

"Here's your report." Jake slid a white, letter-sized envelope across the coffee table. "They haven't found anything after three days. I don't think they're digging in the right location. Snookey's map was wrong." He pointed to the envelope. "Details are in there."

Jake glanced towards the kitchen, and noticed Grace leaning against the doorway. Her shoulders slumped with the news.

"What will they do next?" Taki asked, gesturing to the envelope.

Jake sensed his client's impatience and pushed himself up in the chair. His feet dangled. "I've been on this case a long time, and still can't say what Snookey will do one day to the next." He took a breath. "But I know for certain, he won't give up searching for the vaults and what they stole from your uncle."

Taki's chest heaved several times while he stared at the envelope.

The shrill whistle of a kettle interrupted.

Within moments Grace placed a serving tray between Taki and Jake. She quietly poured tea and offered a plate of anpan and coffe jelly before she took a seat. They held their bowls and politely bowed. Each took a sip, commenting on its good taste. They drank in silence, taking small sips.

Taki finished with an audible deep inhale then wiped his bowl with a tissue. "Let us get back to business," he said, placing his bowl in the wood tray.

Jake continued. "As I was about to say, Snookey is obsessed with finding what he's looking for. He won't quit."

"The clock," Grace finally said, "We haven't told you about it."

"I was about to." Taki patted her hand. "One of the American soldiers who robbed our uncle knew there were two maps. He told us the vaults had been moved and he would return their contents to us. It was obvious, he was overcome with guilt."

Jake nodded. "Snookey didn't mention a clock."

"The second map is hidden in the clock," Grace said. "After the GI's stole my uncle's valuables they shipped them here from California. He knew where the second map was hidden because he never hid the vaults where Snookey told him. He changed the hiding place. He didn't tell the others."

"Give me his name," Jake said.

"He's gone," Taki answered. "The papers reported him missing several days ago. His wife said he never came home from work."

Jake pulled a notebook from his breast pocket. "His name?"

"Dixon, Herkey Dixon. He was in the army with Snookey," Taki answered.

"I know the name." Jake kept his notebook open as he slid out of the wingback chair and leaned against its seat cushion. "I need to know more about what I'm looking for. This case has become more dangerous. I may not be able to continue." From the corner of his eye, he spotted a slight movement of the drapes, which divided the room.

"You didn't ask when you took the case," Taki said. "Now, I am dealing with something more serious."

"What?" Grace asked.

"Murder." He looked directly at her then Taki.

"Who?" Taki asked.

"Snookey killed Herkey Dixon and attempted to kill two other people."

Grace jerked back and began to say something, but abruptly her voice tailed off as Taki put an arm around her shoulder.

"These men are sinister," Jake said. "Mr. Dixon feared Snookey. There were other men who planned the theft, people higher up. Unfortunately, I don't know their names."

"What do you need from us?" Taki asked.

"The truth. Everything."

"Then you'll finish the job?" Grace asked.

"Depends."

Jake noticed Taki and Grace exchange quick looks just as he heard someone gasp behind the curtain dividing the room. Jake's experience told him the case was more complicated than his clients wanted him to know, they always were. He hoped the new visitor wouldn't make it worse.

"There is more we can tell you," Taki said, "My wife's uncle was a war hero…"

Jake cut him off, motioning to the adjoining room. "They also may wish to have tea."

Grace rose, her head bowed, leaving the room.

Jake took a sip of his now cold tea, frowning at the taste. He heard whispering in the next room. A younger Japanese lady entered.

"My niece, Geta Tamura," Grace said.

Jake rose up on his toes and extended his short arm upward. "Jake Ozaki."

She placed her hands on her thighs and bowed. He quickly pulled his hand back, politely returning her bow.

Taki explained she was the Seaman's housekeeper, and they were the gardeners for the property.

The two ladies sat flanking Taki, nearly touching. Jake leaned against the taller wingback chair.

"My aunt died before she returned home. All they had was gone," Grace blurted.

Taki pulled her close.

"They took everything from our family," Geta added. "I have lost my daughter because of what these men did."

Jake didn't speak for a moment, then looked at each of them. "I need one of you to start at the beginning." His tone was firm. He glanced at his watch, knowing he could not be gone much longer from the circus. He was also annoyed that he failed to detect being followed. It wasn't until he stepped from his VW that he saw the truck driven by Sam Simon parked on the street.

Taki cleared his throat. "After Pearl Harbor, Grace's family was relocated from Pomona, California to a prison camp, to live in a horse stable. They left everything behind. Taking only what they could carry."

"My uncle was a proud man," Grace interrupted. "He was an American war hero in the First World War. In the internment camp they tortured him, accused him of being a spy. He felt dishonored. The Army claimed he committed suicide by biting off his tongue." She gripped her skirt tightly, forcing her hands down into her lap.

Jake put his notebook down on the doily covered arm of a chair. "Roosevelt condemned all of us Japanese Americans," he said softly, guessing the story to come.

Taki continued, "When her nephew, Uno was released at the end of the war he had changed. He lost his mother and father. His home had been looted and nearly destroyed. Their family business was gone."

79

"They were jewelers," Grace said, as she dabbed her eyes with a sleeve of her cotton dress. "My uncle had valuable jewelry and gold in a safe at their home."

"And that's what Snookey is looking for," said Jake.

Taki nodded. "We were afraid to tell you."

"How is Snookey involved?"

"He was one of the soldiers helping relocate families," Taki said. "They knew my uncle had hidden his valuables. They found them."

Picking up the empty teapot, Grace motioned to Geta and both retreated to the small kitchen.

Grace stood close to Geta, speaking in a low tone. "I notice June is escaping more often from the prison she lives in."

"She's in love with Woodrow, a taxi driver, but torn by her vows," Geta answered. "She's also angry, I don't know why."

"She's so young and beautiful to waste her life in that place," Grace said.

Shaking her head, Geta spoke in a whisper while tears formed in her eyes. "My daughter is confused. She ran from here very upset, saying she would never come back."

"Children," Grace said, shaking her head.

"Our tea must be coming from Tokyo," Taki shouted. "Our guest is waiting."

Hiding her annoyance, Grace gathered the tray, rattling it unnecessarily. "Coming husband," she answered.

She lifted the teak tray, and while looking at Grace asked, "Will Captain Semans and his wife return home soon?"

"When the weather improves. They enjoy California so much," Geta answered.

Grace bumped her hip onto the door just enough to swing it open. "We're coming," Grace said to Taki in a gentle voice.

As the tray was slid on the table, Jake glanced at his watch, asking another question. "How did you three escape internment?"

The three exchanged glances. Finally, Taki asked, "Will it help find what belongs to us?"

"It might."

Taki nodded to Grace. "Start at the beginning."

"We lived in Japan," Grace began. "Geta was a young girl when Captain Semans met her. He took her many places and bought her things. We were her only family and attempted to stop her from seeing him." Grace paused and squeezed Geta's hands. "One day she came to us, telling us she loved him and she was to have his child."

"He could not marry me," Geta interrupted. "He had a wife in America." I gave birth to our baby and named her June. She was three when Captain Semans took all of us to America."

"We were happy living with Grace's uncle in Pomona, California," Taki said. "We learned English and were planning to become American citizens."

Jake tapped his pen on his notebook. "Did you become citizens?" Jake looked at the three, huddled together on the couch. They quickly averted his eyes.

"That's why you called me, not the cops," Jake said. "You're afraid of the police."

"They distrust us," Taki said.

Jake looked to Geta. "Where's your daughter, June?"

"She lives in the monastery."

"How do I talk to her?"

"It is a cloistered order. They do not talk to anyone," Geta said.

Jake noticed the look that was exchanged between Grace and Taki. Did a signal pass?

After making several notes Jake sat silently for a moment before he spoke. "Then Pearl Harbor," Jake said.

"Ten months after we arrived in California our families were told we were to be taken to an internment camp." Grace stopped, taking a breath. "We had one day to secure our possessions." She held up one finger. Her hand shook.

"Ethnic cleansing is what it was." Jake's voice rose slightly. "Germans and Italians were included in that same order, which was not enforced. Before that this country banned marriage between Asians and white Americans. We weren't wanted, especially by California farmers who resented Japanese Americans."

Taki made a slight gesture with his hands. "White farmers wasted their land. We Japanese grow more on less ground."

"Pearl Harbor was an excuse to uproot us, take our land," Jake said. He waved his hand in the air. "I got off the subject. I need to know how you escaped."

Taki looked at Geta then spoke. "Captain Semans showed up the day we were to leave for the camp. He had a private plane. He brought us here. He wanted, June, his baby."

"Your aunt and uncle Koba stayed behind. Why?"

"The soldiers said they found radios and maps in my uncle's house. They accused him of spying," Geta said. "Captain Semans argued with the soldiers but to no avail. The American soldiers also took my aunt and their eighteen year old son, Uno, to a temporary camp in Pomona."

Jake held up his hand, stopping her. "I should have been told more about Jimmy Koba's family before I spoke to Uno. I got nothing from him. Kowing this may have helped."

"You were still a stranger to us," Taki said.

Jake repeated himself, "I should have been told." He inhaled, fighting off anger and frustration, wrestling with dropping the case. The trouble was, he needed the money. They paid his daily fee and inflated expenses in cash, without question.

82

"We regret doing so," Taki said.

"What was Jimmie Koba's address?" Jake asked.

"You have been there," Taki said. "It's the same as Uno's. He returned home and never left."

Taki waited for Jake to make notes and went on. "We left with Captain Semans. They stayed behind and were given a number and made to live in a horse barn."

"Like animals," Jake said. "Thought we were all spies."

"Animals lived better," Grace said. "We stayed with the Semans here, until the War Relocation Authority began looking for Japanese on the east coast."

"They sent us letters every week," Grace added.

Jake moved to sit on a footstool, where his feet rested on the ground. "What happened?" he asked.

"The Captain hid us in a monastery run by the Passionist Nuns," Geta answered. "He donated money to build it. We lived there until the end of the war."

"They wouldn't search there," Jake said, nodding.

Grace tried to hide a smile. "We lived there and worked in their gardens, but we never spoke to the nuns. All they do is pray and work."

Taki stood. "Speaking of gardens, I would like to…"

"It is near freezing," Grace said, quickly covering her mouth.

Taki glared at his wife. "It will only be a moment. I am sure our guest would like to see what our home was like in Tokyo." He flicked on the outside lights, illuminating several acres of heavily treed gardens.

Stepping out the door, Taki explained their employer, Captain Adam Semans, and his wife, built the lavish Japanese gardens to be a centerpiece of their elaborate parties.

Jake ran his hand over the many stone lanterns while he walked the twisting pathway.

83

Taki nodded to one of the Japanese lanterns. "They represent the simplicity of life."

"So far it hasn't been," Jake said while shaking his head.

"Our delicate flowers are sheltered in the green house," Taki said, as he hurried to catch up. "Despite their absence, we find comfort with our bridges, ponds and gazebos."

"I am honored. Please guide me," Jake said.

Taki bowed. "I shall show you a secret of our garden."

Jake returned the bow and waved his hand in a sweeping motion to continue. He wondered what secrets this family had. Did Taki use the garden as a ploy to bring him outside for another reason?

In a far corner of the garden they walked on a rough section of a cobble stone path, which twisted past a kidney shaped pond.

"These broken stones were designed to distract the visitor," Taki said, as they slowly walked, watching their steps on the uneven surface. When the path evened, they looked up.

"The garden rewards us with a surprise," Taki said, smiling broadly.

Jake stopped to admire the large teahouse. The roof's sharply upturned corners were tucked peacefully among lush cedars and drooping, bare willow branches.

Taki looked at Jake. "The tea room is our tradition. It is our place of total calm and relaxation."

Jake was already nodding his head. Knowing he was overdue at the circus he made sure Taki saw him glance at his watch.

Lowering his voice, Taki looked back to the main house. "I did not want to say this in there."

Jake pointed to a wood bench near an overhead light.

"Grace's uncle Koba was different from the rest," Taki began as soon as he sat.

"Different from who?

84

"Other Japanese in California."

"Why do you say that?" Jake asked, knowing his tug-a-war for answers was about to end. This was his chance to get to the whole story. He knew information had been withheld when he took the case, but he needed the job.

Taki hesitated, and lit a cigarette between cupped hands. "He wasn't afraid of American laws. Uncle Koba was a capitalist. He said great wealth was made by those who took great chances."

"He broke laws?"

"Only a few he thought unjust."

Jake sat quietly. His arms gripped his legs that he pulled close to his chest, trying to stay warm.

Taki dropped his half-smoked cigarette to the ground, twisting his shoe longer than needed on the stub. "What he did was for his family. He harmed no one." Taki stood, pacing, rubbing his hands together. "He owned gold."

"He was a jeweler," Jake said. "He could."

"Koba owned a great deal more than allowed. He wasn't using it for jewelry."

"He didn't turn it in?"

"Koba said the government thought Americans were hoarding gold, said it was an unfair law."

Jake looked up at Taki. "What did he do with it?"

"He kept that a secret."

"Did you see the gold?"

"He showed me once. Gold bars, coins, gold certificates from all over the world."

"Many Americans refused to turn it in," Jake said. "They moved it out of the country."

"Koba told me many times, that by breaking the law you also lose its protection." Taki lowered his head. "You see why we did not call the police. We wanted the gold for ourselves."

"That may be the reason he was killed," said Jake. He also knew he had another suspect to worry about.

85

Taki walked a few steps away. "We may have been greedy but we had nothing to do with Uncle Koba's death."

"Who else knew? Did he do business with anyone that might know?"

Taki thought a moment, walking toward the teahouse, his back to Jake. "There were a few people he did business with. Sometimes they came to the house. We did not know them...except for Captain Semans."

"Your Uncle Koba knew Captain Semans before this?"

"They did business together before we came from Japan." Taki answered.

"What kind?"

Taki ran his hand over one side of his face. "Not sure, something to do with buying farmland. He did not discuss with us."

"Just so I have this clear, Captain Semans lives here and fathered Geta's child. Now all of you live with him." Jake stopped. "Sorry for being blunt," Jake said, as he jumped from the bench, following Taki.

No answer came from Taki. He continued to walk with both hands shoved deep into his jacket pockets. His head was so steeply dropped, he nearly looked headless.

"What kind of business?" Jake asked.

"As I said farmland. That is all I know."

Jake hurried to write in his notebook. "California?"

Taki turned to face him. "What?"

"Was the land in California?"

"As far as I know."

"I need to know, is there more family in Pomona?"

"Uno's his only son." Grace said, suddenly appearing on the path.

"He's very bitter," Jake said. "He wouldn't speak to me."

"Or anyone," Grace said. "He thinks we are trying to steal his father's gold."

"I must try," Jake said. "I have someone in place, he may talk to."

As they walked near a wing of the Victorian home, Jake looked into one of the rooms. A light from a single lamp dimly lit the large study. "Is that your private room, Taki?"

Taki shook his head several times. "Captain Semans' private office, no one is allowed in, not even Geta."

Jake noticed a large, multi-colored map of California covering one of the walls. "He must like California?" Jake said casually.

"Oh, my, yes," said Grace. "He owns land there."

Jake nodded his head and continued to walk. Near an elevated planter he reached into the cold soil, smearing it on his hands and jacket.

Returning to the house, Jake appeared to then notice the dirt on his hands and jacket. "May I use a restroom?"

Entering the house, Grace pointed to the kitchen. "Borax soap is on the shelf."

Jake, for the first time that evening, smiled. "I shouldn't, food is prepared there."

Understanding, Taki showed him to a long hallway leading into the main house, pointing to a bathroom at the far end.

Jake bowed. "I may be a while." Again he showed Taki the dirt-smeared jacket. Walking down the hallway he sensed being watched. He turned back, they were.

Taki pointed down the hall. "Past the table."

Jake forced a smile and waved as he turned. He moved slowly looking for the room he wanted. Hearing Taki's footsteps on the wood floor move away, he hoped he was alone. The bathroom was to his right. He passed it and turned left. The door was unlocked. Opening it enough to squeeze through, he entered the dimly lit office of Captain Semans.

Chapter Fourteen

The tower bell in the monastery chimed once, introducing the day. Sister June Tamura awoke as usual and pulled on her black habit, cinching her belt over her small waist. A simple veil covered her black hair. As she did every day, she knelt beneath the crucifix in her room, whispering several Our Fathers and Hail Mary's. After an unhurried sign of the cross, touching her forehead, both shoulders and stomach, she stepped from her room, feeling like an intruder, joining a procession of nuns heading to chapel. Her bare feet, hidden under the tunic, stung from the piercing coldness of the tile floor that raced up her legs and spine. She tried to hide the shivers that came.

Falling into place, June bowed her head while pressing her palms together prayerfully. This morning, as every morning, she repeated to herself, pray and work, pray and work, as she obediently marched, unacknowledged. Clustered tightly, the flowing river of black robes swelled in size as rows of doors creaked open.

June would not return home, having learned the truth, which horrified her. Instead she would live in silence, at the monastery. The penance for her indiscretions, as well as her family's, would begin today.

They entered the chapel as a small group of sisters exited. For the last three years she had been a dutiful member of this prayer group, however, nothing was known of the others. June initially expected to have an encounter with God during the three hour period, instead, acquired the skill of sleeping as she knelt.

Today, that would change. Instead of kneeling, she intended to pray laying face down, pleading for forgiveness for herself and her family, before the life-sized Christ, who hung before them nailed by his feet and hands. As she genuflected, she dipped her fingers into the font in the chapel's foyer, blessing herself with holy water.

June approached the foot of the cross on her hands and knees, asking for strength, and to know the suffering He had endured for her sins.

Prone on the elevated oak floor, she forced her forehead into the wood, stretched out her arms and crossed her ankles.

Chapter Fifteen

Jake slipped into Captain Semans' private office. There was enough light, from the table lamps, he wouldn't need his pocket flashlight. He inhaled the rich smell of polished wood, admiring the carved arched beams of the high ceiling. The overt display of wealth disturbed him.

Knowing Taki would soon become suspicious, he had to move quickly. Standing at the door he glanced around the room. The deep carpet would cushion his footsteps, but would leave his tracks. He'd cover them when he left.

Bound volumes of county plat maps were stacked on a long worktable in the center of the room. Maps of Los Angeles and Orange Counties lay on a desk near a fireplace. He guessed the life-sized portrait hanging over it was Captain Adam Semans. Individual land tracts were shown with details of fence lines and pipelines, which crossed the properties. An oversized land survey map was pinned to a corkboard. From its top, a red grease pencil hung by a string.

Jake dragged a heavy wood chair through the carpet to the map and placed four books under its legs. Standing on it, he saw large sections of Pomona, California divided into thin red squares, each numbered. Aerial photos, curled at the edges, were pinned along the frame. The same was done, on an adjacent display, for Orange County. He looked at his watch. Several minutes had passed. After pulling the chair back, he carefully returned the feet into their original impressions. There he noticed the mahogany file chest. Just above his eye level, the drawer tag read, "Land Titles". Hopping back up on the same chair, Jake reached out his left hand, balancing against a bookcase. With the other, he pulled open the drawer. Tan file folders hung from metal tracks, arranged numerically. Jake looked back at the map's large numbered squares. He realized the files mated with those numbers. Somewhere in the house, a door slammed. He was out of time. After sliding the drawer closed, he jumped down and headed to the door.

He heard nothing in the hall as he pressed his ear to the door. Opening it a crack, he took a peek and moved into the hallway, quickly brushing dirt from his jacket.

Taki, Grace and Geta stood in the kitchen when Jake stepped in.

"It all came out," Jake said, forcing a grin.

Taki walked him to the side door, casually handing him an envelope. "This is what we owe you, so far."

Jake walked from the porch tapping his breast pocket, reassured the case was worth keeping and would be profitable.

Something, however, troubled him. The interview had given him more information but it had also opened more questions. There was more to learn about Grace's Uncle Koba, Captain Semans and Uno. A gut feeling told him there was more to the case than missing illegal gold. A trip to California was necessary. He needed someone to do grunt work, nothing dangerous.

Jake's VW cranked over and was running smoothly within a few minutes despite the bitter cold. Easing away from the curb, he watched his rear view mirror. The two were still there.

Circling the block, Jake returned to the Semans' house. The pick up truck remained there. He drove, head on, directly at the motionless truck. The high beams of his VW glared into the cab when he stopped within a few feet of its front bumper.

Through the truck's frosted-over windshield, he spotted two figures huddled together. He laughed as he dropped out of his mini-bus. "Need help?" he said, with a tone of arrogance.

The door slowly opened. "Won't start," Sam said.

"You might have frozen to death," Jake said, looking up into the cab.

"Came to see a patient," Doc mumbled.

"That's twice in two days I run into you," Jake said.

"Small world," Doc said.

Sam popped open the hood. "Battery's dead."

"No jumper cables, but I'll take you into town," Jake said, nodding to his VW.

* * * *

The VW bumped through several potholes on Main Street, parking in front of the always open, Town Talk Cafe.

"Buy me some coffee," Jake said, turning off the ignition.

Solitary diners hunched over a white Formica counter in the brightly lit room. A green-aproned employee flung a dingy, cotton mop under tables, not bothering to move the chairs. Doc dropped a few quarters on the counter, waving off a waitress who leaned against a doorway smoking.

"Coffee, we'll help ourselves," Doc said in a low voice.

"Don't forget the tip," she shot back.

Sam and Doc quietly stared into their coffee, finally pushing the cups away. The aroma of Pine-Sol and coffee clashed.

"I don't have much time," Jake said. "I'll get to the point."

He explained he was a private investigator, retained to locate stolen property thought to be hidden at the old airport. He also confirmed, Vince, Snookey, and someone unknown to him, pulled Doc's car from the river.

"You know what happened to my car?" Doc asked.

"I couldn't save Herkey's life, I tried," Jake said, shaking his head. "What I can do is help you clear that up and put Vince and Snookey away."

92

He stopped to look into his empty cup and left to refill it. When he returned, he went on. "In exchange, I'll need your help."

Doc looked at the dwarf in disbelief. "What do you want from us?"

"And why should we believe you?" Sam asked.

"The digging you witnessed the other day . . . Vince and Snookey are looking for something they stole from my client's family," Jake said. "It's not there. They're moving to another site."

"Where?" asked Doc.

"Don't know."

"What kind of help?" Sam asked.

Jake grinned, tugging at his tie, which reached halfway to his belt. "Nothing dangerous."

"We don't know you," Sam said. "You might work for Snookey."

Jake lifted his cup up in a toast. "And why believe me? I'm the guy who's bailed you two out twice. The third time will be when I explain to the cops what happened to that body you have frozen in your car."

Sam and Doc looked at one another. "We'll need time to think," Doc said.

"I'll tell you this." Jake sat up straight in the chair. "I suspect there is more to this case than my clients know. I can't leave the circus to prove it. There are a few things I need you to look into." Jake slid a photograph in front of them. "This is a photo of our three friends." Sam and Doc immediately recognized Snookey, Vince and Herkey, all in military fatigues.

"They were stationed in California," Jake said. "What I'm working on began there."

Jake noticed the time and jumped from the chair. "Give me a phone number, I'll call." After stuffing Doc's business card into his breast pocket, he rushed out.

Chapter Sixteen

The sharp tolling of the monastery bell floated over the valley's floor like silken threads. Its resonating tenor gradually breached June's solemn thoughts, as she lay prone before the crucifix.

The past three hours had granted her immunity from her earthly torment, cleansing her mind and soul. Gradually she pulled her deadened arms close to her chest, resting them there. Her extended legs remained rigid. She wanted to move them but couldn't. Her ankles twitched slightly. Pinpricks of pain tortured every muscle.

In the chapel's stillness, she heard the shuffling feet of nuns. Her forehead remained pressed against the polished wood floor, imprisoned by unseen shackles. Her chest, flattened, firm against the floor, struggled to expand and labored for air, her voice, she dare not use, muted to less than a whisper. June sensed, more than heard, another group enter. No help came. With hands pressing against the floor, she strained, only to lift herself enough to allow her lungs to expand slightly, partially filling with air. Pain was no longer bearable. Exhausted arms could no longer force her chest from the wood floor.

She saw herself running from Captain Semans home to Woodrow's car after she'd discovered her life and her family's lives had been a masquerade.

In the quiet came a faint rustle of garment, then a gentle touch to her shoulder. Two hands forced their way under her chest and waist, rolling her over.

June nearly choked as the first deep breath of air filled her lungs. Lying in the lone shadow of the crucifixion cross, her chest jerked up and down rapidly. The gentle smile of her rescuer calmed her as if it were a sedative. While resting in the arms of the smiling nun, their eyes met and held. Warm hands stroked the side of her face. The pain and tears ebbed as she gradually rose to her feet.

* * * *

With her head bowed, June walked along the chapel's narrow aisle. Uncertain of her wobbly legs, she guided one hand along the tops of pews. Rushes of nausea forced her to stop frequently.

Approaching her room, she thought of the relief of letting herself collapse in her cot.

Near her door, a hand touched her elbow. Surprised, June stopped. A soft voice from behind said, "Can we speak?"

At first she thought it was imagined, left over from her meditative state. June turned to the voice, answering immediately. "My room."

The visitor flashed a smile. "When?"

"After evening vespers."

"Sure." The other sister whispered, rushing off.

In her room, June dropped to her knees. No prayers came, only questions.

Chapter Seventeen

Jake slid from the raised seat of his VW, dropping to the frozen ground, expecting to see the big top being dismantled. Instead his pulse quickened at the site of Snookey and Vince standing inside the tent. Snookey stood with a forward lean, watching him, as if making up his mind. Jake fought off the urge to run.

"We're shutting down the show," Snookey suddenly yelled to him. "Vaults aren't here." He waved his arms towards the large pit. "Ran metal detectors over this a thousand times. Nothing's here, not a damn thing."

"The tent?" Jake asked.

"Tent stays. It'll hide this." Snookey spat at the hole in the ground.

Behind them, a wood door laid across two sawhorses. Vince hunched over the makeshift table removing the back panel from an oversized clock.

Jake eyed the round three-foot high timepiece. He knew its source. "That's a train station clock," he said to himself. He recognized it, having seen it during a search of Doc's home prior to Snookey torching the restored train terminal.

"Where did ya get it?" Jake asked.

"Don't matter," shouted Vince. "The owner won't need it."

"Yeah, his times up," Snookey said laughing.

Jake forced a laugh, a little harder than he should have and felt their eyes fall on him.

"After Herkey moved the vaults, he hid a map of the new location in the clock," Vince said, while sliding his hand from inside it, gripping a brown envelope. "He told us that before he died."

"He was a dumb bastard. Without the map he'd forget where he buried 'em," Snookey said.

Vince pulled a folded sheet from it and dropped the brown envelope to the table.

It read:

Silbaugh will deliver two vaults to the location. The California shipment is late. Delay completing the Koi pond and garden house.

Vince grunted, reading the note a second time. "Hell, we're looking for the wrong kind of vault."

Snookey grabbed the note. "I was looking for what you told me, vaults." Snookey jerked his head toward the large hole and tossed the note to the table. "Then what in hell are we looking for?"

"Burial vaults," Vince said, calmly, then laughed. "Silbaugh makes concrete burial vaults. You know…for dead people. They're on Morgantown Street."

"Water tight," Snookey said.

"Makes sense," Vince said, shoving the clock off the table, kicking it several times.

"I'll be there tomorrow," said Snookey, then asked, "The dates?"

"For what?" Vince asked.

"When you shipped the stuff from California?"

"Middle of May, '43," said Vince, after thinking for a moment. "I put everything on a train in Pomona, shipped it here to Herkey. He must' a decided to keep everything for himself and bought the vaults for storage." Vince's voice lowered. "Before we pull up stakes, I want Sam Simon and Doc Martin buried in the hole. Use our friend."

Jake stood below them, nearly forgotten, watching Vince pat Snookey on the cheek several times. Unnoticed, he removed the empty brown envelope from the table, sliding it into his breast pocket.

"Got that?" Vince said to Snookey. "Don't need 'em anymore. Find where Herkey moved the two vaults. A damn fishpond and a garden house, can't be that hard. You got me now?" Vince spoke with his back turned, leaving the tent.

Snookey stood frozen, holding the note. A growl came from the trailer. "Check on the cats, they're hungry," he shouted to Jake.

Jake looked up at an angry Snookey. He knew Snookey well enough to know that Vince would eventually pay for the insult.

"On my way to the slaughter house boss," Jake shouted over his shoulder.

Jake raced to a phone booth at The Nickel Inn to warn Sam and Doc.

* * * *

Pulling into the bar's parking lot, he thought of the two envelopes in his pocket. Quickly pulling them out, he looked at the two. The one he just removed from the table, which held the map and the other, that contained his payment from Taki and Grace Ozaki.

They were identical.

Chapter Eighteen

Doc glanced at the horses in the arena below as the phone rang.

"Don't answer," Sam shouted.

"Better, might be Lenora."

Remaining silent, Doc pressed the phone to his ear. Then covered the mouth piece and looked at Sam. "It's Jake, the midget."

Sam shuffled to the kitchen shaking his head. He sipped from a bottle of Iron City thinking of Jake's offer to settle the problem with Herkey's frozen body.

Not saying a word, Doc walked in and swung a chair from under the table. He dropped into it, rattling the photographs on the wall.

"That was quick. What did he want?" Sam asked, not looking up.

"Vince is definitely back. He and Snookey are behind all this, Herkey, the circus, the digging…this whole mess."

Sam took a long swallow. "You and me, we're going to the cops tonight. I don't want anymore of this."

"That's not all he said." Doc put his hand on Sam's arm. "Snookey's sending somebody to kill us. They just killed two other men. Remember the guys we saw in the tent with Snookey?"

Sam nodded and shut his eyes. "He already tried."

"Yeah, he did," Doc said. "Jake thinks this time he's sending a cop."

"Rizzo?" popped from Sam's mouth. "I never trusted him."

"Jake said it's a hunch. He's not sure."

"What's Jake want from us?"

"Wants us outta town."

"To where? Pittsburgh?"

"Too close, he'd find us." Doc stopped, hoisting a bottle of beer over his head, draining it. Some leaked, running down his chin. "There's something else."

"Always is," Sam said, leaning back.

"Jake thought Snookey was looking for a steel vault," Doc said, running his hand along his face. "Like a bank's."

"In the tent."

"Yeah, turns out it's a burial vault. Two of 'em."

"Wants us to find them?" Sam asked.

"No. He knows they came from Silbaugh's."

"Good." Sam stared at the ceiling. "Then we'll leave town."

Doc nodded. "We'll take Lenora up on her offer to go to California. But first he wants us to find out where Silbaugh delivered 'em in 1943."

"That's fourteen years ago," Sam said, getting up from the chair, walking to the observation window. The arena's lights blinked out, a row at a time. Sam turned back to Doc. "Burial vaults, you're a doctor, should be easy for you."

"Meaning?"

"Dead people, doctors, burial vaults, you're in the same business."

Doc eyed Sam. "I know Silky, the owner. It won't be easy. He keeps that private, but I can get it. We'll need Lenora."

"Then, we leave town?" Sam asked.

Doc nodded.

"For how long?"

"Jake thinks a week, then he'll wrap this up, if we find out where they were shipped."

* * * *

Silbaugh Vaults sat alone at the top of Morgantown Street. Matching life-size angels with wings extended, flanked a concrete burial vault near its entrance. A lawn, so green it looked painted, sloped away from the building's red brick façade.

100

Lenora almost laughed at the gaudy display as she steered her DeSoto over a small bridge, through a set of white gates, leading to the parking lot. Doc adjusted his tie and nervously smoothed down his red silk vest. He grunted and twisted, turning to look back at Sam. "You and Lenora act normal. Tell them you're here to buy a vault." He winked at Sam and patted Lenora on the shoulder. "I'll do the rest. This'll be a cinch."

The single glass door opened, although a 'closed' sign hung from a window. A bell, sounding like it came from a bicycle, greeted them. Lenora spotted the wire attached to the door, tracing it until it disappeared into the wall near the high ceiling.

Doc winked, "They know we're here."

Lenora coughed several times and retrieved a magazine from a table, waving it at a cloud of cement dust hanging in the air.

All three stepped carefully onto the waiting room's ragged and duct tape patched maroon carpet.

Before anyone greeted them, a heavy thud shook the wall of an adjacent room. They rushed through the double doors into an adjacent larger office. Someone was sprawled on the floor, kicking the wall. Their bound arms tightly secured to their ankles, contorted them into a fetal position.

"Silky!" Doc shouted. He dropped to his knees, beginning to pull the pillowcase from his face. "What in the..."

"Leave it on," a voice said from the doorway.

Sam and Lenora turned to see the red and black-faced clown, dressed in bib-overalls, aiming a gun at Doc.

Each remained silent, not removing their eyes from the gun. Snookey moved into the room, shifting the pistol to his left hand. Looking at Lenora, a slight smile rose in the corners of his black painted lips. "You brought a friend." He shook the gun at her. "Turn around."

She stood still.

101

Snookey looked down at Silky, ramming his boot into his side. "Now."

She turned her back to him.

"Drop the coat."

She let it slide from her shoulders to the floor. He walked close to her, inhaling deeply, guiding his fingers along the collar of her dress. He gently lifted her hair, letting it fall through his fingers.

"What a pity," he said, shaking his head, looking down at Doc.

"What do you want?" Sam asked, stepping toward him.

Snookey took a few quick steps, putting his mouth and gun within inches of Sam's ear. "What do I want?" It sounded like a hiss. While looking at Lenora, he stepped away from Sam. "I want you two in the shop." He grinned at Lenora.

Doc struggled getting to his feet. "What about her?" he asked.

"Nice tie. Give it to me," Snookey said.

He grabbed it from Doc, and threw it at Lenora's boots. "Tie her ankles," he said to Sam. Snookey pulled a roll of electrical tape from his pocket, tossing it to Sam. "Now her wrists."

Sam finished tying Lenora, leaving her on the concrete floor next to Silky. Snookey poked at Sam and Doc, forcing them through a door into the shop.

Rows of large portable concrete mixers were scattered throughout the shop. Close to each sat wood forms, coated with a thin crust of concrete.

Snookey gave them another shove. "All the way to the back."

The deserted shipping area was filled with concrete burial vaults, stacked four high, each separated with wood four by four's. Two open vaults sat on a large flat bed trailer, backed into a loading bay.

102

"What do you know? This looks good. One for both of ya," Snookey laughed. "Get in."

"In those?" Sam said, staring at the cold rectangular boxes.

Doc edged his hand close to his jacket pocket where he carried a low profile handgun.

"Face down," said Snookey.

Doc was about to reach for his Luger when Snookey pressed his handgun into Doc's neck. "Take your hand off it."

Snookey removed the 9mm, laughing.

"Now, climb in." Snookey gave Doc a push. "You wanted to see the circus? I'm gonna take you."

* * * *

Lenora struggled, twisting her leg and foot inside her boot. Feeling it give slightly, she yanked again, harder. Nothing budged. Over and over she pushed and pulled her leg inside of her boot. The prosthetic loosened slightly. She felt it wobble. A dull ache at the end of her leg throbbed. Trying again, she took a deep breath, knowing the pain would be sudden.

In her mind's eye, she saw herself falling, that day, from her mount. Her boot stuck in the stirrup wrenching her foot from her ankle. Unable to move, excruciating pain ripped through her leg. Her horse lay nearby, tangled in the jumble of shattered fencing. She watched as the gun rose to his skull. His head dropped to the turf silently.

Counting to three, gritting her teeth, yanking and twisting, the prosthetic foot worked free. Her leg pulled easily from the boot and she kicked it aside. Pushing up from the floor, she hopped across the room to her purse. Opening it with her hands bound behind her was difficult. She rummaged through the purse searching for her pocketknife. Unable to find it, she turned the purse over,

103

dumping the contents to the floor. She fell to her knees, fighting off panic, and spotted the tangerine bone handle of her Case mini-knife. Jabbing and poking, she cut her hands free of the tape.

Silky lay nearby struggling. Lenora pulled the sheet cover from his head and peeled duct tape from his mouth and cut his hands free.

"Call the police," Lenora said, hopping to the large double door Snookey fled through.

Stopping to rest, she held her breath, easing one of the doors open. Not hearing or seeing anything, she ventured into the shop.

As the door swung shut, Silky sat up gasping for air, his voice weak. "He cut the phone lines."

Using the maze of stacked vaults as cover, Lenora guided herself, hopping through the shop, looking and listening for signs of Snookey. Pausing, she thought of returning for her prosthetic foot and boot but quickly dismissing it as a waste of time.

Pain charged through her good leg. Rapidly fatiguing calf and thigh muscles slowed her pace to a shuffle. Her stump, dragging behind, forced her to brace her arms against the vaults for support.

Tottering, near collapsing, and fighting off panic, she spotted a short stool mounted on casters. Attached to it was a leather tool belt. No longer able to stand, she dropped to her knees and crawled to it. With the last amount of energy remaining, she pulled herself onto a sitting position and pushed herself behind the unfinished vaults. She hoped to rest and listen for telling sounds. None came, only dull clanking from the roof's exhaust fans.

The trembling in her legs subsided enough for her to continue. Relying on stealth, she planned to approach Snookey from behind. The hammer, which hung from the tool belt, would be targeted for the back of his skull. She went into action, quietly pushing herself, using her stump

104

and good leg, maneuvering through a labyrinth of stacked vaults.

Spotting blood on the floor near her, she stopped. Her blood had seeped through the cotton hose used to protect the stump. Taking a peek at the raw skin, she shuddered and pulled the bloodstained sock back into place. She removed the boot from her good foot, sliding it over the inflamed stump for protection. For the first time since the accident, she was thankful for the prosthetic foot. It may save all their lives.

Nearing exhaustion, she slumped over, resting her chin on her knees. Staring at the ground, she saw it for the first time. Her hands, foot and stump were coated with it. The stool's metal casters had cut thin, stringy lines through the fine powdery cement dust covered floor.

After pushing herself back to the double doors Snookey used to escape to the warehouse, she found a faint trail of shuffled footsteps leading to the loading dock.

Lenora spotted Snookey as she neared the dock. His back was to her, standing on the edge of an open burial vault. Rolling closer, she saw there were two vaults loaded on a flat bed truck. Snookey aimed his pistol down into one of the vaults. Rising from her stool, she grabbed the hammer from the tool belt.

"I called the police," she screamed. At the same time, she hurled the hammer, end over end, at Snookey.

Surprised, he turned to her as the hammer grazed off his shoulder, knocking him off balance. Losing his footing, he fell onto the edge of the truck's wood side guards, hanging there for a moment, finally dropping to the bay's concrete floor.

Lenora fell from the force of her throw. She crawled several yards to the dock's edge. Looking down, Snookey laid twisted, un-moving, his painted on smile and cruel eyes glared at her. She fought off the urge to carry on her revenge against the defenseless assailant.

"Doc, Sam, it's me," she shouted.

Her words echoed back as the only response.

After climbing to a standing position, she found Sam and Doc lying face down inside the vaults.

They rolled back and forth, shaking their heads, making muffled noises, through their gags. Lenora hopped over the dock bumpers, onto the truck's wood deck, jarring to a stop against its side rails. Leaning into each vault, she cut their taped hands and feet.

Doc stood, brushing his jacket and shaking his head. "What happened?" He looked to the ground. "I'll be go to hell."

Near the truck's rear tires, the clown's red-and-black face stared blankly at them. His arms sprawled over his head, the gun, just out of reach.

"Said he was gonna bury us alive," Sam said. "He was standing on top the vault when he fell."

Sam retrieved Snookey's gun, aiming it at him while Doc checked his pulse.

"Still alive," said Doc.

"Leave him. He was planning to kill us," Lenora said.

"We came to get an address," Sam said, pointing up at a row of file cabinets. "Looks like a place they'd keep old shipping records. Give me a minute."

He climbed the wood stairs to a loft overlooking the shop.

Sam moved past a long row of tall, olive colored file cabinets, each drawer tagged with a year. Following the sequence, he found two drawers marked 1943.

"Get up here, Doc!" he yelled, while straining to pull open a drawer. "Give Lenora the gun."

Upstairs, Doc looked at the overstuffed drawer and yanked out an armful of files. "Too damn many of our boys came home from the war in coffins."

106

Doc glanced back at the truck Snookey remained motionless. "Let's get this done. I need to take Lenora to my office."

"We're looking for somebody that bought two vaults at the same time," Sam said. "Look for two vaults delivered to the same place that's not a cemetery."

Neither spoke while ruffling through white and yellow sheets of musty, tissue-thin paper.

"Aha, if there's more than one, they wrote it bigger and circled it, like this," Doc said, holding up a paper.

Both took time to glance down, checking on Lenora. She sat quietly, aiming a gun at Snookey's prone body.

Finished with the top drawer, they pulled out the last one, K - Z.

Standing at each side of the file, Sam and Doc hurried, haphazardly flipping through pages. "Two's the most anybody ordered," said Doc. "They went to the cemetery in Hopwood."

Sam nearly missed the large circled "2" in the center of the page as he fanned through the file marked "S". Moistening his thumb, he retreated back several pages.

"Hold it, got something." Sam ran his fingers down the page and stopped. "Adam Semans, same address we followed Jake to."

A scream and a gunshot came from the loading dock. Sam grabbed the file as they rushed to the stairs. Snookey was dragging his injured leg, hunched over and limping, attempting to run to a beat-up jeep.

Lenora lay on the ground, gripping her stump of her leg. "I looked away he grabbed me . . . I tried to shoot . . . he took the gun. "

A moment later the Jeep, almost leisurely, drove past them. The large tarnished red and black face filled the window. "You're all dead," he shouted speeding off.

Chapter Nineteen

Bright fluorescent light spilled from Doc's exam room while he finished wrapping Lenora's injured stump.

"It'll be tender. You won't be able to wear your prosthetic for a while. Otherwise, you're fine," Doc warned her.

Lenora sat on the edge of the exam table, eyeing Doc, "I can't stay in bed while this heals. I'm planning to go see my new horse in California."

"Try these." He handed her a pair of crutches that he pulled from behind the door. "Just a few days."

"I hate doctor's offices, you know that," Lenora said, sliding from the table.

As she did, the phone in Doc's private office rang. He stopped at door and leaned against the doorframe. "I'm closed today, everybody knows that. Let it ring."

After several sharp rings it stopped, leaving behind deep echoes.

"Might be important," said Sam.

"The one in the corner…when it rings, that's important," Doc said, pointing to a red phone.

It could have been a thunderclap that shook the office when the red phone suddenly rang with a dull clink, as if the bell was silenced with a wad of cotton. Doc flashed a look of alarm while he hurried to the phone. He stood over it, not touching it, deciding. After several long rings, he lifted the handset. The caller spoke first. Doc cupped his hand over the mouthpiece. "It's Jake." He dropped into a chair, wedging the phone between chin and shoulder, rapidly scribbling notes. After nodding several times, Doc hung up and stared off at nothing while tapping his pen on the paper. Finally looking up, he faced Lenora and Sam, sitting quietly across from him.

"He called from a pay phone at the Nickel Inn." Doc exhaled and dropped his pen. "We need to leave town.

Snookey plans to kill us tonight. Jake said don't pack, there isn't time."

"We'll go to California," Lenora said, propping herself up on the wood crutches. "We leave now. No arguments."

"Sold," said Doc. "Jake asked us to check on someone there."

Lenora struggled on her crutches. "I'll call my pilot," she shouted, hobbling to the nurse's office.

Sam waved a large file folder in front of them. "Remember why we went to Silbaugh's?"

"The two burial vaults," Doc said. "Let's have a look at those shipping papers that nearly got us killed."

Sam dropped the folder on Doc's desk. "They were shipped to Adam Semans' home, the house we followed Jake to."

"He's a rich man," Doc said. "Why hide something in a burial vault? He's got banks for that."

Sam ran his fingers along the faded page where Semans' address appeared. "How's Semans involved in this?"

"Who signed for 'em?" Doc asked. "Because they were delivered to his address doesn't mean he ordered 'em. Does it?"

"Can't tell." Sam nodded, understanding.

"Can't tell! What's that mean, can't tell?"

"Can't read the carbon copy," Sam said, holding the tissue like paper to the light. "Who ever signed this didn't press hard enough, only a few thin lines show up."

"I might be able to do something." Sam took out a pocketknife and grabbed a pencil from Doc's desk.

"Not now you won't." Lenora leaned on her crutches in the doorway. "I just got off the phone with my pilot. Planes ready in two hours. You two can..." She stopped and raised her wood crutch, pointing to the front window. "Someone just walked up to the entrance..."

A knock rattled the glass door, before she finished.

"I'll see who it is." Doc whispered.

Lenora shook her head. "This isn't good."

"There's a back door," Doc said, pointing to a hallway.

"I took a peek," Sam said. "Cop car's parked across the street."

Doc looked at Sam. "Rizzo!" they both said.

"Remember what he did at the train station," Sam said.

"I thought he was gonna shoot us," Doc said.

"We can't run. My cars out front," Lenora said.

"He knows I'm here, lights are on," said Doc. "He's got keys to all the buildings."

Another knock shook the door.

"He's checking on us," said Doc. "Better if he only found me here." He guided Lenora and Sam to a back door. With a jerk, he opened it, frigid air rushed in. "Don't make a sound," Doc whispered, tossing them a blanket. "Keep each other warm."

"Hold on. I'm on the way," Doc shouted toward the front door. He quickly stepped into an exam room, dumping Lenora's used bandages and gauze into the trash. He also turned off the heater.

The door shook again.

"Hold your horses, I'm on the way."

Rizzo stood at the door, shifting his weight from one foot to the other. Doc stepped to the glass door. Unlike in the past, he was no longer greeted with a smile.

"Saw the light. You alone?" Rizzo asked.

"Just got here," Doc said through the glass.

"Working late?"

"Little bit."

Rizzo grabbed the handle. "Mind if I come in?"

Doc felt his pulse quicken. He twisted the dead bolt, opening it with a loud click.

Rizzo pushed the door open. "Cold in here."

"Said I just got here."

"Yeah, you did."

110

"Now what?" Doc said, not offering to move from the entry.

"Can I look around?"

"For what?"

Without answering, Rizzo stepped past Doc.

Doc smelled bourbon on his breath.

"Take just take a second."

"Your shotgun, you didn't bring it this time."

"Do I need it?" Rizzo said.

Doc remained in the entry while Rizzo walked down the hallway, his arms swinging, unnaturally bowed, around an array of gear hanging from his duty belt. Before looking into the first exam room he slid out his baton and looked inside without entering. The next was not searched. Instead, he stopped in the hall, tapping the thermostat with his nightstick. "You didn't turn on the heater."

From down the hall, Doc answered, "Wasn't gonna be here long."

"I see." Rizzo took a quick glance at Doc and then stepped into the last exam room.

"Expecting a patient?"

"No."

"This table has a sheet on it. The others didn't."

"Shouldn't be, nurse must have done that." Doc felt his pulse pounding in his temples. Hoping Rizzo over-looked the trashcan.

Rizzo leaned over, poking his baton into the over-hanging sheet. He slowly pulled it off the table. Rolling it up, he smirked, tossing it on the padded tabletop leaving the room. "Took it off for 'ya." He glanced to the end of the hall. "Back door?"

"You know it is," Doc reached into his pocket for the keys. "Need to look?"

Rizzo turned away not answering. He stopped in the narrow hallway. "We're still looking for Herkey. Any ideas?"

111

Doc fought the urge to take a swallow, knowing Rizzo was measuring his reactions.

"How 'bout your house?" Rizzo asked.

"What?"

"Your house, the fire. Any news."

"They think it's arson, but the insurance will cover it unless they prove it's me." Doc heard himself fumble for words, knowing he said too much.

Rizzo exaggerated taking a long deep sniff. "You made coffee," he said, looking around the office.

"Yesterday's. Just warmed it. Want some?"

He waved away the offer, showing a faint grin, then slid his nightstick into its loop. "You're not going anywhere, are you?"

"Wish I could." Doc forced a laugh.

Opening the door to leave, Rizzo turned back. Their eyes met in a stare. "How'd you like the circus?"

"Didn't care for the clown." Doc's voice was stern.

Shadows of a leafless tree fell across Rizzo's face, tattooing it with thin stripes as he started to speak. Words hovered at the edge of his lips, then he nodded, taking one last look and walked to his cruiser.

After locking the door, Doc stood with both hands braced against the steel frame. "You bastard, you're scouting for Snookey."

Rizzo took one last look and walked to his car.

Watching for a moment, Doc saw Rizzo hunched over lighting a cigarette. After a few quick puffs, he picked up the radio's handset.

Doc rushed to the back door. Lenora and Sam stood shivering behind a dumpster. Once the door opened they hurried in. Within minutes, the squad car rolled through the back alley.

Chapter Twenty

This evening Sister June's pace was faster than usual as she returned to her room after vespers. Her thoughts, throughout the day, were of the mysterious nun who rescued her at morning chapel. More puzzling to her, the nun asked to meet this evening.

She removed her veil, letting her hair fall to her shoulders as she entered her room. Only imagining what it looked like, she slid her fingers against her scalp, lifting her silky black hair away from her neck, letting it fall repeatedly. After a final shake she was satisfied.

Unsure why she felt the way she did, June sat on her cot longing for the visitor. Twisting strands of hair around her fingers, she reflected back several days ago, before she returned to the monastery.

She was still in her ball gown early that morning, and had been searching for a letter opener. Captain Semans' private office door stood wide open. Unable to resist, knowing it was forbidden ground, she looked on his desk. A drawer had not been pushed closed. In the far back were several stacks of envelopes tied together with heavy cord. Looking at them, she saw they were written in her mother's hand in Japanese, all addressed to Captain Semans.

Confused but curious and eager to see what her mother, Geta, a common housekeeper in his house had to say to a wealthy man, she pulled the knot loose, letting the letters fall loose in her lap. Stopping, realizing what she was about to do, she hurriedly gathered them together, re-tying the bundle. After tapping the letters several times, she placed them back into the drawer. As she slid the drawer, about to push it into a locked position, she yanked it open.

The letters had been arranged in chronological order by the postmark. As she expected, the early letters were cordial, praising him for the generous gifts to her and to her aunt Grace and uncle Taki while Captain Semans visited

Japan. She knew the Captain was well educated and had learned to read and speak Japanese during his yearlong visit. After reading several more, she fell back into the chair. Her fingers twitched slightly, holding the thin page in her lap. Each had grown in tenderness, her mother expressing more emotion and affection than she had ever witnessed. Reluctantly, she realized these were love letters from her mother. In the final letter, her mother informed him she was carrying his baby.

The thought exploded in her, she gasped for air in the suddenly dry, arid room. Captain Semans is my father. The next thing she recalled was running to the jitney driven by Woodrow.

June jerked at the faint knock as the wood door opened slightly. June quickly stood. Her guest eased into the room, gently shutting the door behind her back, keeping June in view.

Was this an angel? June asked herself as she looked into the deep blue eyes that had comforted her earlier this morning as she had lain on the chapel's floor.

Hello," the visitor whispered.

Their eyes met for an instant. June took a deep breath, not knowing what to expect, and answered, "Hi."

The shy visitor kissed a bulky, black rosary, wrapped loosely around her right hand, then blessed herself with the sign of the cross. Both quietly stared into each other's eyes. June feared her caller regretted the visit and was about to depart. After a moment, her guest reached over her head, removing her veil. Her face flushed red as straight silver hair fell from beneath. June extended her hands. They came together, embracing. With a slight nod, she guided her visitor to the cot. They sat together, each with their hands folded in their laps looking at the gray wall in front of them.

"You look much better," the visitor said with a dulled voice, deadened by years of silence.

114

"I am."

"Has your pain grown less?"

"Some. More prayer is needed."

"I prayed for you."

"Thank you," June said, patting her visitor's hands.

The visitor smiled. "You work in the kitchen."

June held up her hands as if she were squeezing dough. "I make bread,"

The nun's eyes twinkled as she laughed, quickly covering her mouth.

"I'm June."

"Irma, Sister Irma." Her voice cracked.

"I'm glad you came."

Irma's gentle face brightened.

Irma slid her hand from her lap to touch June's knee. "What troubles you?"

"My family," June said.

After a silence, Irma grasped June's hands. "Where is it you wish to be?"

June hesitated. "Nowhere."

Irma held June's hands in both of hers. "I think there is. We all have left behind another life."

"I'm happy here."

"You must also be happy somewhere else," Irma whispered, as if someone would overhear. "You've been sneaking out of the monastery."

The words blasted in June's ears.

"I have asked forgiveness."

Irma remained silent for a moment, finally asking, "Have you confessed this to a priest?"

June shook her head slightly.

"You haven't taken your final vows. Perhaps this is not the place for you."

"I'll never leave again," June said, raising her voice, then catching herself.

Irma shifted, turning to face June. "Tell me what worries you."

"My family…they've committed great sins and have deceived me. I can't face them."

Irma bowed her head.

Outside, the tower bell rang, puncturing the long silence that followed.

Irma eased her hands from June and rose to her feet. "I'm sorry, I need to go. I'll be missed."

June felt her hands shaking, standing beside Irma. "Please come again, when you can. It helps to talk."

Chapter Twenty-One

The twin engine, Douglas DC 3 stood at the doors of the private hanger. A fuel truck pulled from under its long wing, passing the approaching car.

"My former husband, the dear he now is, rarely uses the plane," Lenora said, stepping from her DeSoto. "It's part of my settlement." Her words were nearly drowned out by a distant plane taking off into the dull blackness.

Entering the main cabin, they met the pilot and copilot. Both appeared to have stepped out of a Marine recruiting poster.

The pilot poked his head out the plane's door. "No luggage?" he asked, before he pulled it shut.

"Last minute decision," Lenora said. "We'll pick up what we need at the ranch."

"LA was seventy-five today. You won't need winter clothes," the pilot said, turning to leave.

"How long will it take?" Lenora quickly asked.

"Maybe twenty hours, with a light head wind and a couple fuel stops. Figure we'll land around six, California time."

The spacious interior, originally designed to carry thirty-two passengers, accommodated ten in an open lounge area. The centerpiece, a small kitchen and a well stocked bar, divided the cabin.

Lenora leaned against one of the many white leather armchairs, extending her arms. "What do you think of my ex's version of the Sistine Chapel? And don't pretend you didn't notice."

A mural scene of white sandy beaches lined with drooping palms and thatched huts done in soft pastels wrapped the entire cabin. Bare breasted native girls frolicked in sand and gentle surf of azure water. A blue sky, dotted with cotton ball clouds, arched overhead.

"Could be worse," Sam said, dropping his lanky frame into a chair.

Doc whistled softly. "Tasteful, we've never been in an airplane. Is this common?"

Lenora laughed. "It's an artistic mortal sin."

"Repaint it," Sam said.

"Can't. He did it to spite me."

"I find it soothing," Doc said.

"That's neat," Lenora answered, waving him off. She winked at Sam. "I, myself find the stars and moon relaxing on a long flight. It can be romantic."

Within moments they sped down the runway, lifting off over a ragged field that had been strip mined, now treeless and barren. The lights of Pittsburgh were soon under them as they banked west. Doc looked at Lenora, she was already asleep. The stump of her leg hung over the arm of the recliner.

The landing gear locked into place with a jolt as they climbed slowly and leveled off at fourteen thousand feet. Doc helped himself to food and drink from the amply stocked teakwood bar. The cabin lights dimmed to a soft yellow blush. The only sound came from the constant drone of the engines, trying to tear themselves from the plane's wings.

Uneasy, Doc sat rigid, leaning his head against the small rectangular window, watching veils of misty clouds float by the night's copper-colored moon. Below, scattered patches of light appeared like islands, to flicker in the stillness of murky darkness and then slid away. Half dozing, with partially closed eyes, he watched the pilot exit the cockpit and move through the cabin. He pulled pillows and blankets from a hidden compartment, piling them in an unoccupied chair. Doc watched him walk to the rear of the plane where he unlocked a narrow door and went inside. A few minutes later, a toilet flushed. Doc felt the pilot's eyes inspecting him as he silently passed.

118

The cabin temperature cooled. Doc leaned his head against the small pillow he wedged between two seats and pulled a blanket over his shoulders. The monotonous hum of twin propellers eventually relaxed him, something the liquor failed to do. Encased in the metal cocoon, his mind drifted back to just over a week ago. His lost Cadillac had mysteriously returned with Herkey Dixon's dead body in the trunk, which he now stored in a freezer. His home had been burned to the ground. He and Sam were nearly eaten by circus tigers, and now they were working with a Japanese midget private eye. Flying to California to...

Doc jerked, his heavy, crystal glass slipped in his hand. By reflex, he gripped it tightly before it fell.

The DC 3 rocked several times, then leveled. The pilot's reassuring voice came over the intercom. "Nothing to worry about, just a few rough spots."

Finishing his drink, and too exhausted to pull himself up, he lodged the heavy tumbler between his leg and the chair's arm. The name, Uno Koba, popped into his mind. Twenty-four hours ago, he had not known the name. Now he was flying three thousand miles to talk to him, about the death of his father, Jimmie Koba. Uno's father, died in a World War II internment camp. How was this connected to the excavation done by Snookey and Vince at the abandoned military airport?

Doc looked out the small window, seeing only blue-black nothingness. The plane rocked and shuddered a few more times. This time, the pilot didn't bother to reassure his passengers.

Chapter Twenty-Two

The silver DC 3 glided over rolling hills of the Central California coast toward a vast expanse of open field. The glistening Pacific Ocean was off to the west. At the small airstrip, two men dressed in Levis, work shirts and scuffed western boots watched the plane approach the grassy runway. Their sharply creased, white straw, cowboy hats were tilted back revealing blanched foreheads normally shaded by the wide brims.

The plane dipped below the crest of a mountain, blending in with the white rocky cliffs, and touched down smoothly on the worn out grass runway. Before long it rolled past the two men, sending up plumes of white dust. At the far end of the runway the DC 3 turned, taxiing past several open-faced hangers and an idle steamroller. It rolled to a stop near a whitewashed structure that had once been a railroad boxcar, now the airfield's terminal. On its flat roof was a faded sign, Flying M Ranch Airfield, Los Olivos, California.

The two observers waited until the twin propellers shuddered to a stop before they rolled the short stairs to the rear of the plane. The door swung inward at the same time the steps arrived. Sam stood in the doorway, taking a deep breath of warm California air. A calloused hand shot out to him.

"Tom Miller. Nice to meet ya." He said his name as if it were one word.

* * * *

Before Sam answered, Tom introduced Mitch, his ranch foreman. Both of their faces were hidden by the shadows of their big hats.

Sam turned back, seeing Doc assisting Lenora to the plane's door. Tom Miller quickly rushed inside to help. Without asking, he lifted her in his arms, carrying her from the plane to a waiting open-air Jeep. Sam gathered the

120

crutches and stepped slowly down the stairs, then hurried to catch up.

Lenora looked off into the distance, to a set of stables. "Where's my horse? When do I get a look?"

"How 'bout right now?" Tom smiled, then glanced at Lenora, and turned the Jeep sharply, heading toward a cluster of neatly maintained stables which looked more like roadside motels set among jutting white boulders and live oak trees.

Sam grabbed the seat in front of him, fighting to remain in the backseat.

The Jeep rolled to a stop under a cluster of tall oaks. "We keep our three year olds here," Tom said.

Lenora, using her crutches, swung herself to the stable. The Dutch door was half open. Approaching, she shouted, "Where's my baby?" Once she spotted him, she turned back to Tom. "He looks lean. How's his training?"

"Have a look," he said. "You're the vet. You tell me." He tipped his hat, grinning at Lenora. "We'll throw a saddle on him in the morning. Can you ride?"

She looked at Doc who held up his hands in defeat.

Tom swung open the lower half of the door. Lenora abandoned her crutches, hopping into the stable. She ran her hand down the front of the thoroughbred. "Look at that deep chest, plenty of room for the lungs and heart to grow."

Tom winked at her. "I smell a Triple Crown in this one."

"Be serious," Lenora said laughing, guiding her hands along the horse. "Shoulders have nice angles. He's a show jumper. It's in his blood."

The clang of a bell got their attention.

"Dinner," Tom said.

* * * *

After dinner, all four sat in a spacious wood paneled den, which doubled as Tom's office. Cedar rafters crossed twenty feet above them in a steeply pitched roof. Dead eyes

121

mounted into the heads of brown bears, mountain lions and deer, stared sightless into the room. Behind a curved oak desk hung a gallery of ornately framed and matted photographs and paintings of horses and riders. Lenora appeared in many, showing her trophies and ribbons.

The houseman entered, pouring each guest a fresh glass of California white wine.

Lenora hung up the phone. "Our clothes will be delivered from Santa Barbara tomorrow."

Tom finished his log entries and closed the ledger on his desk as the phone rang. He picked up on the first ring. "Now's a good time. Bring him over," he said and hung up.

Sam raised his eyebrows, looking at Lenora.

Holding up her hand she smiled. "It's okay. Its Tom's foreman, Mitch, is bringing over your tour guide."

Within a few minutes, the back door opened. Mitch walked in and dropped into a deep chair, throwing one leg over its arm. Standing next to him, hat in hand, was a tall, slender young man wearing a snug fitting suit jacket buttoned in the middle over a washed-out pair of bib overhauls. His deep-set, brown eyes never left his shoes.

"This is Hector. He'll take you to Pomona," said Mitch.

Tom walked to Hector and patted him on the shoulder. "One of our best riders. Aren't you, Hector? He started here as a groom."

Hector managed a small grin, looking up only long enough to make quick eye contact with everyone.

"He's from Pomona and speaks English and Spanish." Mitch paused, looking at his boss. "Should he drive one of the ranch's cars?"

"Yeah, take the new Ranch Wagon. Break it in, why don't 'ya."

Sam sat back, quietly wondering where this was leading them. More trouble, he guessed.

Chapter Twenty-Three

Jake Ozaki jerked awake from a troubled sleep in the back of his VW Mini-bus. Hovering on the edge of consciousness, he heard Snookey shouting his name. At first, it felt like a dream, like the others, blurred faces surrounded him, spinning rapidly on a carousel. Snookey appears from the dizzying blur of up and down horses, pulling the trigger of a crossbow. The steel bolt came at him in flashes of stop-and-go slow motion. Its feathers rotating, air rippling in its wake. He swung his arm wildly in front of his face, grabbing the cold metal of the arrow.

Jake sat up, his face wet with sweat. The pistol he kept under the pillow was in his hands, gripped by its long barrel, pressed to his forehead. His dreams came often, progressing farther each time. He was unsure where they separated from reality, or if they did.

This time, his finger rested on the trigger.

Snookey stood at the rear window of the VW pounding the glass. "Time to work. I got a plan."

Jake pulled open the curtain. "Okay, okay, hold your horses."

"We're gonna set up one of the balloons."

"Why?" Jake grumbled, jumping down from his car. He turned up his jacket collar against the sharp wind while running to catch up with Snookey.

"Damn good day to fly," Snookey finally answered. "It's gonna be clear and warm, in the fifties."

Jake's pace quickened. His short, squatty legs scrambled through the deeply rutted field to the maroon trailers parked alongside the big top tent.

His hands shook, inserting the key into the heavy padlock. "This is a bad idea, Snookey," he shouted, swinging the wide doors open.

From it they carried a large wicker basket, and set it in the open field. Next to come was the deflated balloon, folded and wrapped inside a heavy canvas. Cylinders of propane gas and the burners were rolled out on a cart and staged near the basket.

Jake remained quiet while they both unrolled the canvas, exposing the neatly folded cloth of a red and gray stripped balloon. He worried he'd be forced to ride in the balloon with Snookey. Fearing heights and Snookey, he preferred to remain on the ground.

"Unfold it. Get some air in it," Snookey yelled.

Jake took hold of it, opposite Snookey, stepping backward several steps. Each pulled until the folds opened, revealing the entire profile of the balloon, which was the size of a house.

Jake whistled. "That's one giant balloon."

"Envelope. It's called an envelope," Snookey said, while pulling at the folds.

"What's your plan?" Jake asked.

"With this, I'm gonna find where the vaults are buried."

Jake's eyes opened wide.

At the narrow end of the envelope, where the basket attached, the fabric wrapped over a large metal ring. Snookey grabbed it with two hands, raising and lowering it slowly, fanning air into its vast chamber. As he did, he shouted to Jake to set up the power generator and electric fan.

The round, bulky fan was positioned near the envelope's opening, forcing a steady current of air to flow into it. Within minutes the cloth rippled as air stretched the balloon's panels open while it remained on the ground. Soon, it bobbed with the dawn's breeze, barely grazing the frozen, petrified field, taking the shape of an enormous light bulb.

The morning's darkness began to evaporate revealing shredded thin clouds. A sliver of light from the winter sun hovered on the edge of the horizon, bringing early sparkles

124

of frost to life and silhouetting leafless branches of oak and maple on a nearby ridge.

Snookey stood on a small out-cropping of rock, hands on hips, as a buccaneer might on the bow of a marauding galleon, surveying the sky. "Day's gonna be calm." He hopped from his perch and attached the basket's lines to the nearly filled envelope. "I wanna be in the air when the sun clears the tree line."

"Where you takin' it?" Jake asked.

"I'll do some sightseeing and drop off something."

Snookey hurried back to the trailer, disappearing inside. Within minutes, he reappeared dragging a large, black, canvas bag laced on one side. Jake watched him drag the awkwardly shaped bag to the basket and hoped Snookey didn't open it.

"Lift the other end," Snookey shouted.

Jake held his breath, gagging, feeling bile climb to his throat. Overwhelmed by the stench, he dropped the bag and backed away, taking deep, heaving breaths. "Did you have to kill him?"

Saying nothing, Snookey lifted the unwieldy bag in both arms, like a small child, and dropped it into the wicker basket. After throwing in two cement blocks, he climbed inside and shoved the blocks into the canvas bag without looking at the body.

"This stuff's not on the market yet," Snookey said, tapping the gas burner centered at the base of the balloon a few feet over his head.

Nauseated, Jake turned his back to walk away, when he heard the loud, **WHOOP**. Looking back, he saw the blazing, yellow-blue flame of a blowtorch coming from the gas burner. Snookey turned a valve above his head, adjusting the flame to a smooth even blue tip, heating the air trapped in the envelope.

Within minutes the oversize, red and gray balloon gradually lifted the wicker basket several feet from the ground, stretching its anchor ropes.

"Where you think you're goin'?" Snookey shouted down to Jake. "You're my co-pilot."

"Not in that, I'm not."

"On the ground, drive your van. Follow me."

"Why?"

"When I come down, pick me up."

"You got the balloon, fly home."

"No can do." Snookey gave the gas valve a few more turns, heating more air inside the envelope. Soon the basket pulled the anchor lines tight. "I'll ride the wind currents. I'll be damn lucky to get back to a few miles of here."

Jake nodded and gave the thumbs up sign. "Which way you going?"

"Towards town, keep an eye on me," Snookey said, releasing the tie downs. As he floated free, he shouted, "When I go down, come lookin' for me."

Jake climbed into his van and began the chase. Prickles of fear dashed up his spine, thinking of what Snookey was planning to do with the body in the black bag.

* * * *

Once airborne, Snookey pulled a jacket over his heavy sweater as the temperature dropped. At two hundred feet he leveled off and a light wind began to push him towards the center of Uniontown, nearly ten miles to the east. Below, a few cars moved along deserted streets, early Sunday morning.

In a short time, barren fields and yellowed grass passed under him as he floated toward a distant coal tipple. Snookey gave a few blasts to the overhead burner, heating more air, gaining elevation, easily gliding over the mine's six story tower. Snookey wrapped both arms around his chest, attempting to ward off the chill. Colder temperatures came with the new altitude, altering his direction of travel, taking him off course, away from town. New, stronger winds pushed him over a blackened, coal ash covered landscape. Bleak coal patch houses, burning coke ovens and smoldering ash dumps sped under the rapidly moving balloon.

Soon he was carried away from the mines and over the wide and fast Monongahela River. A tugboat, pushing several barges loaded with coal, was working its way up river to a Pittsburgh steel mill. Once they passed, Snookey positioned the balloon over the center of the river. He hoisted the black bag, over the side of the wicker basket, tipping it momentarily, then dropped the bag into the fast moving river. It floated briefly, finally sinking below the surface into the murky, choppy water.

With less weight the balloon rapidly rose. Snookey grabbed the long rope, which dangled from the top of the envelope, and yanked it several times. Hot air released, slowing the assent. Checking the altimeter, while raising and lowering the balloon, he found a wind current that would put him on course toward his destination.

Snookey smiled. Down below he spotted Jake's van speeding through vacant parking lots and alleys following him.

Backtracking and after numerous course corrections, Snookey and his balloon were finally approaching downtown. He spotted the area of town he wanted a few miles to the north. With several tugs of the rope, he released enough heated air to drop into a northern airflow direction. He dropped lower than wanted, however, he was drifting in the right direction. At the current speed, Snookey felt confident he would be able to maneuver the balloon over the home he hunted. Near the southern edge of town, he floated over an area of abandoned warehouses and scrap yards. Neighboring them were haphazardly erected shanty houses roofed with rusted tin sheets. No discernable road led to the area, only a dirt footpath. Laundry hung, thrown over tops of chain link fence. Dogs ran in circles in grassless yards, jumping wildly at the slowly descending balloon. Snookey shot a few bursts of flame into the balloon, rising higher and climbing away.

After bypassing the downtown business district, Snookey swung the balloon back on course, heading in the direction he intended. Near freezing, he lowered the balloon to a warmer zone. The wind current lessened, and soon he floated over a neighborhood of modern day castles. English Tudor, Victorian and Romanesque style homes lay cloaked in a forest of heavy pines. Although dangerous, the lower level gained him a bird's eye view of the stately homes and lush gardens owned by the region's coal barons, and wealthy businessmen.

Again, Snookey lowered the balloon, slowing his travel speed as he skimmed the treetops above the large estates. Just ahead, on a large parcel of property, he spotted what he searched for.

Chapter Twenty-Four

Lenora waved good-bye to Sam and Doc the following afternoon, as they left The Flying M Ranch. Hector drove while Doc slumped in the front seat. Sam relaxed in the back, watching the soft blue Pacific Ocean stretch to the western horizon. He inhaled, smelling the interior of the new car. He had worried it would smell like horse manure, like everything else at the ranch.

"How long to Pomona?" Sam asked.

"Four hours…maybe more." Hector hiked his thumb to the picnic basket next to Sam. "Tom said to stop for lunch in Ventura."

Doc reached into his jacket pocket, pulling out a pad of paper. "Jake gave me an address. The guy's Japanese, Uno Koba. His father is somehow involved with what's going on back home."

Sam leaned forward, looking over Doc's shoulder. "What are we to do with Uno Koba?"

"He was eighteen when his father was killed. We find out what he remembers about the day Semans showed up at his house."

"If he won't talk?"

"Jake's got a letter that's gonna make him talk," Doc said. "It's in a post office box in Pomona. He gave me a key."

"Anything else?"

"I didn't want to worry you," Doc said, holding his gaze over the Pacific. "He said to be careful. This is where the whole mess with Vince and Snookey started."

"Shit. I knew it," said Sam as he turned in his seat, looking through the rear window of the station wagon.

"Lookin' at something?" Doc asked.

"Checking, if we're being followed."

"Is there a map in here?" Doc asked, opening the oversized glove compartment. Spotting the partially concealed handgun, Doc slammed it shut, hoping no one noticed.

Hector remained quiet, his eyes steady on the road.

Sam saw it and the box of shells next to it. He knew Hector was aware of Doc's discovery. He wondered what other surprises awaited.

After passing through Santa Barbara, Highway 101 turned back to its course near the ocean. In a short time they spotted a wood pier jutting nearly seven hundred yards into the breaking waves of the Pacific.

"That's Ventura Pier," Hector said, breaking the long silence. "We'll eat lunch out at the end."

They pulled closer to the deserted pier.

"Water deep?" Doc asked.

"Out there? Yeah, real deep," Hector said. "Might see some sharks." He pulled the car off the road and stepped out.

"Can we eat in the car?" Doc asked.

"Tom said eat on the pier."

Walking to the pier, Hector abruptly stopped and returned to the car. "Forgot something," he shouted over the crashing surf.

Sam watched Hector swing open the passenger door. His back shielded what he retrieved. Sam looked around, hoping to find other visitors on the pier. They were alone. The car door slammed shut and Hector jogged toward them. His coat that once flapped in the sea breeze was now buttoned at his waist.

130

Chapter Twenty-Five

Snookey found the house he looked for and released more air from the balloon. He hoped the areas affluent residents would be asleep in the early morning hours. Hovering close to the steeply pitched roof of Captain Semans Victorian home, he was cautious of the hot embers, which rose from its many chimneys. Suspended over the expansive estate, he looked down at the brilliant red and gold arched bridges, fishponds, and gazebos that dotted the barren winter landscape of the Japanese gardens.

Snookey spotted his target. The large, ornate Japanese teahouse was nearly hidden among a cluster of pines. Adjacent to it was a pond, surrounded by jutting rocks and a few wood benches. He hovered over the structure. Everything matched the description he'd found hidden inside the railroad clock in Doc's home, prior to him burning it down. He pulled the note from his pocket and read the message again.

Pomona shipment late. Delay completing Koi pond and teahouse.

Somewhere under the pond or the teahouse were the burial vaults filled with gold bars he'd removed from Jimmy Koba's safe nearly fifteen years ago. Snookey saw it as the perfect crime. He had simply followed orders, relocating the family to internment and seizing the gold they illegally hoarded. Soon it would be his.

A plan to resurrect the vaults stirred in Snookey's mind along with whom he would bury in their place. The way he saw it, he had one too many partners.

Snookey gave a quick look to the south, noticing Jake's VW parked near the Victorian home. There were no signs of anyone. He'd make a quick get-a way. The wind shifted suddenly, jerking the balloon backwards, brushing the basket into the tops of nearby elm trees. Snookey reached up, opening the gas valve, blasting hot streams of gas flame into the overhead envelope. The balloon climbed into a wind current which carried him away.

* * * *

Below Jake, watched the sudden outburst of gas flair-out as Snookey twisted the valve several times. The balloon sped away, its wicker basket skimming treetops as it gained altitude. A hunch told Jake, Snookey found what he looked for.

After cranking over the ignition, Jake hurried to catch Snookey as he sailed away into the clear, blue sky. With a foot heavy on the throttle, he caught up to the fast moving balloon, following at a distance.

For the next several miles, Jake watched the balloon maneuver, changing elevations and directions, attempting to return to the circus tent. After nearly a half hour, Snookey failed to locate a westerly wind stream. The red and gray balloon retreated, losing altitude, and floated over an abandoned block of coke ovens.

Jake sat below watching Snookey turning the burner valve. This time nothing happened, the tanks were empty. With no flame to heat the bag full of air, the basket slowly descended between long rows of coke ovens, which resembled brick and rock beehives. In minutes the large red and gray canopy draped over Snookey and the basket. Jake took his time driving across the barren, ash and coal covered ground. He'd had made up his mind what he would do with Snookey and the elusive vaults.

Chapter Twenty-Six

Rolling waves crashed against the aged wood pilings below them. Hector sat at the far end of the pier, his back against the railing. The open lunch basket sat between them on a sun bleached picnic table.

Doc finished his sandwich and looked over to Hector. "What did you forget back at the car?"

"Nothing," Hector answered, while tossing breadcrumbs at a flock of seagulls clustered near is feet.

"You have a gun in the car," Doc said.

"It's a ranch car, they all have guns. We use 'em to shoot snakes."

"Why'd you hide it in your coat?"

Mumbling in Spanish, Hector bowed his head, then looked at Doc and Sam. "Tom told me why you're here. Somebody's trying to kill you."

Both nodded, still watching Hector.

"I'm a good shot," he said. "I got it just in case."

With both hands, Doc slapped the table, chasing off the sea gulls. "We got ourselves a guardian angel, Sam." Doc patted Sam on the back. "How does that make you feel?"

"Since you can't shoot straight Doc, makes me feel damn better."

Doc winked. "Does me too." He slid his hand back onto his jacket pocket. "But from this range I wouldn't miss." Doc eased his handgun out, showing only the white pearl handle.

Hector stood. "We need to get to Pomona."

* * * *

The warm November sun sat a few degrees above a row of Queen Palms on an adjacent knoll in Pomona. Below, in the palm's long shadows, the Ford Ranch Wagon drove through a heavy iron gate. Bold script letters arched across the top, "Los Angeles County Fairgrounds".

Hector sped past rows of vacant horse stalls and pens. Never hesitating, he navigated the maze until they reached the large racetrack.

"My parents live here," Hector said, getting out of the car. "The fair just ended. They'll be in Mexico seeing family."

Doc and Sam stretched their stiff, aching legs, walking toward the track's massive, sloping steel roof, which loomed out over the grandstands. Inside was a large expanse of lush, green grass, circled by an oval dirt track. Not far from there stood three long, whitewashed stables.

"Looks peaceful," Doc said.

Sam's eyes narrowed with suspicion, wondering how long it would last. Was this idyllic scene a Hollywood set? What surprises waited?

Doc looked at Sam's contorted face. "Relax. Nothing's gonna happen."

"I feel it coming, like a mine cave in. Something is gonna happen. You watch."

Doc waved a hand at Sam and turned away to shout to Hector, "Who's taking care of the horses?"

Before Hector answered, a squat man, driving a dull red Massey Harris tractor turned the corner of the grandstand. He jumped to the ground, losing his straw hat, rushing to Hector, hugging and patting him on the back.

Hector introduced Fernando, his cousin.

"We'll stay a few days," Hector signed to him.

Fernando nodded, with a smile on his weatherworn face, and pointed to a passageway under the grandstands.

"He'll take us to the apartment," Hector said.

Fernando swung open a green, Dutch door under a sign, PRIVATE. He waved them inside.

Sam ducked into the cramped and musty apartment. He caught Doc's eyes and shook his head.

134

Hector dropped his carpetbag next to a worn sofa. He motioned Sam and Doc to a narrow door. "You two sleep in there."

"You take it," said Doc.

Hector patted the sofa. "Growing up, this is where I slept."

"Where's Fernando sleep? Doc asked.

Hector smiled. "In stables with the horses."

* * * *

That evening, after stable rounds, Hector and Fernando took over the galley kitchen to prepare a simple late dinner. Sam and Doc set the table, pulling dishes and silverware from a green and red glassed pantry.

While alone, Doc stepped close to Sam. "I told Jake about Lenora, that she knows everything what's going on. He has the ranch phone number, if he needs us, he'll call her."

"How 'bout us? Sam asked. "What do we do? Knock on some guy's door we never met, then ask him why Snookey's digging up a Quonset hut three thousand miles from here."

"Jake said be careful with Uno," Doc answered. "He thinks there's something strange about him and he's keeping secrets."

Sam shook his head. "What's Jake asking us to walk into? What if this is a set up to kill us?"

"Don't know," said Doc. "All we know is Uno Koba is connected to why Vince and Snookey are digging in the circus tent." He paused, glancing back at the kitchen. "Remember, Jake gave us his word he'd take care of Herkey's body."

"We'll do this," Sam said giving Doc several quick nods. "If Herkey's still in the trunk, we go to the cops. That's the deal."

They were interrupted by the clank of a heavy cast iron pot, filled with pinto beans being placed on the table. Fernando carried a large, red clay dish, inside were steaming flour tortillas wrapped in heavy cloth. Sam and Doc watched Fernando and Hector spoon beans onto open tortillas and quickly wrap them, eating them like hotdogs.

As they ate, there was a loud knock on the door.

Chapter Twenty-Seven

The monastery's kitchen was sparse, over-heated and dimly lit. Sweat covered Sister June Tamura's face as she finished placing balls of bread dough on a large rectangular pan and slid it into the heated oven. In the next room, she spotted her replacement rearranging the cooling racks. Stepping away, dusting flour from her hands, Sister June glanced toward the high windows. Scarlet ribbons of early light streaked across the horizon as the night stars began to fade. The promise of sunrise dispelled the darkness she had once felt. Today, new hope came, her destiny was the monastery, serving and praying. She knew it.

* * * *

Sister Irma had spent a sleepless night thinking of June. She worried June was making a decision to commit her life to prayer and solitude for the wrong reasons. Sister Irma had made up her mind to speak to her again.

* * * *

June rushed from the kitchen. Her bare feet tingled from the cold tiles. Hurrying to her room she cut across the courtyard grass. Nearly metallic, a thin crust of ice floating in the oval fountain grabbed her attention. Looking down at the face, which stared up at her, she asked, "God, You know my heart. Can I give you the selfless love you expect from this order?"

A gust of wind rippled the water, blurring her face. Walking away, fingering the beads of her rosary, she wondered if that was a sign. After looking around, Sister June ran to the dormitory. She had little time before the six-thirty mass.

Approaching her door, she stopped dead still. The door was open a few inches. Someone had entered her room. For a moment she stood outside the door, and gradually opened it.

"Sister Irma," June whispered.

Irma smiled, holding a finger to her lips.

June closed the door softly. Both stood in silence.

"I thought we might talk again," Irma began.

"Yes," said June, as she seated herself at the edge of her small bed.

Irma cleared her throat. "June, we are permitted to speak at our daily recreation time."

June nodded. "Yes, but this is not that time."

A grin crossed Irma's face. "It will be fine. There are allowances, since you do not attend."

June exhaled. "I enjoyed our last visit."

"I did as well," Irma said as she sat next to June. "Tell me what troubles you."

"I discovered who my real father is."

Irma squeezed June's hands in hers. "When I saw you returning to the monastery?"

"It was that same morning." June's voice quivered. "He is the man my family lives with. He saved my mother and her aunt and uncle from internment." June paused, wiping her eyes.

Irma sat quietly, staring into June's eyes, waiting for her to continue.

"My father is also responsible for destroying our family. He deceived many people," June said. "I learned what he did to my mother's family. I can never let her find out. It's a secret that I must keep. My mother continues to love him. It would kill her if she knew. I will never leave this place. I can't. I must keep what I know a secret."

"You should speak to a priest, tell him what you know," Irma said.

The tower bell chimed, announcing morning Mass.

Chapter Twenty-Eight

When the second knock came, Hector was standing at the door.

"Hector, are you there?" they shouted, knocking again.

Recognizing the voice, he opened the door. "Olivia?" Hector said, stepping back. "I hardly recognize you. You grew up."

"Five years, Hector. You've been gone five years."

He looked at the girl who was tall as he, and just as thin. She stepped closer allowing him to inhale her fragrance.

"What are you now...seventeen...eighteen?" Hector asked.

Olivia stepped away and completed a graceful pirouette. "I'm nineteen. Can't you tell? I even have a job." Exhaling, she gave him a quick smile and pointed to a phone booth near the grandstand ticket windows. "There's a call for you."

Hector looked back into the apartment at Sam and Doc. "No telephone. We use the pay phone." He ran a short distance to the booth. The hinged door was open and he grabbed the handset, which dangled on the cord.

The call was from Tom who got directly to the point. "Still got your gun?" he asked.

"Yeah, why?"

"Lenora got a call from a private detective, a Jake Ozaki, from Pennsylvania. There may be a problem."

Hector closed the door. The booth's light blinked out. He banged his palm against the light cover. It flickered, then remained on.

"What do you mean?" Hector asked.

"A friend of theirs was found dead," Tom said.

"Want me to bring 'em back?"

"Not now. Hold on." After a short pause, Tom came back on the line. "Put Sam or Doc on, Lenora need's 'em."

Within seconds, Sam and Doc hurried to the phone. Holding it between them they listened to Lenora. "Thought you should know a coal barge captain found Herkey Dixon's body floating in the Monongahela River. He said it was dropped from a hot air balloon."

"There's a mistake. Can't be," Sam said more to Doc than Lenora.

"How do you know?" Doc asked.

"It's in the papers," Lenora answered.

"You're positive it's Herkey?"

"His wife's picture is in the paper. She said it was."

"Any mention of my car?" Doc asked.

"No. Nothing. I guess that's good," Lenora said.

"What did the story say?" Sam broke in.

"Herkey was reported missing five days ago and a mystery hot air balloon dropped him into the river two days ago. They were unable to identify the balloon or who was in it. They're looking for witnesses. The rest was an obituary on Herkey."

"We gotta get back there!" Sam said.

"Sam's right. We need to go to the police."

"Did you talk to Uno?" Lenora asked.

"Planned to tomorrow," said Doc.

"Good. I hope he cooperates. It will take a few days to get the plane ready. I'll be in Pomona in two days. We'll go home."

Chapter Twenty-Nine

Inside the trailer, Snookey leaned back in his chair while Jake stood on a small stool shaking coffee grounds into a coffee pot. The trailer sat inside the darkened circus tent, surrounded by mounds of dirt and twisted metal that remained from the demolished Quonset hut.

"It's late, he might not be coming," Jake said.

Snookey looked out the window with a sober stare. "He'll show. This is what he wants to hear. He'll show."

"You're sure the vaults are there?" Jake asked.

"I'm positive."

The sudden glare of headlights swung across the trailer's dirt smudged windows, and within minutes a truck slid to a stop in the loose gravel. Jake hopped from the stool, feeling his gun's ankle holster jar when he landed. At that moment, Vince removed his fedora, entering the trailer. His long overcoat hung open, exposing a semi-automatic hanging under his arm.

"This better be good," Vince said, looking at the cigar he took his time to light.

"I found the vaults," Snookey said. "Herkey never buried 'em here."

"Should not have trusted him," Vince said.

"Thought he was clever," Snookey said. "He buried them in Semans' Jap garden."

"You sure?" Vince said.

"Yeah. He was keeping it all for himself."

Vince moved to the trailer's door, looking at the piles of debris surrounding the excavation site. "He wasn't smart enough to plan this. Semans is behind this," Vince said, dropping the match to the wood floor, smashing it with his boot. "Where in Semans' garden?"

"Under a Japanese tea house," Snookey answered.

Vince laughed. "Hell, Semans got what he wanted in California. We were supposed to get Koba's gold. That was the deal with Semans. He crossed us. We're take'n back what's ours."

"Digging equipment, we got." Snookey said. "How do we get on his property?"

"I gotta think," Vince said, walking to a widow, staring at the backhoe. "We're gonna fix a gas leak," Vince said to Snookey as he left the trailer. "Be ready to go when I call."

Chapter Thirty

Hector looked at Uno Koba's address. "Reservoir . . . I know the street. When 'ya want to go?"

Sam held the slip of paper, waving it close to Doc. "Should we call first?"

"What for?" Doc said. "Let's surprise him."

Later that day, Hector pulled the Ford wagon to the curb across the street from Wayne Sweeper Manufacturing, several miles from downtown Pomona.

"Doesn't look like much of a place," said Doc.

Hector pointed to a small house across the street.

"That his house?" Doc asked, climbing from the car.

"That's it." Hector nodded to Sam as he opened the metal gate.

Sam looked at the open fields and large areas of dry brush. He was ready to climb back on Lenora's plane and return home and take his chances with the police. The faint sound of Bing Crosby drifted past, coming from a distant radio. It reminded him of home, sitting in his kitchen listening to his wife's old albums.

A straight, narrow sidewalk led to the porch of a gray, two-story rock home. Adjacent to it was a cinder block barn with wide steel doors secured with heavy pad locks.

Sam looked into one of the open, steel-bar covered windows on the barn. "Over here, take a look."

A stench of rotting and decay reached out from inside the buildings as soon as they leaned close to the window.

All three stepped away, balancing against the wall, taking quick breaths of fresh air, before looking inside.

From the high roof, streams of weak light entered through dust-covered, wire mesh windows exposing dozens of heavy wood boxes. All similar, each four by eight foot and nearly three foot deep, stood on thick legs in uniform rows. A flat sheet of un-painted plywood covered each one.

"Looks like he's got a hobby," Sam said.

"Mushrooms maybe," Hector said.

Sam went to the double doors. Two heavy pad locks secured the tall wood doors. Looking across the yard he spotted a small pole barn and shouted to Doc and Hector.

Inside it, food scraps, shredded newspaper and rags overflowed from wood crates. Nearby, steel drums spilled over with a hodge-podge of fruit rinds, peelings and buzzing flies. On a work table, next to a white enameled butcher scale, sat stacks of carryout paper containers.

Doc waved in disgust. "We're wasting time." With a quick tilt of his head towards the stone house, he marched to its front door.

From habit, Hector gripped his pistol inside his jacket pocket.

"Anybody home?" Doc shouted, peeking through the screen door.

Only ticking and chimes of a clock answered.

Doc looked at his watch. "Five o'clock. He should be home from work."

Hector tapped the steel mailbox, shaped like a street sweeper, and removed a stack of letters and bills.

"Let me have a look," Doc said, and pulled a tan, window envelop from the pile. "Looks like a paycheck."

Hector looked at the return address. "This came from Wayne Sweeper across the street."

* * * *

The doors were locked and guarded by heavy, rusted gates by the time they arrived at the sweeper plant's main entrance. Nearby, cars filled a walled parking lot next to an expansive, aged two story, brick building. A long line of roll-up doors opened to an alley cluttered with steel bins overflowing with curled metal shavings, axles and wood pallets.

144

The three walked, cautious of each step, through the alleyway. Sam moved ahead, looking for somewhere to hide and view inside the large plant. Banging metal and occasional shouts echoed inside the three-story structure. He settled on a spot behind a stack of flat steel sheets and waved for Doc and Hector.

Crouching, they spotted through hazy light from overhead saw tooth skylights, a clumsy procession of disfigured equipment, lumbering, single file like ancient mastodons. The oddly shaped creatures rode on two widely spaced forward wheels. Between them, near the ground, like a large gaping mouth, was a giant, open hopper.

Two men rushed, attaching large circular brushes to each side of the street sweepers. Others bolted over-sized mirrors to front fenders as the machines crawled along the assembly line.

"How do we find him?" Sam asked.

As they were about to enter the shop, a golf cart with a red flashing dome light pulled into their path. The driver's green baggy coveralls were smeared with paint and grease. A nametag, Sid, was sewn over a pocket. Wayne Sweeper, Pomona, Cal. was stitched across the back in tall, yellow, narrow letters.

"Looking for something?" he asked.

After Sid led the three to a large break room in the center of the plant, he rode off in his cart, leaving them there. Sam and Doc sat on one of many long and narrow benches that stood beside the lunch tables. Hector paced the room examining rows of cigarette and candy machines, stopping occasionally to pull a handle.

"That him?" Hector asked, pointing toward the shop.

Looking out the room's glass windows, they saw the short trim Japanese man approaching. He wore the same uniform as Sid, however, his was starched and pressed, pens clipped in each breast pocket. The name patch read, Uno.

145

Before the room's double doors swung shut, he said, "You have come here for nothing."

At the same time, Hector stepped around Uno, leaving the room.

"Sid told you who we are?" Doc asked.

"You came about my father, Jimmy Koba."

"We did, to help," Sam added.

"How so? Who sent you?"

"Can we talk here?" Doc smiled as he looked around the glassed room, filled with gray metal tables, benches and glaring florescent lights. It reeked of stale coffee and soured milk, which had, over years, blended with metal cutting oils and hung in the air like incense. The thin walls and glass were no defense against the grinding of heavy machinery that assaulted the room.

Uno glanced at the wall clock. "Twenty minutes, plant has a break. Make it fast."

"You know a private detective named Jake Ozaki?" Sam asked.

Uno laughed. "He once worked here and belongs in a circus. My so-called family hired him, not me. I told him, like I am telling you. I cannot help." Uno crossed his arms on his chest. "Are we done talking?"

Speaking softly, Sam stepped close to Uno. "He's looking for what was stolen from your father during the war."

"Theft was common," Uno said. "We Japanese were only allowed to take what we could carry. When we were taken to the camps, the valuables we left behind were stolen."

Sam raised his palms in defeat. "We don't know what was taken, diamonds, gold, silver. Your father was in the jewelry business. We took a guess."

"Jake Ozaki asked us to talk to you," Doc said stepping between the two. "It would help Jake to know what you

146

remember from the morning your family was taken into camp."

He's close to finding what they took from your father," Doc said. "He asked us to locate you. What you remember may help."

Sam nodded. "The Pomona police have no theft report."

"I don't want anything they stole."

"It belongs to you," Doc said.

Uno banged the metal table, knocking over paper cups and rattling ashtrays. He stalked to the far end of the room. "The American soldiers said my father killed himself in prison camp, said he was a spy. What I care about is his honor, not what may have been stolen."

Sam and Doc stepped back.

Uno balled his fists while veins in his neck rose. "He was a hero for this country in World War One. He won medals. He was no traitor." His voice trailed off.

"He was a hero," Doc said with a calm voice. "We'll help prove it."

Uno spoke in a soft tone, moving closer to Sam and Doc. "He was murdered, but not for what my family thinks, something more valuable."

"Did you say this to the police?" Doc asked.

"Military Police supposedly investigated. I told them, they didn't listen. They said they found evidence in our house that proved he was a spy."

"What was it?" Sam said.

"In our attic. They claimed he had radios, cameras, maps of oil refineries, and military bases." Uno shook his head. "They were not his. I know my father."

"You tell Jake this?" Sam asked.

Uno took a deep breath. "No. He wants the gold the soldiers took. My family hired him to find it, that's all. They're paying him a share of what he finds. He doesn't care about my father."

147

Sam whistled softly. "This is somehow connected, the circus, Snookey, what Jake's looking for and what what's we should be looking for."

"You can clear his name," Doc said. "Accusing your father of spying may have been a cover for the theft. Jake has something to show you."

Uno shook his head several times. "No use. I have tried. Lawyers take my money. Army takes reports. Nothing changes."

A shrill bell rang in the plant. Several doors flung open, filling the room with men carrying lunch pails and crumpled paper sacks. Uno nodded for Sam and Doc to step into the empty shop floor. "I must go back to work."

"Can we talk more, after work?" Sam asked.

"No." Uno leveled a cold stare at Sam. "Do not bother me. Go away. There is nothing you can do."

"There is," Doc said.

"I'm done wasting time," Uno said, turning to walk away.

Doc worked his hand into his pants pocket. "Jake gave me something."

Uno raised his arms into the air with his fists tightly clenched. "I am calling our security guard."

"No," Doc said. "Here." From his pocket he pulled a long key. "Jake found something that proves your father was framed. It's here in Jake's post office box."

With cat-quick reflexes, Uno yanked his pay envelope, which poked from Doc's shirt pocket and waved it in the air. "You already know where I live, bring your proof to my home, seven in the morning."

* * * *

Inside the Pomona post office, Sam's footsteps echoed in the deserted, red tiled corridor. "Here we are, box seventy-nine," he shouted back to Doc.

148

Breathing heavy, Doc hurried to catch up. Nearing the box, he stretched his arm out, hurrying to hand Sam the key.

"Why didn't Jake show this to Uno?" asked Sam, opening the small door.

"Said he got this after he spoke to him. Uno refused to see him again."

Inside the box was a single, tan envelope addressed to Mr. Jake Ozaki, PO Box 79, Pomona, California.

"What do you suppose it is?" asked Sam.

Doc touched the envelope and nodded. "Open it."

"In the car."

"No. Don't trust Hector," Doc said, looking over his shoulder.

With his pocketknife, Sam slid the blade under the flap, slicing it open. With care, he dropped the black and white photos into his hand.

They stared in disbelief.

Chapter Thirty-One

The cold sky, thick with clouds, promised rain.

Taki and Grace Sasaki had stepped onto the front porch of Captain Semans' home when the gray truck, towing a large backhoe, pulled to the front of the house. As Snookey and Vince stepped down from the cab, a patrol car pulled next to the trailer. The police officer motioned the truck's occupants to remain behind, while he marched toward Taki and Grace.

Smiling, he held up a folded sheet of paper. "There's a gas pipe line under this property with a leaking valve." He shoved the paper into his back pocket. "I'm officer Rizzo. I'm here to see that you cooperate with the gas company until they repair it."

"What do you want us to do?" Taki asked.

"For your safety, everyone must leave the property."

Rizzo pointed at Snookey and Vince, undoing the chains that anchored the backhoe in place. "They say it will take two maybe three days. You have a place to go?"

"When must we leave?" Grace asked.

"Thirty minutes, anyone else live here?"

"Captain Adam Semans and his wife are in California," Grace answered.

"Geta, our niece, lives here," Taki said, putting his arm around Grace.

Rizzo nodded. "Pack your things."

At the trailer, Snookey signaled the backhoe was free, as he tossed the wheel chocks to the gutter. Vince revved the diesel engine several times, sending out plumes of black smoke while he drove it from the flatbed.

Snookey held open the maintenance gate as the excavator rumbled past the Victorian home. He'd waited fifteen years, now he stood a few hundred yards from reclaiming what he had been cheated out of.

Vince maneuvered the hulking, oversized machine into the dormant gardens between a bamboo fence and green house, finally stopping near a tall, lichen covered mound of granite boulders stacked in the shape of a Japanese lantern. Splintered tree limbs, crushed shrubberies and overturned stones, that once outlined the path, were scattered in the wake.

Snookey jogged to catch up with Vince who hunched over in the open cab relighting his cigar.

"Herkey's note said to delay digging the pond and tea house," Snookey shouted over the idling engine. "I figure he buried the vaults somewhere near them."

"Which way?"

"Follow the path for about a hundred yards," Snookey shouted, stepping out of the way.

Vince nodded, sticking the stub of a cigar back into the corner of his mouth and turned the backhoe toward the Japanese teahouse. The narrow, curved footpath, bordered by dwarfed pines and ornate teak benches were tipped over and crushed by the backhoe's over-sized tires. In a while, Vince left the winding path, and straightened his course, plowing over dormant bushes and carefully trimmed trees.

Snookey remained on the path, running ahead to give directions, fearing Vince would wonder aimlessly, destroying the garden and call attention to themselves. When he reached the teahouse, he waved and shouted to Vince.

Vince pulled to a stop next to the bamboo teahouse. It stood peacefully, tucked among lush, drooping cedars and tall pines, centered in the serene garden.

Chomping on the stub of his cigar; Vince revved the backhoe several times, lowering its stabilizer arms, firmly positioning it on a patch of dry foliage. The hydraulic boom arm and bucket lifted and swung out, resembling a scorpion's tail. In a clumsy, surreal motion it struck its prey, collapsing a corner of the teahouse.

Within an hour the house and its foundation were demolished. Heavy bamboo wood, delicate latticework and twisted copper gutters had all been pushed onto the adjoining pond.

"Vaults better be here," Vince shouted over the rumbling diesel.

"This gotta be it." Snookey said. He pointed to the large house of Captain Semans in the distance. "Semans' not gonna be happy."

"He took what he wanted from Jimmy Koba," said Vince. "Now we're taking what's ours. We're even."

"Rizzo will take care of the Japs in the house," said Snookey. "They won't be calling Semans until we're done."

* * * *

From his VW mini-bus, Jake watched Rizzo guide Taki, Grace and Geta into his patrol car and drive away. He followed, at a distance, unseen, until they pulled through the open flap of the giant, red and gray tent.

Jake waited several minutes before pulling into the circus grounds. His mind searched for a safe place to hide his clients from Rizzo.

Feeling confident, he entered the big top tent through the same concealed entrance he had used to help Doc and Sam escape. He climbed over and between piles of dirt and twisted steel siding of the Quonset hut's remains and reached the maintenance trailer unseen. As he pushed open the door, Rizzo glanced in his direction, but quickly went back to the outdated LIFE magazine he read. Jake held a finger to his lips, quieting his clients. They hid their surprise at seeing him, giving no hint they knew him.

Jake forced a laugh. "Looks like you're being held captive."

152

Rizzo dropped the magazine, without an explanation he walked outside.

Jake shook his head to the three after the door slammed. After pausing, he looked over his shoulder, making sure Rizzo was gone.

"There's no gas leak," Jake said. "Those two digging in the garden stole your uncle's gold, they think it's buried there."

Taki, Grace and Geta jumped to their feet. "Officer Rizzo will arrest them," Taki said.

"Rizzo's one of the thieves," Jake said, looking out a window. He watched the cop, leaning against his patrol car using the radio.

"You can't stay here," Jake said. "I'll find a safe place for you when I return."

He pulled a scrap of paper from his pocket and wrote the names and phone numbers for Lenora, Sam and Doc. "If you don't hear from me in the next five hours call these people then call the state police.

Chapter Thirty-Two

Balmy breezes swept Southern California early that morning as Sam and Doc arrived at Uno Koba's house. After knocking several times on the front door they gave up and walked to the large barn at the back of the property. Inside it Uno stood over one of the deep boxes shifting through a mixture of dirt and manure. His face and shirt were streaked with sweat and grime. If he saw them, he didn't let on. After some time, he slid the heavy lid back into place, tapping the corners tight into the rough wood container.

"I raise earthworms." He waved at the large area full of boxes inside the barn, then tossed his work gloves on a bench, motioning them outside.

Sam was first to step from the barn, hurrying to the fresh air. It was more than the odor. The boxes reminded him of empty caskets, representing the unrecovered bodies of coal miners from the mining accidents he witnessed.

Under a drooping canopy of queen palms, Uno rested his foot on a picnic bench. From the pocket of his shirt he pulled a crumbled pack of cigarettes and shook the last one from the pack. His other hand slid into the side pocket of his coveralls to retrieve an ornate, jade cigarette lighter. He ducked behind a palm tree to light it against the steady wind. After taking a puff, he looked directly at Doc. "Yesterday, you told me there was proof that may clear my father."

Doc gave a quick nod, pulling several small scalloped edged photographs from his jacket pocket, handing them to Uno.

Uno grabbed them. "Where did these come from?"

"Jake Ozaki, got them from your neighbor," Doc answered.

Uno's hand trembled as he held a photo out to Sam and Doc. "Yesterday you asked me why my father killed himself." He pointed to the soldiers in the photographs. "That's them. They killed him." Uno shuffled through the stack several times. "My father fought and was willing to die for this country," Uno said, glaring back to his house. "We said the Pledge of Allegiance every day. They still took us."

"This was your father's house?" Doc asked.

Uno nodded. "The FBI or INS or what have you, kicked down our door in the middle of the night and searched our home many times. They said he was a spy. They cut open our couch and chairs, never finding anything." He paused, taking several long drags from his cigarette, staring at the snow covered San Bernardino Mountains a few miles to the north. "On the morning we were to be taken away," Uno paused to hold up the photographs of the men he recognized. "These soldiers show up and said they found radios and maps in our home. My father's business partner was here to take us to his home back east."

"Where back east?" asked Doc.

"Pennsylvania." Uno answered as he studied the other photos.

"You know his name?"

"Adam Semans. He wanted to be called, Captain Semans."

Startled looks ran across both Sam's and Doc's faces.

"Get the other names?" Doc asked.

Uno pointed to the photos. "Yeah, here…I'll never forget. This one, the Sergeant, he's Vince, the two privates, Snook and Rizzo."

Sam and Doc nodded in unison. "We know them," said Doc.

Uno laid the four photos on the table. They showed Snook and Rizzo lifting radios and microphones from the rear of a Jeep. In another, Rizzo was placing them into

155

sacks, and in the last two, Rizzo and Snook carrying the sacks into the house.

Uno took a seat; then motioned for them to sit. He flicked his half smoked cigarette into the dirt, grinding it with the sole of his heavy boot. "Just like that, they took our lives. An evacuation is what the government called it. They took away our name...gave us a number on a tag. Looters came in and took away everything else."

Uno's voice went to a whisper. "Over there," he pointed, "Is where we were taken, not far from here, Los Angeles County Fair Grounds. The Army gave us three cots and crammed us into a horse stall. Urine and manure is all we smelled. We used lye it didn't help. Our meals were slopped into tin plates from garbage cans."

"That's where he died?" Sam asked.

"Yes, soldiers kept him in isolation, to question him."

"Did you speak to him?"

Uno took a deep breath. "I found where they tortured him."

"You and your mother, they kept you at the fair grounds during the war?"

"In four months, we were transferred to a permanent camp in central California, Manzanar. It was worse, desolate, not like here." Uno snapped his fingers. "Just like that, our lives were taken away. I was to go to UCLA medical school."

Uno sat on the bench, rubbing his hands on his thighs and knees over and over, watching the sky. He glanced over to Sam and Doc, an odd look was on his face. "Many American Indians refuse to carry a twenty dollar bill. You know why?"

Doc and Sam gave a quick shake of their heads.

Uno suddenly stood. "Andrew Jackson's picture is on it. The Indians blame him for taking away their land."

Doc stood in front of Uno. "Jake Ozaki wants to get back what was stolen from your father."

156

Uno's shoulders stooped. "Will that bring him back?" His voice shook as he spoke.

"No, of course not," said Doc. "These photographs can clear his name. It's unforgivable, what happened to your family. These were crimes committed against Japanese Americans by the government. We can't do anything about that, but we can do something to the soldiers who stole from you."

"They got away with it for fourteen years," Sam said. "Can you help us?"

Uno walked silently towards his house. Turning, he spoke, "I saw the sadness on my father's face. He was disgraced, humiliated. The soldiers took him away and interrogated him. One day they told us he killed himself, he bit off his tongue. We buried him that afternoon. It was easy for the army to convince people he killed himself."

"You don't believe that?" asked Doc.

"The soldiers killed him, they cut out his tongue and watched him die." Uno paused, letting out a deep breath. "They wanted what was in our safe. I'll show you."

Doc and Sam exchanged surprised looks with the unexpected reply.

In the house, Uno pushed aside a beaded curtain and led them into a small kitchen.

"Are you afraid of small places?" Uno asked while he opened a pantry closet.

Before they answered, a bare light bulb clicked on in front of their faces. White painted shelving and hooks covered three walls. With his palm, Uno pushed a metal hook to the side. A wall panel swung away, exposing a set of narrow wood stairs. He ducked his head and disappeared into the blackness. Several sets of lights blinked on. Uno stood in the basement, waving them down.

Hovering over the small opening, Sam and Doc stood together, their faces almost touching. Doc finally spoke. "One of us should wait here."

157

Sam nodded. "I'll go." He inhaled musty air with his first step.

The basement's floor was uneven brick laid directly over dry, hard packed dirt. Uno stood in front of a black, five-foot high, open vault door. Sam walked stooped over, avoiding low ceiling joists and cobwebs floating above his head.

"See for yourself," Uno said, aiming a flashlight into the safe the size of a small bathroom. "He kept it all here."

Without stepping in, Sam looked into the empty room.

"Two-foot thick concrete walls, reinforced with steel bars," Uno said. "The only way they got in was with a combination."

"The soldiers got the combination from your father." Sam said.

Uno hesitated, then nodded slowly.

"Could he have moved the money?" asked Doc.

"Not before the solders came. There was no money, just gold."

"Gold?" Sam said, stepping into the vault. Using Uno's light, he surveyed the empty shelves. "How much?" he asked pulling open an empty drawer.

"My father did not trust printed paper money. The shelves were filled with gold coins and bars from Peru, London, Chile, United States…many countries. He started buying gold before World War One."

"You're sure it was all here?" asked Sam.

"I saw it. I knew the combination."

"How?"

"Does it matter?"

"Probably not," said Sam.

"I have some."

Sam's eyebrows shot up. "Show us."

Uno stepped from the kitchen, leading them to a small sewing room on the second floor. After pushing away a floor lamp, he removed a small, square piece of wood flooring. "I hid this before the soldiers came."

He lifted the dusty, wood cigar box from beneath the floor. "My father liked cigars." Uno pointed to the peeling label on the lid, **Cuban Gold.**

While Uno untied the cords from the box, Sam kept his eyes on him while Doc looked to the street from an open window. A sudden gust jarred the house, raising the room's curtains from the wall.

"Santa Ana's. They come every year," Uno said, not looking up.

A blast of hot, dry air slammed against the house again. From outside came a sharp cracking sound of splitting wood. A jagged, heavy branch torn from a Eucalyptus tree scraped and rasped against the house, sliding to the ground.

Uno undid the last knot, and slid the brass latch aside, opening the box. "Peruvian Soles, about five grand. I got six more boxes. That's all that's left."

"What was your father doing with the gold?" Doc asked.

Uno hesitated while rewrapping the box. "Buying land. Doesn't matter now, does it?"

"Where?" Doc asked.

"Here in California. He said it was worth more than gold."

"How'd he do it?" asked Doc. "Japanese couldn't own land."

After guiding the box back into the hole and replacing the wood floor, Uno slipped a hand into the top of one of his socks, removing a cigarette from a pack near his ankle. After a few puffs, he walked to the window and closed it, calming the blowing drapes. "These devil winds can blow for days . . . dry up everything like straw. Some bastard will toss one of these," he held up the cigarette, "into a field and burn Los Angeles...you watch." He shook his head,

159

looking at his shoes. "It was legal. He had a silent partner, an American. He bought the land with my father's money."

"Captain Semans?" Sam asked, knowing the answer.

"He took my aunt and uncle back East. They escaped."

Uno's face reddened. His eyes were alive with fury when he raced from the room, taking the stairs two at a time.

Sam whistled softly. "I have a bad feeling."

Sam and Doc hurried, following Uno to the street. Doc yelled, "One more question."

Uno stopped in the middle of the narrow street, doing a quick about face. Standing ramrod rigid, he glared at them. "Go ahead, ask."

Sam watched Uno, not knowing what to expect. He was a trapped animal, dangerous.

A blast of hot, dry air from the west rippled their clothes. Carcasses of fronds, ripped from palm trees, dropped, slapping the street, scraping and rattling along the pavement, following the path of the devil winds.

Fighting against powerful gusts, Doc walked toward Uno shouting, "How did they open the safe?"

Uno stood silent and sighed deeply. He rapidly shook his head. "What does it matter? I don't care about the gold. It will not bring my father back."

"No, it won't," Doc said, attempting to keep Uno calm.

"I told 'em," Uno shouted. "They beat my father. I told 'em the combination."

"It's okay," Doc shouted into the wind.

"Yesterday, you said Jake worked here," Sam shouted, stepping closer to Uno.

"He was the security chief," Uno said.

Surprised, Sam and Doc looked at each other.

Uno's shoulders slumped, as if he were ready to collapse in the street. "The soldiers said they'd stop." He laughed, but not a real laugh, then bowed a mocking curtsey and turned, walking casually to the sweeper plant.

160

The shift whistle blared.

* * * *

Sam unfolded carbon copies of the shipping orders they had removed from Silbaugh Vault, laying them on Hectors kitchen table.

"The name's here," Sam said. "Just too faint to read."

"The gold Uno says is missing could be in the vaults Jake said were delivered to Adam Semans," Doc said.

"Humor me," Sam said, tapping the carbon papers. "If Uno and Jake are right, we need to know who signed these."

He rummaged through a small desk drawer until he found a pencil. Using his pocket knife, Sam shaved a fine powder from the lead point onto the lacy thin sheet of paper. Leaning over, he gently rubbed the graphite over the faint, unreadable name and blew it away, revealing the signature.

They looked at each other. It was a name they didn't expect, Herkey Dixon. "That's why Snookey and Vince killed him and stuffed him into your trunk," Sam said. "Herkey was in the Army, stationed at the same air base where they dug up the Quonset hut. He was part of this from the beginning. My guess, he was supposed to bury the vaults there. Instead he crossed Snookey and Vince."

"He didn't have the brains," said Doc. "Somebody else planned this."

Outside, under the fair ground grandstands they heard the heavy slapping of shoes running.

"Mister Sam...Doctor Martin," Hector shouted. "Miss Lenora called from the ranch. She's on the phone." He pointed to the distant phone booth at the far end of the steel grandstands.

161

Arriving at the battered pay phone, Doc reached for the handset and squeezed inside. He held it to his ear while Sam leaned in close.

"Jake called me," Lenora began without preamble. "A barge captain found a dead body floating in the Monongahela River. He said it was dropped from a hot air balloon."

"Anybody we know?" asked Doc.

Lenora cleared her throat. "Herkey's no longer frozen in your car."

Sam and Doc exchanged tense looks.

"How come?" Doc finally said.

"Jake said Snookey thought he was dumping someone else. Instead, Jake switched bodies and Snookey dumped Herkey in the river."

"What happened to the other body?" Doc asked.

Lenora took a deep breath. "He said not to get upset. It's in your car."

"What?" Doc shouted.

"Jake said it was safe. He plans to use it as proof against Vince and Snookey. It's the only crime he can prove against them…He said not to worry."

"Worry!" Doc shouted. "Did he forget Snookey and Vince robbed Jimmie Koba?"

"He said officially that wasn't a crime," said Lenora. "Nothing was reported. The unknown body in Doc's car is the only thing he has that will put them in jail."

The winds funneled, gaining strength beneath the grandstand. The phone booth rocked a few times after Sam and Doc stepped from it. A section of metal siding flew past their heads, shattering a glass pane of the phone booth.

162

Chapter Thirty-Three

A light drizzle dimpled the tight surface of the nearby pond as Vince dropped the bucket of the backhoe into the ground, ripping and tearing away the dormant grass and shrubs. The ruins of Captain Semans' demolished teahouse had been pushed into the pond. Its cardinal red, arched roof jutted from the water like remains of a broken ship washed ashore.

The light shower turned into a downpour as the day passed. Each time the bucket rose from the deep, narrow trench it oozed muddy water and clay. Snookey trailed behind, sloshing through the flooded ditch ramming and poking a steel rod into the trench. Rain dripped from the brim of his hat and the bandages wrapped around his ribs loosened and fell away. Blood soaked through his shirt giving it a brown tinge.

"Vaults aren't here." Snookey shouted over the growl of the diesel engine.

Vince swung the boom from the hole, dropping it to a mound of dirt. "We'll dig up the whole damn place. They're here."

"Face it, Herkey conned us again," Snookey yelled.

"He's not that smart."

"Semans is," Snookey said at the same time he jammed the long steel bar into the rain softened dirt. He jerked back, feeling the steel rod stop suddenly in his hands.

"Rock?" Vince asked.

Snookey pulled the rod up, ramming it down several times. "Don't think so, sounds hollow."

"Septic tank?" shouted Vince.

"Might be," Snookey said, continuing to poke the rod into the trench.

With no warning, the boom dropped into the trench, narrowly missing Snookey.

"Let's take a look-see," Vince shouted while he jockeyed the clawed bucket, carefully maneuvering it, pulling away heavy layers of soil and clay, outlining the long rectangular shape of what Snookey struck. Within minutes the teeth of the bucket, as though it was a surgical instrument, scraped against the concrete vault, removing a thin layer of skeletal roots that encrusted the exhumed concrete box.

"Looks like it," Vince shouted, staring down at Snookey.

"Got to be one more," Snookey yelled. "Put the bucket under it. I'll throw a chain around it, and yank it out."

With the vault partially lifted, Snookey looped a heavy chain around the box. Another chain was attached to the backhoe's bucket and hooked to the vault. While Snookey climbed from the deep trench he gave a thumb up.

As it rose from its grave of fourteen years, the exhumed vault swayed. The chain dug into the concrete, grinding into its sides. The rear wheels of the backhoe lifted, straining as the vaults weight shifted. Mud and water poured from beneath its lid. The load tipped to one side. Vince quickly swung the boom to the side, lowering the box to a mound of dirt above the recently dug trenches.

The rain continued to pour down, quickly filling the hole. Vince hopped from the backhoe. He grabbed the steel rod from Snookey, and jumped into the trench, sinking in over his ankles into water and mud. After he regained his balance, he jabbed the rod into the spot below where the first vault had been. It traveled less that a foot then stopped. Vince stabbed randomly, each time it stopped with a sharp thud.

Vince fell to his knees, scrapping away mud and dirt with his hands until he exposed raw concrete. "This is it. He buried 'em on top of each other."

"I almost gave up," Snookey said, jumping back into the hole after dropping down more chains.

164

* * * *

Both vaults sat close to one another at the edge of a deep trench. The rain continued to lash down washing their concrete walls. Vince and Snookey stood deep in mud, gripping pry bars. They wedged them under each of the vault lids. Nothing budged.

Vince slung the pry bar to the ground. "Dynamite," Vince shouted.

"No," Snookey said as he hunched over and poked the long blade of his pocketknife into the seam between the lid and case. "They won't pry open. There're sealed with epoxy."

"I got a sledge in the trailer," Snookey said.

* * * *

Darkness had begun to fall when Jake returned alone to the Semans' estate. He parked his VW bus in an over-grown alley several blocks from the home and pulled on a poncho to walk in a steady downpour to the back of the estate's gardens. He scaled the eight-foot, ivy covered rock wall using a nearby tree. After hopping down, he stood in the Japanese garden.

He imagined its springtime beauty, when everything was in flower. The peaceful setting was sacred to him and he hoped someday the peace and beauty would be restored after today's intrusion.

Moving slowly so he would not be heard, he pushed away somber branches of willow and ginkgo, stripped for winter. Soon, he heard the persistent stuttering rhythm of a diesel engine. Moving toward it, he recognized a path he and Taki had followed in the expansive garden a few days ago. Shouting voices of Snookey and Vince forced him to stop. He ducked behind a large Japanese lantern sitting at the edge of a drained pond, hoping to spot their location.

165

The rain beat down harder, plunking off his canvas poncho. Fearing the sound would carry, he pulled off the rain gear, letting the rain quickly soak through his clothes. Moving through the garden, he followed their voices until he reached the area where he recalled seeing the elaborate teahouse. Approaching its location, he spotted Snookey and Vince standing where it once stood. Its demolished remains were scattered over the garden's dormant foliage and nearby pond.

What Jake saw next caused his heart to beat faster, the two vaults he'd spent nearly a year searching for were real. He had begun to have doubts. What they contained would change his life. He'd have respect, not pity.

Stooping behind several moss-covered boulders, Jake watched them attempt to open the vaults. Hissing, torrential rain, beating against the ground, made it impossible to hear what they said. Jake planned to take them by surprise. He crouched low and retrieved his compact semi-automatic from an ankle holster, then threaded on the silencer, giving it one final turn, making sure it was snug. The palm of his hand nestled perfectly around the nine-millimeter's black, wood grips. He took a deep breath, ready to go. What he saw caught him off guard.

While Vince's back was turned, Snookey pulled a handgun from inside his soaked jacket. He waited for Vince to turn back to him, when he did Snookey pulled the trigger. Vince jerked back, staggering onto one of the vaults, pointing aimlessly to the sky. Snookey shot him two more times in the chest.

Vince fell against the vault and dropped, sprawled on a mound of dirt. Snookey rushed to him, putting the muzzle of the gun's silencer to his temple, pulling the trigger.

Lines of blood ran from his chest, puddling in pools of muddy rainwater. Snookey crouched, placing his fingers on Vince's neck for a moment. He then stood and with one of his mud-covered boots, kicked him several times in the head and chest. Vince's body jerked, unfeeling, from the blows.

Jake got to his feet, taking several backward steps, staring at what he'd witnessed. With his free hand, he touched the back pocket of his sopping wet pants, checking his spare clip. He stood motionless, deciding.

A flashlight beam appeared from near the main house. "Everything okay back here?" someone shouted.

Instinctively, Jake squatted behind the boulder, resting his gun hand against it, taking aim at the glaring light. The light swung back and forth as it approached.

In the shadows of the rapidly darkening sky, Jake saw the faint outline of a rain parka pushing through a cluster of white pines.

Jake recognized the visitor and abandoned his plan.

Chapter Thirty-Four

Fifteen years earlier:
1942, May, six months after Imperial Japan attacked
Pearl Harbor.

Private, First Class Henry Snook's assignment was to
round up Japanese detainees in Pomona, CA. Instead of
reporting to the bus station, he arrived at seven am at one of
the family's homes. Waiting, he propped his freshly shined
boots on the Jeep's dashboard while lighting the remnants
of a half-smoked cigar he'd pulled from a shirt pocket. For
the past several months his unit conducted searches of
Japanese homes in the area with no success.

Civilian and military officials were concerned about
the loyalty of the more than a hundred thousand Japanese-
Americans residing in California. Rumors of spies and
sabotage were circulating. The recent shelling of a Santa
Barbara oil refinery by a Japanese submarine escalated the
hysteria.

Up until today, Private Snook's unit failed to uncover
contraband items such as radios, maps and explosives.

"Snookey," someone shouted.

Turning, he saw a large truck pulling up behind him.
Jumping from his seat, he watched the two passengers
approach.

"Now what Sergeant?" Private Snook asked the taller
stocky soldier.

"You know what to do," Sergeant Vince Pergalsky
answered, hiking his thumb at the stone house. "Semans is
on his way. He'll take the rest of the family. We'll make it
look good." Vince leaned into the rear of the Jeep, lifting
out two radios. "Get these Jap radios into his
house...couple days, Koba's dead."

"You're sure the gold's here?" Private Art Rizzo
asked.

"Better be," Vince said. "We'll be living like kings or we'll end up in Leavenworth if we don't do this right."

Private Snook stubbed out his cigar against the Jeep's tire. "What's Semans get out of this, if he doesn't want the gold?"

Vince shook his head. "Hell, if I know. He's got something in mind…said the gold was ours. All we gotta do is take care of this Jap, Jimmy Koba."

"That so," Snook turned away, wiping his shirtsleeve over his forehead.

"Yeah, that's all," Vince answered.

"Rizzo stepped between them. "I don't trust Semans."

"When Koba's dead, Semans gets what he's after," said Vince. "We keep him alive until we get our gold."

"Why's he keep gold in the house?" Snook questioned.

"…And not in a bank?" Vince asked, grinning, lightly slapping Snook on the cheek. "In '33 Roosevelt made it illegal to own more than a hundred bucks of it, thought people might hoard it. We're just enforcing the law and confiscating it."

Rizzo slapped Snook on the back. "Best part, who's gonna know. He's not gonna call the cops."

The screen door of the front porch swung open and slammed closed, getting everyone's attention. Jimmy Koba, wearing his World War I dress uniform, stood alone, at attention, staring into the distance. He lowered two suitcases to the wood plank porch.

"What are you doing here?" he asked the soldiers.

"Escorting you to the assembly center," Vince shouted.

"I will take my family," Koba said calmly to the three approaching soldiers.

"We got to look around the house first…be sure you didn't leave any valuables behind," Vince said, holding the door open for Snook and Rizzo as they entered carrying bulky canvas sacks.

Vince grabbed Rizzo by the arm. "Get everybody out of the house. Put 'em in the front yard with everything they're taken."

Jimmy Koba shouted into the house, speaking in Japanese.

Vince shoved him on the shoulder. "Talk American."

Before he could, his wife and eighteen year old son, Uno, stepped from the house carrying suitcases and boxes tied shut with laundry rope.

Two Yellow Cabs pulled up, stopping in the middle of the street. The lead cab's passenger door flung open as it skidded to a stop. Adam Semans stepped from the car and took a deep breath. "Jimmy, you all right? Where's Geta and the baby?" he shouted, hurrying to the house.

Vince blocked the door with his arm. "Can't go in. We're searching for contraband. Private Snook, bringing everybody outside."

Semans stepped close to Koba, stopping to notice the evacuation tag looped through the lapel of his jacket. "I'm sorry for this Jimmy. I don't know what's going on. You and your family are going with me. There's a plane in Alhambra. I guess they need to be sure you're not a spy."

Geta stepped from the darkened house carrying her three-year-old daughter, June. Soon after, Geta's aunt and uncle, Taki and Grace followed. Semans took the child from Geta, holding the toddler in his arms.

"June is my daughter," Semans said to the assembled family. "And that makes us all family. I'm taking all of you to my home." He pointed to the idling cabs. "We'll build gardens. It'll feel like home."

Snook and Rizzo came out the door, pushing past everyone on the porch, carrying two way radios and rolls of maps.

"These were in the bedrooms," Snook said.

Vince crouched over and examined the items. "Looks like Jap radios." He rolled open a map, examining it. "It's a

170

map of the California coastline." His finger traced down the heavy paper, stopping on several red circles the size of a half dollar. "These marks are oil refineries in Long Beach."

Jimmy Koba looked at Vince in disbelief. "This does not belong to me. I am not a spy. I fought for this country. I am an American."

Snook pulled his sidearm, pointing it at Koba's chest. "Face on the ground." Rizzo stepped over Jimmy Koba's back, handcuffing his wrists.

"Cuff his wife and boy." Vince shouted. "They're accessories."

Semans stepped away from Geta and her aunt and uncle as they loaded their bags into the waiting cabs. "This is a travesty. He's not a traitor," Semans shouted as he hurried towards Vince.

"It's out of my hands. FBI will take over." Vince looked at Koba's luggage and boxes. "They can only take what they can carry by hand. Put the spies in the Jeep."

Koba's son, Uno, took a quick step toward Semans, shouting, "I know what you are doing. I never trusted you." He spit in Semans face as he was yanked away by Snook. "You won't get anything," Uno screamed.

Semans wiped his face with a silk handkerchief he yanked from his jacket's front pocket.

"I'll fix this," Semans said, watching Jimmy Koba being lead to the Jeep. "I'll come get you."

* * * *

That afternoon Vince returned to the Koba house, after depositing Jimmy Koba, his wife and son in a horse stall at the Los Angeles Fair Grounds internment camp. From the curb, he whistled sharply then shouted, "Status report."

Rizzo stuck his head from an upstairs window. "Nothing up here."

"Same here," yelled Snook. "House is clean.

171

"Meet in the kitchen," Vince shouted, stepping from the Jeep.

Vince slammed the back door entering the small screened-in porch. He pounded his boot on the heavy wood floor, hearing a deep hollow sound. "This place got a cellar?" he shouted.

"Don't know." Snookey answered.

"Find out," Vince said, walking into the kitchen, tapping the walls. "Get some tools to tear out the front and back porches."

Snookey and Rizzo looked at him.

"Do it, soldiers!" Vince commanded. "We only got a few days 'til the army transfer Koba to Manzanar. Up there he's out of our custody. Right now, he's locked in a dark hole."

"Beat it out of him," said Snook. "Save us a lot of work."

"Might get something from the boy," Rizzo said.

"My way first," Vince said while he tapped the wood floor. "After we get what we need, Semans wants Koba dead. Make sure he has an accident. For now we look for a basement."

"I need to eat," Snook said, taking a step into the kitchen. He opened the icebox, finding it empty. He moved to the pantry closet, it was also bare.

"Damn Japs don't waste anything. Probably gave it to the neighbors," Rizzo said.

Snook stood in the pantry and pounded his large fist against a wall.

"Hear that?" Vince shouted. "Do that again."

"Yeah, I heard it." Snook gave a quick nod, then slammed the wood paneling again.

Vince grabbed Snook's arm and pulled him from the pantry as he stepped in. Not saying a word, Vince hunched over near the wall, like a safe cracker examining a safe, and

172

pushed against the wall several times, rattling it. It creaked, and swung open, exposing a set of dark stairs.

"Knew it," Rizzo said. "Japs are sneaky."

Snook lit a match and was the first to enter the basement.

"Careful," Vince warned. "If the gold's here the place might be booby-trapped."

A light bulb flashed on in the staircase. Then several more lit the basement. "Found the lights," shouted Snook.

All three rushed into the small musty basement. In front of them was a black safe door. Vince turned the dial several times, then gripped the handle, yanking it up and down several times. "Any of you know how to open one of these?"

"Say we blow it off," Rizzo said.

Vince pointed upward. "Too many ears up there. We'll draw attention to the house. We got time. I'll get the combination."

Chapter Thirty-Five

Pelting rain fell from a smudged, gray sky as Rizzo stepped from the pines onto the cobble-stoned path of the Japanese garden. "Is it done?"

Shining a flashlight on Vince's dead face, Snookey nodded. "It's getting dark. Let's get him in the hole, then open up the vaults."

"Feels like I'm back in the army when Vince told us about the gold," Rizzo said.

"Fifteen years. It's finally ours," Snookey laughed.

Snookey drove the excavator to Vince's body, which sprawled over a mound of dirt where the once majestic teahouse sat. He dug the bucket under the body, scooping it up. Vince's head flopped, hanging so his flaccid face stared back at Snookey. Yanking a lever, he swung the body over the ditch, dropping it. Swinging the backhoe about, he pushed the piled dirt and rock into the grave.

From behind a cluster of boulders Jake watched Snookey and Rizzo bury Vince's body. Jake's knees stiffened from the cold, and a burning numbness ached in his thighs. Rizzo's appearance altered his plan to overtake Snookey and recover the stolen gold.

"It's a two-way split now," Rizzo said, standing over a vault, grasping a sledgehammer. "Let's bust 'em open like a piggybank."

Snookey leaped from the backhoe, rushing to join him. "Semans and Herkey must 'a planned to double-cross us the whole time."

"The gold's ours," Rizzo said, watching Snookey. "Neither of us needs to get greedy."

Jake hunched lower behind the rocks, forcing himself to remain motionless. Men were dying, and if these two discovered him, he'd be dead, too.

Snookey picked up the other sledge.

174

Rizzo tapped the heavy, steel head against the concrete lid. "Hit it here."

"Gotta be worth half a million bucks," Snookey said, rubbing his hands together. He gripped the long, oak handle and swung the sledge into the burial vault.

Rizzo followed, striking the same spot. The repeated pounding crumbled the concrete. After several more blows, it was pulverized into powder. A dinner plate-sized hole appeared, exposing interwoven steel rods, which reinforced the heavy duty vault. Continuing to beat on the same spot, they knocked away more concrete, exposing a two-foot diameter hole. On his knees, Rizzo held his flashlight over the gap. "Think I see 'em."

With his other hand, Rizzo reached between crossed pieces of steel. "It's here! They're wrapped in something, maybe burlap." He pulled a heavy pocketknife from his duty belt. Laying flat on his stomach, with both arms deep inside the vault, he slit the coarse material. With one hand, he grabbed a gold bar. "Suckers are heavy," Rizzo said, then immediately fumbled it back to bottom of the vault. A dull clink echoed from the black hole.

Snookey stood over him. "Let's get this done."

"Just nervous," Rizzo repeated several times.

His hands were shaking from the cold when he finally managed to guide a gold brick through the vaults cage-like bars. When he did, Snookey grabbed it and used his wet shirt to wipe off the thin layer of mud, which coated its top.

"Fifteen years, but we got 'em back!" shouted Rizzo.

"Yeah, I wanna look at it," Snookey said. "Gimme your knife."

"What for?"

"Something's not right. Give it to me," Snookey yelled.

Jake inched closer, legs and knees aching, watching Snookey wipe the muddy blade across his pants. He scraped the sharp edge across the gold brick, like someone

175

peeling an apple, slicing away a thin layer, examining the gold bar.

Snookey's eyes closed, a crooked and twisted look crossed his face. Without a word, he tossed the brick and cuttings into the dead, heavy bush, then grabbed handfuls of mud, tossing them in the direction of the Semans house. "You cheat'n bastard."

Rizzo took a few steps to retrieve it.

Jake backed further into the underbrush, knowing something was wrong, hoping he wasn't spotted.

"It's a fake, don't bother," Snookey shouted.

"Can't be. I took it from the safe myself."

"Gold-plate. You saw gold-plated lead," said Snookey.

Rizzo grabbed another brick, cutting it. He held the shaving in his hand, letting them fall to his feet. "Somebody went to a hell of a lot of trouble."

In disbelief, Jake crawled to where Snookey had tossed the bogus gold. Examining it, he saw a thin layer of gold enveloping a metallic, dull gray interior. Knowing the new risks, he no longer could work for his clients. Too many people were dead. He planned to look out for himself.

"We got took," shouted Snookey.

"People see what they expect to see. I learned that as a cop."

"I fell for Semans' scam."

"Who's got the real stuff?" Rizzo asked.

Soaking wet, Snookey walked to the open trenches, and tossed a gold brick into the soft mud. "The girl, June, from the monastery, she's close to his family. She may know something. Semans cares for her."

"We'll make a visit to the pretty nun," said Rizzo.

Still hidden in the garden, Jake retreated, stepping through water soaked foliage, back to his mini-bus. A new plan popped into his mind as he drove away.

* * * *

176

Jake slammed a fist against the dashboard of his VW bus. He'd come close to finishing the job. After driving past Snookey's trailer, he made a U-turn and returned. Stopping alongside it, he jumped to the street and removed the small cap from the trailer tire's air valve. After finding the right-sized pebble, he forced it into the cap, threading it back onto the tire's stem. Immediately, he heard a faint hiss of air escaping. After doing the same to the tire beside it, he took one last look to the garden gate, no sign of Snookey and Rizzo.

* * * *

Jake pulled his beat up mini-bus into the circus tent. Taki, Grace and Geta waited outside the trailer and rushed toward him.

"We wish to return home." Taki said.

Jake held his stubby arms out. "Too dangerous. We must get out of here. They found the vaults but no gold."

Taki pushed aside Jake's arms. "Take us home."

"They've killed more people today. They'll use your family to find the gold, they won't hesitate to kill all of you," Jake said.

Taki nodded and gathered the two ladies to his side. "What do we do?"

Jake pulled Doc's business card from an over-stuffed billfold and looked up at Taki. "I will find a safe place for your family. Then you will buy me an airplane ticket to Los Angeles. I have a strong hunch the gold never left home."

Jake pulled a phone next to him. "Operator, long distance to California." Waiting, he motioned his three clients to his VW bus and glanced out the window, hoping Snookey and Rizzo would be delayed by the flat tires.

After a moment of clicks and finally ringing, the call was answered in Los Olivos, California.

"May I speak to Lenora Perkins?" Jake asked.

177

Chapter Thirty- Six

The Santa Ana winds grew into a ceaseless gale, rocking palm trees, carrying branches and limbs like missiles.

Hector steered the Ford Ranch Wagon from the curb near Uno's home. Doc strained, twisting to take a last look at the barn behind Uno's gray stone house. "Something bothers me about that place."

"Mean the rotten smell?" Hector asked.

Doc continued to stare. "Hell, I don't know, it just does."

"Jake warned us Uno was strange," Sam said.

Doc turned back and propped one of his thick legs on the red padded dash. "I'd like a closer look inside his barn."

"Why not ask him?" Sam inquired.

"Better he doesn't know," Doc replied.

Sam pulled upright, leaning over the seat, staring at Doc and shaking his head. "Holy Moses, you want to break and enter. Lenora gets here tomorrow. We go home. We're done."

Hector nodded. "That's a one man job."

"Why?" Doc asked.

"Less chance to be seen, amigo."

"Maybe," Doc said.

"Those locks, I can pick 'em like that." Hector snapped his fingers.

* * * *

Alone, Hector stood, several blocks from Uno Koba's house after driving the three miles from the fair grounds. Noticing the moon was so bright, he changed his plan and decided to approach the barn through an overgrown back alley.

He leaned into the battering wind, occasionally stepping behind a palm tree for relief. Gale force winds weaved between houses, whistling, and sounding like distant freight trains.

While at Pomona High School, it had been second nature for him to pick a locked door and search a home for valuables. Thoughts of breaking into the barn began to plague him. Robbery was not his intent, only to look around and report to Sam and Doc. No harm in that. The risk was small, still, he was on edge.

Spotting Uno's house, he patted his breast pocket, checking his lock pick and small flashlight. The gray block barn sat near a row of tall cypress trees and provided cover from the alley if a distant neighbor looked from a back window. After squeezing between rows of tall Oleander, he hopped a chain link fence knotted with ivy, landing in Uno's back yard.

Hector crouched low, running along a row of Bougainvillea to a stack of firewood. Stopping to rest, he wiped his shirtsleeve along his dripping forehead. Dim lights from distant houses momentarily distracted him. He watched them for a moment, nothing happened.

Kneeling, he turned back to Uno's house. No lights appeared. From habit, he ran fine sand paper over his lock picks, cleaning off bits of corrosion, getting ready for what he hoped would be a quick job. He could see the barn's double doors were visible from the house and he'd be exposed for a short time. His heart pounded as he sprinted. Rustling Jacaranda trees hid his heavy breathing after he reached the barn's shadow. He surveyed the house, nothing changed, there was no sign of Uno.

Hector held the flashlight in his mouth. With a practiced, light touch, he gradually maneuvered the tension wrench and pick inside the lock's keyway taking a deep breath, he lifted the pins one at a time.

179

The twin upper and lower padlocks popped open in minutes. After entering the barn, Hector pulled the doors closed, leaving the shackles hanging from their hasps. After pushing rolled-up wads of cotton into his nose, he tied a heavy red bandana across his face, leaving only his eyes exposed to the putrid odor. Lighting was sparse. In each corner, a light bulb hung, seemingly suspended in the barn's dusty air. Hector shut off his small light, allowing his eyes to adjust to the dimness. The size and shape of the worm boxes, that filled the barn, reminded him of a pool hall.

It was quiet in the darkness. Thick cement walls insulated him from the howling winds. *Devil winds make strange things,* thought Hector, as he moved to a window, taking another look at Uno's house. He strained to see even the slightest speck of light from an interior room. If he did, he planned to escape immediately. He had no fear of the smallish Japanese man, confident he could overcome him with the boxing he'd learned on the streets of Pomona.

Satisfied he was alone, Hector checked the sides of the barn, rapping his knuckles on walls, searching for unseen doors. With the handle of a shovel he tapped the floor under the large tables, discovering the entire barn had a concrete floor covered by a shallow layer of fine dirt. He continued, finding no hidden rooms. In a hurry to leave the tomb-like room's horrible smell, he gave another quick glance toward the house.

A dull red light came from a small round window.

Hector questioned himself, dismissing the speck of light as something he hadn't noticed earlier. Content, he swung the weak beam of his flashlight into the roof's high pitch. Strands of webs floated from un-painted, wood rafters. Forcing a laugh, he said, "Good thing I don't believe in the boogie man."

Hector ran his shirtsleeve over his eyes that burned from the barns acrid odor. An unexpected shuffle of feet

180

came from behind him. A hoarse voice said, "Start believing."

A sharp flash of jagged pain ripped the inside of his head. His eyes blurred, while at the same time a sudden dullness overcame him as he collapsed to the dirt floor.

Chapter Thirty-Seven

Looking out from the window of the circus trailer, Jake motioned for Taki, Grace and Geta to follow him to his VW bus.

"Snookey and the cop, Rizzo, killed Vince after they dug up the vaults. They're headed back here."

"They have the gold?" Taki asked.

"It was fake. The three of you must hide. They'll come after you next, thinking you know something."

Several tense seconds passed before Taki responded. "How can that be? There must be a mistake."

"No mistake," Jake said. "I have a strong hunch where it is."

"I must know." Taki said, glancing at his family in the rear of the VW. "We must resolve this soon."

"For now, its better that you don't know," Jake said.

"Where are you taking us?" Taki asked.

"The lady I called will let you stay at her house until it's safe."

"What will you do?" Taki asked.

"I'm returning to Los Angeles to find your uncle's gold."

"What about my daughter, June, at the monastery?" Geta asked.

"The place is a fortress, she's safe. Leave her there."

Following Lenora's directions, Jake drove, speeding along potholed route 51 which followed the wide, sweeping Monongahela River toward Pittsburgh.

His passengers remained silent, too frightened to speak. Taki sat next to him, staring into the darkness. Dreary, hazy lights of steel mills flickered on the river beside them. Jake's few questions concerning the gold were answered with only a nod. Taki's eyes revealed nothing.

The glaring, white lights of the Liberty Tunnels appeared as they bumped through an intersection of

182

crisscrossing streetcar tracks. Once through the nearly half mile tube, the skyline of downtown Pittsburgh lit the black sky.

Jake saw the Mount Washington signs and slowed for the sharp exit ramp. His hands knotted on the gearshift, slipping the transmission into low gear. For the next several miles the VW bus's small engine strained to climb the steep hills to reach Lenora's home at the crest of Mount Washington. Along one of the steep slopes they spotted an incline car, back lit by a full moon, inching its way up, passing them. At the top, they saw the incline's terminal. Knowing they were close, Jake took a last look at the directions that rested in his lap. After driving past several large, homes, he spotted the tall entry columns and hulking gargoyles Lenora described.

The high, wood and leaded glass door swung open. A butler with a white napkin tucked into his collar appeared in the doorway. Jake stared up at the bowling ball shaped man blocking the door. Before he spoke, Jake announced, "Lenora said we could stay here for a few days."

"Indeed she did," he answered. Sniffing several times, the butler stepped aside, giving the four a hesitant glance as they entered the foyer.

After pulling the napkin away from his shirt, he pointed to a sitting area where a black telephone sat on a gold, gilded Victorian desk. "The telephone number for which you asked is there."

Jake climbed up into the matching desk chair. Before calling Pomona, California, another idea came to him that might bring Captain Semans from hiding. Looking a Taki, he asked, "Can you reach Captain Semans?"

Taki reached into his jacket pocket, producing a small notebook. "I have the phone number of his hotel in San Diego."

Jake smiled. "Call him. Tell him about the digging at his gardens. Let him know they found the gold and it was fake."

Chapter Thirty-Eight

Sam and Doc jerked back when someone knocked on the door of Hector's apartment.

Olivia peeked her head in. "There's a phone call for one of you."

"They give a name?" asked Doc.

"Jake. He said he has news."

Nodding, Doc stood. "Wait here for Hector. I'll get it."

Olivia stood in the doorway, nervously grabbing her arms behind her back. "Hector show up?"

Doc held up his index finger. "Hold on. Let me get this. We're worried too." He patted her on the shoulder as he passed.

At the phone booth, he picked up the dangling phone. "Give me the news."

"I found the vaults buried in Semans Japanese garden," Jake said.

"Good, then we're done." Doc let out a deep breath and let his broad back collapse against the wood phone booth.

"Snookey and the cop, Rizzo, dug 'em up."

"Rizzo, huh?"

"Yeah. Surprised me. Guess he's a silent partner."

"I'm not surprised. What about Vince?"

"Dead. Snookey shot him after they dug up the vaults."

Doc stood erect. Beads of sweat formed on his forehead. "What happened to the gold?"

"It was fake."

"Did it ever exist?" Doc asked.

"I plan to find out. I'm on my way to Los Angeles...how's your end?"

"Talked to Uno. He seems nervous, like he's about to flip out."

"Talk to him again, push him. Don't take any chances."

"My gut tells me he knows something."

"Think you're right. Got to go," Jake said.

"Hold on." Doc shouted. "How did Herkey's body get from my car to the river?"

"You heard?" Jake said.

"Bad news travels fast."

"Snookey dropped him from the balloon. He killed the cab driver, Woodrow. Snookey saw him with you and thought he might know how to find you. I switched his body with Herkey's. Snookey thinks he dumped the cab driver."

"Switched bodies, did I hear that right?" asked Doc.

"Woodrow is now in your car, frozen."

Doc slammed down the phone.

* * * *

Olivia steered her beat-up, black Hudson along Town Avenue towards Uno's home. "You think Hectors at Uno's barn?" she asked.

Doc remained silent. Sam took a deep breath. "He was going to look around the barn."

Olivia looked at Sam. "He's in trouble again, isn't he?"

"We don't know that, but he's been gone for three hours," Doc said.

She gave a short whistle, dropping her head. "I knew it," she said, and guided the car onto Reservoir Avenue.

Hector's Ford Ranch Wagon was parked on a narrow side street, a few hundred yards from Uno's home. She pulled behind it. Sam climbed from the Hudson's back seat. A blast of warm, dry wind knocked him off balance, pushing him into the Ford. He grabbed the door handle for support and found it unlocked. Sam slid into the front seat and checked the glove box. Hector's gun was missing.

186

Doc raised his voice over the howling wind. "Olivia, go back to the Fair Grounds, Hector might call. Be back here in an hour."

Bracing their hands against the trunks of the palm and Jacaranda trees, they navigated towards Uno's house.

"I see the house, lights are on...somebody's home," Sam said, shielding himself behind a utility pole.

"What are we gonna do?" Doc asked. "Uno scares me. We can't ask him to search his barn."

"That's my plan," Sam said, leaning sharply forward, walking into the harsh Santa Ana wind.

Standing behind an overgrown Bougenvilla they spotted Uno crossing his living room wearing a black sleeveless tee shirt.

"Seems harmless," Sam said.

They both stood at the front door. Before Sam knocked, Uno jerked open the door, and spoke through the screen door. "What do you want? I told you everything this morning."

Sam stepped close to the screen. "I think I lost my watch in your barn. Can we look around?"

Uno paused, examining Sam. Finally, he pointed to Sam's empty wrist. "No marks. You don't wear a watch."

"Pocket watch." Doc pulled a silver watch from his vest, dangling it from a chain. "His is just like mine."

Uno made a move to close the door. "It's late. Maybe tomorrow?"

"We're leaving in the morning," said Doc.

Uno looked back into the house, then pushed open the screen door, motioning them in. "Make it quick."

Sam felt the small hairs rise on the back of his neck and gave Doc a concerned look when Uno slammed the wood door shut behind them.

Shaking his head, Uno pulled a lace curtain back to peek out his picture window. "Devil winds...bad things happen when they blow."

187

"Swell. Do you mind if we look in the barn for the watch?" Sam said, shoving both hands deep into his pockets.

Another sudden gust of hot, dry air shook the house, causing the lights to blink. Uno smiled, while he motioned them to a back door. Sam and Doc nodded, watching him carefully, as they passed him in the narrow hallway.

"I'll join you," Uno said, stepping from the porch. "The barn is not well lit."

Walking several steps behind, Doc pulled Sam's arm. "Don't take your eye off him," he whispered.

Sam patted him on the shoulder, acknowledging.

Uno looked around the wide open field before he hunched over to open the two matched padlocks. He entered the darkened barn alone, turning on the few lights.

"If Hector's not here, what do we do?" Sam said under his breath to Doc before entering.

Doc shrugged his shoulders.

Uno pushed the two doors shut behind them. "Have a look. Don't wake up the worms." Uno laughed. His smile went no deeper than his lips.

Sam and Doc covered their mouths and noses with their hands, walking up and down narrow aisles between worm boxes, pretending to search for the watch.

Finally, Sam leaned against one of the barn's supports. "Not here. Let's go, Doc."

"There a basement?" Doc asked.

"This is it," Uno said, pulling the barn doors open to leave. "I guess you are done here."

* * * *

Walking away from Uno's house, the sudden yelping of coyotes caused Doc to jerk and look back. As he did, he spotted Uno staring at them from his lace-covered window.

"Still watching us?" Sam asked.

188

Doc turned back. "He just lit a cigarette."

"Glad to get out of there," Sam said.

"Must be the rotten food he feeds the worms."

"Maybe worm crap," Sam said, taking a look back.

"Doesn't care about his dad's gold."

"He cares about his dad's honor."

"As I would," Doc said, slapping Sam on the back.

"Hectors probably back at the track."

"Hope so. Lenora's flying in tomorrow and we go home."

"We did what Jake asked us," Sam said. "He's coming back here. Let him deal with Uno."

Doc abruptly stopped. "Something bothers me about the barn."

"What's that?" Sam said.

"Footprints. The dirt didn't have any."

Sam looked at him, but before he spoke, Doc went on. "It was raked. The whole floor was raked. There were no footprints until we walked in."

"Hector never got in?" Sam asked.

"Why rake the dirt floors?"

A glaring pair of headlights pulled to the curb behind them.

Chapter Thirty-Nine

The Ford Ranch Wagon coasted to a stop behind Sam and Doc. Lenora lowered the window slightly, waving them into the car. "Decided to surprise you and flew in early."

"Your foot's better?" Sam asked, bending to get into the front seat while Doc struggled into the back.

Lenora nodded. "I can wear my prosthesis and I couldn't leave you two alone."

"We have a problem," Doc said.

Her smile quickly turned grim. "I met Olivia. She told me about Hector. No one has heard from him."

"He was supposed to look inside Uno's barn for us, but he didn't come back," Doc said. "We're planning to watch the barn. It's a hunch, but it seems to be our last option before we call the cops."

"Call 'em now. Why wait?" Sam said.

"And tell 'em what? We asked him to break and enter someone's property?" Doc said.

Exposing her long brown legs, and her prosthesis, from under her pleated blue skirt, Lenora turned in her seat, looking at Doc, then Sam. "Olivia said the Pomona police don't think much of Hector and will turn him over to immigration." She held her lip between her teeth, watching them both, then added, "There's something about Olivia....don't ask me what...I just met her. Its women's intuition, but something feels wrong."

"She had a crush on Hector," Doc said.

Lenora waved her hand at them both. "She's worried. That's probably it."

"For now, no cops," Doc said. "If he doesn't show up tonight...we got no choice, for his sake."

"We go home with you tomorrow," Sam said, looking at Lenora.

Relying on moonlight, Lenora steered the Ford wagon away from the curb. "Where to?" she asked.

She stopped near Uno's house, backing the long station wagon next to a long row of tall, wind beaten Eucalyptus trees. After pulling the hand brake, she took a long breath. "Now what?"

"We wait," Sam said, leaning close to the windshield. "This is good. We can see Uno's house and barn."

Doc nodded and slumped into the seat closing his eyes. Sam and Lenora did the same, beginning their vigil.

The moon's glare intensified through the night, deepening the long, stark shadows, casting the barn and house into blackness. The Santa Ana's gained power and howled incessantly across the Pomona valley. Nothing in its broad path escaped its vengeance. Only ragged barks of far off coyotes could be heard over its torturing rage.

Lenora raised her head from against the car's window. Breaking the long silence, she asked, "How is Semans connected to a Japanese man in California?"

"I'll tell her," Sam said. "Back home, we followed Jake, the midget detective, to Semans estate, where his clients, Taki, Grace and Geta live. They're related to Uno." He nodded to the house they watched and paused. "Here's the connection, Semans was business partners with Uno's father, Jimmy Koba before the war."

Doc cleared his throat and tapped Sam on the shoulder. "Here's something else, remember the morning I left you alone at my house?"

"The day before it burned down?" Sam asked.

"You took Woody's jitney to town. Remember the attractive girl in the back seat, Woody picked up at Semans house?"

Sam nodded. "Gave her my coat."

"She's a nun, Geta's daughter, June." Doc went silent as something hit the car's roof with a heavy thud. With a swoosh, a withered palm frond flew from the car, bouncing

191

on the pavement, and was drug by a riptide of wind along the debris covered street. He stared at Lenora and Sam. "This is private patient information I'm gonna tell you and it doesn't leave the car."

They nodded.

"Adam Semans had an illegitimate baby with Geta. He's June's father. He brought Geta to Uniontown along with her uncle and aunt, Taki and Grace."

Sam slapped the dashboard. "All this somehow ties to Jimmy Koba, where this whole mess started."

Doc pointed to the house across the street. "The whole thing with the burial vaults and the circus began right here. Semans gotta be in the middle of this. He's always been the big fish."

* * * *

The full moon had just begun its downward arc when Doc's deep voice broke the silence. He spotted someone walk to the front of Uno's home.

All three were alert when the solitary figure rushed to the porch and knocked on the front door.

Sam sat erect, his face inches away from the windshield. "Who in blazes is that?"

Lenora put her hand on his arm. "What kind of guest wears a riding duster and a cowboy hat?"

A porch light flashed on at the same time the door flung open. The tall, slender caller disappeared inside.

"Who in hell was it?" Sam asked.

Doc could only stare at the house.

"He let 'em in like they were expected," Lenora said.

"Whoever they are, they could be part of this mess," Doc said, shaking his head. He had to raise his voice over the ceaseless roar of the wind. "I wanna get a closer look."

192

Chapter Forty

Through the dusty fog, pale lights of the Monastery appeared as the police car descended Summit Inn Road, high in the Blue Ridge Mountains of Pennsylvania.

"The nuns in this monastery don't talk," Rizzo said.

"You got a badge. They'll talk," Snookey answered.

"They took a vow of silence," Rizzo said, keeping his eyes on the narrow winding road.

"If Semans wants the nun alive, he'll tell us where he moved our gold."

"Maybe."

"She's the only one left," Snookey said. "You let those three get away."

"I told you the damn midget took 'em."

"We'll deal with him later."

"I may not recognize her," Rizzo said. "Been a few years, but she's a looker, I'll tell 'ya that."

"What's her name?"

"June Tamura. Guess it's Sister June now."

Rizzo slowed the patrol car, pulling from the main road to a gravel drive leading to the Monastery's main entrance. The well-lighted tower bell chimed six times.

"She might be at dinner," Rizzo said. "We gonna just march in?"

"This still in the city?" Snookey asked.

"Oh, yeah."

"You're gonna take her in for questioning about the disappearance of her aunt and uncle."

"What?"

"You heard me," Snookey said, staring at the heavy steel bars guarding the monastery's entry doors.

"They won't let us in."

"Turn on your siren and dome lights."

A high pitched, blaring wail accompanied by twin red flashing dome lights, overran the night's serenity. Snookey leaned close to Rizzo. "We may not get in, but they'll come to us."

In moments, the double gates slid open. Three small glaring lights bobbed, moving toward the patrol car. With raised arms, Rizzo stood in front, waving his badge to the approaching group of nuns.

"I'm Sister Irma, the Mother Superior, may I help you?" the smallish nun asked. The others flanked her, knotting their hands at their chests.

"I need to speak to one of your nuns," Rizzo said.

"We are a cloistered order," she said. "I'm the only one permitted to speak to…"

Rizzo stepped closer, pointing to the silver badge on his chest, cutting her off. "I'm a cop. That gives me the right. June Tamura, how do I find her?"

The three nuns drew together. Sister Irma spoke in Latin. They bowed in unison. She then turned back to Rizzo. "May I ask the reason?"

"Family emergency, they want her home."

Sister Irma looked into Rizzo's eyes. "Is this the truth?"

"Sure is," he said glancing away.

She smiled. "This is her home now. However, I will ask her." Turning away, she walked quickly back to the monastery gates. The other nuns grabbed-up their robes, hurrying at her footsteps. Right behind them rushed Rizzo and Snookey.

Sister Irma looked back at Rizzo. "Stay outside the gates. Sister June may be praying in the basement chapel."

"You're interfering with the law," shouted Rizzo.

"Her life is here," Sister Irma answered.

"It's an emergency," Rizzo said.

Like a striking cobra, Snookey grabbed Irma, pulling her veil from her head. Long silver hair fell loose over her shoulder.

194

"Unlock the gate," Snookey whispered, holding his mouth next to her ear.

The two nuns rushed to Sister Irma, replacing her black and white veil. "We have the sword of heaven to protect us," Sister Irma said calmly.

She opened the gate. "Very well, come with us."

After guiding them to a small alcove, she unlocked a narrow wood door. "Come, this way. I will take you to her, but God will punish you."

Descending several stories, they walked single file down a curving stairwell. The air was damp and cold when they stepped into a long narrow Tudor arched hallway. With a flashlight, Sister Irma led the way through a pitch-black corridor. Snookey's and Rizzo's footfalls filled the mausoleum-like passageway with dull echoes.

"Not much farther. It's the last door." Sister Irma said, while she fumbled under her long robe, pulling out a set of oversized skeleton keys. "This room is directly under our main chapel. We must accompany you. Our nuns come here to commune with God in complete solitude, Sister June is here."

Rizzo and Snookey pushed by the nuns, entering the pitch back dark space. Once they did, Sister Irma and the two others slipped, unheard, from the room, slamming the metal door, quickly locking it.

Pounding on the door came in quick bursts, followed by muffled shouts. Sister Irma knelt at the door, as in prayer, speaking into the keyhole. "No one can hear you. These rooms are used to bury our sisters. May the Holy God bless you."

The sisters bowed their heads, making the sign of the cross. In their bare feet, they silently climbed the spiral stairs.

Chapter Forty-One

Olivia stepped into the house, ignoring the stink of simmering fish stew. Uno Koba, dressed in slippers and work clothes, took her hand. She slumped to kiss him on the cheek.

"I haven't seen you in days," Olivia said, putting a soft hand on his chest.

"You could have called."

"I like face to face," she said, wrapping an arm over his shoulder and slinging a hip to one side.

"So talk."

"Can we sit?"

Uno pointed to the living room, where a plastic covered sofa sat on a highly polished wood floor. He grunted, dropping next to her, both stared at a new General Electric television.

Olivia slid forward, sitting at the edge, clasping her hands over her knees. "I've worked here six months, still I hardly know you." She tilted her head and finally smiled while walking her fingers down his arm. "I work here taking care of your worms and you know...." She let her words drift off.

Uno groaned, shifted his bare feet in and out of his carpet slippers. Outside the wind moaned. "There are others who know less about me and have known me longer."

"Do they keep their boots under your bed at night?"

Easing himself up, he laughed, then walked to the portrait of his father, Jimmy Koba wearing his war metals. "Today has been difficult. Shall we go upstairs?"

Olivia wagged a finger at him and patted the spot next to her. "I want to talk, and get to know you better."

Uno shook his head, walking toward her, holding out his hand. "What is it about me that will satisfy your curiosity?"

"Are you rich?" Olivia asked.

"What kind of question…"

She laughed before he finished. "You think 'cause I'm Mexican, I'm gonna rob you?" She played, making two guns from her thumbs and index fingers. "You know why. You're a mystery man, and I'm nosy."

"Are all Mexicans so direct?"

Olivia held her gaze on Uno. "Do you want me to leave?"

"Did you come here to talk?"

"I might have."

"Then, you should have been here sooner, you missed Amos and Andy."

"I should go." Olivia stood, running her hands down the sides of her white blouse and denim jeans. "I hope Amos and Andy can do what I do."

Uno threw his arms up in defeat. His eyes revealed nothing, walking to her.

She repeated, "Well, can they?" Olivia smiled. He stepped behind her, placing his hands on her shoulders, guiding her into the kitchen pantry. He opened the hidden door exposing narrow wooden stairs to a dark basement.

Dim lights lit their walk along the brick floor.

"I can't hear the wind down here," Olivia whispered.

"It's a quiet place. Sometime, I come here to hide," Uno said, while grabbing the base of a low hanging light bulb, aiming it to illuminate the open safe. "It's empty," he said stepping inside, turning on a light switch. "American soldiers cleaned it out. Is this what you wanted to know?"

While the side of her face nearly rested on the dusty surface, Olivia ran her hand over the empty shelf, feeling the deep ridges of bare wood on her callused fingers.

"They took everything?" She could barely force the words out.

"Not everything, my family is rich in tradition and honor."

Olivia stepped from the safe. "There were stories about hidden money and gold."

Nodding, Uno led her back to the basement stairs.

At the kitchen table, Uno stared down at Olivia, sitting across from him propping her smudged face in her palms. He held up two fingers, giving a mock Boy Scout pledge. "I'll give you the Reader's Digest version of the plight of our family."

He stood quietly for a moment, playing out the words in his mind. Jutting his chin out, he swung a leg over the back of a chair as if mounting a Harley Davidson. "We once had money. My father and his business partner bought strawberry farms in Orange County. The money came from gold my father and his father accumulated. His partner sold it to foreign countries. They supposedly acquired the best land in Southern California."

"Strawberry pickers…stoop labor for us Mexicans." Olivia made a sour smile. "You were going to be farmers for the rest of your lives?"

"My father said it was worth more than gold," Uno said with a laugh.

"I know," Olivia said. "We all have dreams. They never come true."

Uno stood, ending the conversation.

Leaning back, she stretched her arms over her head, making no move to stand. Instead asking, "What happened to it?"

Uno rested his palms on the table in front of her. "To what?"

"To the strawberry fields," Olivia smiled.

"During our internment, they killed my father. His partner stole every acre of land."

She sat upright. "What did the police do?"

"For someone so young, Olivia, you ask many questions."

"Curiosity." She reached a hand out to Uno.

198

"The police were not called," Uno said. "He owned the gold illegally."

Olivia tilted her head. "You said it was his."

Outside, pounding wind moaned, sounding like a wounded animal. Uno sat rigid, his eyes riveting on the jagged shadows of oak tree branches whipping back and forth, scraping against the house.

His solemn eyes returned, focusing on her. "In 1933, this country made it illegal for Americans to own gold bullion." Uno let out a breath. "The soldiers that took us away claimed they were confiscating our gold."

"They stole it," Olivia said while her eyes wondered the small room. "Guess nothing's hidden in the walls?" She stood and wrapped an arm around his waist. "Bet you're not telling me everything."

"Life is full of surprises." Uno swung his arm toward the staircase.

She ran up, two at a time.

* * * *

Olivia remained asleep when Uno arose. He inhaled her musky fragrance on the pillowcase. Her feet, which hung over the foot of the bed, jerked as he pulled the covers over her long bare back. Lighting a cigarette, he moved to the window. A full moon illuminated the late night sky, producing quivering shadows of the numerous trees, which surrounded his home. A limb, victim of the blowing wind, brushed against the house and fell, crashing onto the street. From the corner of his eye, he caught the glare of an oncoming car's headlights swerving to miss it.

Uno recalled that dreaded morning. Nearly fifteen years ago. He had been first to spot the headlights of the Jeep that parked at their home.

The satchels nearly slipped from his shaking hands when he stumbled over the edge of pavement raised by

199

roots of the Eucalyptus tree. Numbered tags hung from his father's military jacket and from the fur collar of his mother's coat she wore over her best flowered dress. Swinging from a rope around her waist was a copper teapot.

Jap spies, Jap spies, echoed.

Neighbors, arms snuggly wrapped over their chests, stood mute. Sobs from mother grew. He turned back only to be shoved.

"Pigs, Fascist army pigs!" he shouted.

He heard the hollow thud inside his skull before feeling the blow against his face. Dropping to his knees, his lips tasted blood.

Jap spies, you're Jap spies, echoed again, as if coming from inside his head.

Falling against the Jeep, he tossed his bags inside. The teapot rode in mother's lap. Father, his head held high and arms bound, walked between two soldiers, disappearing among the onlookers.

While jamming the gearshift, the driver spit in the street and the Army Jeep lurched from the curb.

He stared at its green floor until it stopped inside the fairground's gates. Crammed behind the fence, circling the track, Japanese American families watched new arrivals, wanting to recognize family and friends that climbed from the rows of nearby brown busses.

Processing lines for medical checks and contraband wove endlessly between horse stalls and barns that would soon become their prison.

Walking in the circus-like madhouse, somber, flat faces moved trance-like, encircling him, seemingly enlarging, springing within inches of his face, then deftly vanishing. A shove in his back jolted him. An angry, big hand grabbed his collar, throwing him into the barracks. He stared at the unutterable sadness in his mother's eyes as she unpacked her meager belongings. Her gloves, hat and

Sunday shoes found a home on top a suitcase next to the hanging blanket, which divided the stall. Lye and wood shavings thrown on the concrete floor did nothing to hide the odor of urine and manure.

Bedding, blankets and cots were stacked next to a coarse brick wall. Recently white washed, it failed to hide crusty remains of long dead insects.

He laid awake, longing for home, listening to the anguish of frightened families calling out for misplaced elderly parents and children. Shuffling playing cards and murmurs came through a partition, which stopped before reaching the low pitched roof.

Intermittent flashes of lighting lit the barbed wire fence.

A narrow line of light glared in the glass window. Uno turned, seeing Olivia's bare back slip into the bathroom.

"I need a shower," she said, closing the door.

Chapter Forty-Two

The brilliant moon bent downward in its arc, reminding the three of their long vigil. Lenora lifted her chin from the top of the steering wheel. "Are they still there? I haven't seen anyone in a while." She gave Sam a hurried glance, and slumped back into the seat.

"Uno's at the window," Sam whispered. "He's lighting a cigarette. Stay down, he could see us."

"Is that his bedroom?" Lenora asked.

"Could be. It's not the room we were in," Doc said.

"You were there?" Lenora asked.

"He showed us a cigar box full of gold coins," Doc answered. "Said the army took the rest."

Lenora jabbed a finger to the upstairs window. "Somebody just opened a door behind him. He's not alone."

"Just saw a little bit of their backs, couldn't tell much," Doc said.

"It was fast. I couldn't see anything," Lenora said.

"I'm gonna take a peek in the windows," Sam said. "Shut off the dome light before I get out."

Doc turned to work himself from the back seat. "We'll both go."

"I'll move faster. Wait here."

With the strong wind at his back, Sam ran from the parking lot to a narrow, rutted alley, which slipped, between rows of white, frame houses. The moonlight and clear sky gave the late night the appearance of summer dusk, illuminating trash and debris, which overflowed from badly dented garbage cans. Haggard dogs with teeth bared, rushed from under houses only to halt abruptly at chain link fences that surrounded postage stamp sized yards. Returning to the street, Sam ducked behind a row of tall hedge, which hung over the sidewalk, hiding himself and his long shadow. Sweat rolled down the small of his back as he surveyed the moonlit street. He spied the line of Eucalyptus trees near Uno's house. Resting, he glanced to the second floor window of the house. Uno stood motionless, arms across his bare chest, one hand held a cigarette to his mouth.

To reach the trees undetected Sam backtracked along the hedgerow, moving away from his target. Fighting the wind, he jogged across an intersection. From the shadows something skittered toward him. As he turned to look, a large palm leaf crashed into him. Its long wood-like stem armed with twin rows of curved, jagged teeth, ripped across his forearm, drawing a thin line of blood. Struggling to regain his breath, he leaned against a Eucalyptus tree, which blocked the wind and allowed him to remain hidden. His legs ached and trembled. Taking deep breaths, regaining his composure, he looked back at the shadowy images of Lenora and Doc sitting in the Ford Ranch Wagon.

He cursed himself for accepting Doc's invitation to attend the circus and nearly becoming lunch to a trio of hungry tigers. Doc's house would still exist, if he had not answered his call two weeks ago.

Approaching the house, using the giant trees as a shield from Uno's view, he was confident of remaining unseen. It took longer than planned, but he finally arrived. He pinned his back against the house's rock exterior. His chest heaved while he caught his wind. After several deep breaths, Sam began to inch along the wall, moving to a side window. The venetian blinds were angled, slightly open, lace curtains were pulled together behind them. Crouching near the edge of the window, Sam raised his eyes above the window's ledge. Two lamps burned in the room and another across the hall in the kitchen. After watching for a few minutes, no one appeared. Ducking under the ledge, he planned to move to another window at the rear of the house, closer to the kitchen. Before he took a step, the kitchen door slammed, causing him to jump and press back into the dark shadow of the house, wishing himself invisible. Hearing muffled voices, he squatted behind an overgrown bush. On hands and knees, he moved toward the sound, hoping the whistling wind camouflaged his approach. Putting his face next to the ground, feeling the coarse soil against his cheek, he peeked one eye around the corner.

Two people, their backs to him, stood in the yard between the house and barn. The taller visitor struggled to keep a cowboy hat in place while the broad skirt of a riding duster billowed and flapped. The visitor pointed to the end of the alley and walked off. Sam watched the tall figure depart. Its silhouette soon vanished in the gloominess of the barn.

In a moment the screen door slammed. Uno returned to the house. Sam pulled himself up from the ground, luckily spotting the darkened shape of the fleeing visitor turning a corner under a nearby street lamp.

Not giving up, Sam followed well behind. The lone figure stopped, looking back to the house, then, in a hurry, walked in the opposite direction, away from where Lenora and Doc waited. Fatigued, Sam rested behind an overgrown cactus, unsure if his prey had seen the waiting car.

Unable to gain ground on the tall figure, Sam watched from a distance, thanks to the full moon. Uno's late night guest traveled several blocks before stopping at a car parked on a narrow side street. After slapping its roof several times, climbed in and sped away.The black car they drove was familiar to him.

Struggling against the wind, and his pounding heart, Sam reached Lenora and Doc, surprising them as he slipped into the front seat. "His guest left by the back door," he said. "They suspected being watched."

"Did you get a look at 'em?" Doc asked.

"No, but I saw the car they used, you'll never guess."

"We're wasting time," Lenora said. "Let's follow them."

"No rush," Sam said. "I know where they're going."

"Mind telling us," Doc said.

"Pomona Fair Grounds," Sam answered. "Who ever they were, they got in the Hudson Olivia drives."

"Might be Hector," Doc said.

"They had the same build," Sam said.

"This could be a con game they're playing," Doc said.

Lenora had the car running by the time Sam and Doc agreed to return to the Fair Grounds.

Pulling away from the parking lot, a long, sharp cracking sound came from beside them.

Chapter Forty-Three

The bellman left the spacious lobby of the Hotel del Coronado carrying a folded note on a silver tray. He walked to the billiard room, searching for Captain Adam Semans.

"Two ball in the corner." The tall slender gentleman, dressed in white slacks and shirt, announced, chalking his cue. His stroke was smooth and effortless. The ball dropped with a dulled clunk into the braided leather pocket. Semans poked a cigar into his mouth. "I believe you owe me some money, Pike."

The bellman stopped outside the room, waiting for a nod of approval.

Noticing the interruption, Semans asked, "Why does the Pacific have such beautiful sunsets?"

"Don't know, sir."

"Isn't it apparent? It's the clean air of San Diego." Semans waved the messenger to him.

"There's a telephone call waiting for you."

Taking the note, he pressed his lips tightly after seeing the caller's name.

The bellman pointed to a telephone sitting on the room's small bar. "The operator has transferred the call."

Semans picked up the handset. "Taki, what is the problem?" He listened to the recounting of the destruction of his Japanese garden and discovery of his buried vaults. Angered, he asked about the contents. After learning the gold bars he schemed to obtain were phony, he snapped the cue stick, bashing it against one of the room's opulent wood columns.

Propping himself against the bar, Semans searched for an explanation. None came, however, an idea did. Satisfied, he tossed the shattered pool cue to the carpet.

"Bellman, arrange to have a car brought around."

Semans left the room, failing to collect his winnings.

Chapter Forty-Four

Uno stepped from his house. A massive Eucalyptus rested across the hood of a red and white Ford Ranch Wagon. Its doors opened slowly. Three stunned passengers pushed aside heavy, leafy branches, cautiously stepping out from the wreckage.

"Anyone hurt?" Uno shouted.

Sam, Doc and Lenora walked around the car and tree, inspecting the damage. The tree's trunk had crushed the hood, while a thick branch shattered the windshield.

"He knows what we've been doing. Might as well admit it," Doc said.

"Should I call somebody?" Uno shouted.

"We can't stay here," Lenora said to Doc and Sam.

"No choice," Doc said. "Lenora can't walk far on her foot."

Uno waved. "It's dangerous out there, come in."

"Look at him," Sam said. "He's enjoying this."

Uno waved again, smiling, holding his front door open.

"Who do we call?" Doc asked.

Before anyone answered, Lenora was hobbling across the street. She looked back. "I'm tired and I need to use the ladies room."

Uno stood at the open door, pointing to the kitchen table.

"What brings you out tonight?" he asked.

"Still looking for Hector," Sam said. "Thought he might be around here."

"You're wasting time," Uno said. "You'll have better luck at the bars."

"That was our next stop, before this happened," Doc said, nodding outside.

Lenora walked back into the kitchen asking, "Who can we call?"

207

"We have a number for the Fair Grounds," Sam said, reaching into his pocket.

"Mean the phone booth?" Doc asked.

Sam held up a slip of paper. "That's the only one."

"Call it. What choice do we have?" Lenora said.

"Be my guest." Uno pointed at the wall phone. "I don't own an automobile."

Lenora followed Doc to the phone. After they were out of site, she whispered, "His visitor was a woman. I smelled perfume in the bathroom."

"Maybe aftershave?"

Lenora shook her head several times. "Cheap perfume. Olivia wore it when I met her."

Doc gave a glance to Lenora as he gave the number to the operator. After a dozen rings someone answered. He spoke at once. "Who's this?"

"Olivia. Who's this?"

"It's Doc Martin. We need a ride."

"What happened? Are you all right?"

"Everybody's fine. Pick us up at the sweeper plant. We'll be there."

Before Olivia asked more, Doc hung up.

The three stepped to the front porch, leaving Uno sitting at the table.

Doc grabbed Sam and Lenora by the arms, ushering them from the house, down the semi-circular steps. Crossing the street, they hurried to the sweeper plant, hiding from Uno's view in a doorway niche.

"Lying sack of shit," Doc said. "He has a truck in a shed near the barn."

"It doesn't matter," Lenora said. "Olivia will be here any minute."

Doc looked at her. "Tell Sam."

"I smelled Olivia's perfume in the bathroom."

"Over the fish smell?" Sam asked.

208

"I liked the fish smell better, boys," Lenora said smiling. "I know perfume like I know horses."

"Hell," Sam said. "Then she's the one I followed. Now, she's coming to pick us up."

Doc looked around the corner. "I don't like this."

"I'm not getting in the car," Lenora said.

"Now, do we call the police?" Sam asked.

"They'll send Hector back to Mexico," Lenora said. "You two got him into this."

"Not our business," Sam said. "Jake wanted us to talk to Uno. It was Hector's idea to break into the barn. I'm done. Jake's on his way, he can find him, he's the private eye."

Doc took a deep breath, and looked around the wind-blown street. "Somebody's burned down my house and there's a frozen body in my car disguised as a Pop-Cycle, This time I'm with Sam."

"Nuts," Lenora said. "Olivia's on her way. What do you want to do, give up?"

Chapter Forty-Five

Olivia spotted the Eucalyptus tree lying across the Ranch Wagon's crushed hood as she headed to the sweeper plant's main entrance. Turning the corner from Reservoir Street, she saw the oversized, wooden Santa Claus face being battered against the factory wall by the constant wind.

She recalled the plant's Christmas tree that nearly filled the spacious lobby. Nearly a year ago, she had gone there, as she had for the past seven years, delivering tamales her mother sold to the employees.

Unlike previous years, the receptionist was absent from her desk. Instead, she was met by a well-dressed man, introducing himself as the plant's security director. At first she declined his offer to return to his private office. Each time she attempted to bypass him, he stepped in her path. After several stand-offs, he relented, offering to allow her to complete her job once their discussion was done. She agreed.

In the stark office, he wasted no time getting to the point, outlining an investigation of a factory employee suspected of theft. After completing the no-frills review of his case, he requested her help, offering a reward. The cash would buy a small ranch house and several horses, with plenty left over. Something she'd always dreamed of.

Within weeks of agreeing, she won Uno Koba, an assembly shop foreman, over, landing a part time job caring for his worm farm. Gaining his trust was her initial objective. What she was to search for had not been revealed. The task came with the caution to be alert for anything unusual. The security man, pleased with the inroads, rewarded her with a hundred dollar bonus. Nothing eventful happened by the end of the first month, however, she was paid another hundred. She should have suspected something.

Three times a week she fed a mix of food scraps to hungry worms, raked their dirt boxes and packaged worms in peat moss for shipment to bait shops. Her work continued for months without hearing from the security director, except for the five, twenty dollars bills, which showed up in special delivery letters every four weeks.

One afternoon, while raking the barn's dirt floor, she looked up, startled, seeing the agent from the sweeper plant standing in the door. He contorted his face at the strong, rancid odor of the barn, and informed her he would be away for an undetermined time.

After handing her a thick, brown envelope, he requested a signature on a receipt, calling it a formality. That envelope was stuffed with cash, twenties and fifty's. Paper clipped to it was a phone number.

He fooled with his tie then laughed, saying he expected results while gone. The number was to be called weekly with progress reports. Pausing, he tapped her hips, suggesting she use her assets, adding that a woman learns more from a man with her head on his pillow. She understood the message.

Walking away, he slapped a worm box, telling her their contents were worth more than what she had so far produced. He surprised her, revealing the search was for gold bars. Her payment would be doubled with success.

That was the last time she'd seen him for nearly five months, then his telegram arrived. His trip east was unsuccessful and he was returning.

Olivia realized she'd driven past the entrance into the sweeper plant. After a U- turn, she sped back.

Pulling the Hudson near the curb, she looked for the three she was to rescue.

No one waited.

211

Chapter Forty-Six

Exhaling, Doc stepped from behind a vine-covered wall, staring at the black Hudson driving away. "Think she saw us?"

"It's dark back here. Doubt a bat could have," Sam said, bracing against a metal roof support.

"Stay in the shadows," Lenora said. "Make sure she's gone."

After the car's taillights turned the corner. Doc stepped into the street. "Until we know what Olivia is up to, we have to assume she knows something about Hector."

"We can't go back to the fairgrounds," Sam said.

"For now, we use my plane. We can sleep and shower there," Lenora said. She struggled walking against the strong wind, guiding her hand against the building. "There's a mom and pop grocery on the corner. It has a pay phone. We'll call a taxi."

* * * *

The cab ride took less than an hour despite the late-night bumper to bumper congestion along Foothill Boulevard. Lookey-loos slowed traffic to a crawl, stopping to watch the fires burning in the close by Sierra Madre Mountains.

Lenora paid the fare and slammed the cab's front door shut. "Here we are...Rosemead airport."

Doc raised both hands in the air, stretching his short, rotund frame. "Winds aren't blowing, barely a breeze."

Lenora winked at Sam. "This is one of those nights I just want to lay next to someone and look at the stars."

Doc poked a sharp elbow into Sam's ribs.

"It's been a long day. Am I the only one thirsty?" Sam said.

212

Passing through the gate's chain link fence, Lenora pointed to a lone hanger near the control tower. A large black number one was painted on the massive white structure. "We'll be cozy in there. Plane's stocked with food and booze and we'll be alone. My pilots are on call in LA."

They passed rows of single and twin-engine planes tied down at the edge of the tarmac. Along the other side, garage-like shops with metal signs hung over doors promoting airplane repair, sightseeing and flying lessons. A green Sinclair aviation fuel depot stood alone, at the far end, guarded by steel posts and concrete bunkers.

With a ring of keys in her hand, Lenora led them to a man door at the side of the number one hangar. Inside, it was quiet, except for their echoed footfalls on the glossy concrete. Two smaller planes also occupied the spacious hangar. High in the steel rafters, a row of security lights burned, permitting them to navigate safely to her plane.

Near the tail section of the silver DC 3, Lenora unlocked the passenger door and pulled down the short stairs, then stepped aside, waving her guests in. Doc looked around, smiling at the tropical mural that covered the roomy interior. "Been a week, missed the place," he said walking to the bar.

After sliding open a deep drawer, Doc lifted out several bottles and glasses, and poured drinks. Lenora limped up the slight incline to the forward section and dropped into one of many white leather chairs, immediately pulling off her prosthetic foot. Rubbing the stump with both hands, she groaned. Sam moved up and down the aisles, shutting drapes over the small windows.

After a dinner of cold sandwiches and Champagne, Sam and Doc briefed Lenora on all that had occurred since they separated at the Flying M Ranch.

"What are we doing to find Hector?" Lenora asked. "Tom expects him back."

213

"Our best option's the police," Sam said.

"Not for Hector," Lenora said.

"Forty-eight hours, then we call 'em."

"We'll search the barn and house," Lenora said. "I mean every crack and crevice."

"We're forgetting Jake," Sam said. "He'll be here in the morning."

Nodding, Doc pulled his pocket watch from his stained suit pants. "In about ten hours. I say we wait, he's the private eye."

Chapter Forty-Seven

Jake Ozaki un-buttoned the white napkin that hung from his shirt, folded it neatly and tossed it on the plate in front of him. Sliding the curtain open, he pulled himself up to look out the small window.

The DC 7 was in a slow decent over Palm Springs, approaching Los Angeles International Airport. The long flight from Pittsburgh had been turbulent, preventing him from sleeping soundly. Stretching his bowlegs, he kicked at but missed the empty seat in front of him.

The plane bounced and jerked, rattling the ice in the cocktails that were being served. The growl of the planes droning twin engines amplified in the cabin's abrupt silence. After a few uneasy minutes, the hum of passenger conversation resumed.

Jake leaned back in his seat, taking a sip of Scotch, savoring his anticipated wealth. He was about to solve the case, which plagued him for the past year. Without warning, a slight vibration ran through the fuselage from front to rear. Then suddenly the plane bumped and shuddered, as if struck by an earthquake, and dropped, losing altitude. All heads turned to the cockpit door that swung open and banged against the bulkhead. Sharp clicks of an intercom grabbed everyone's attention.

"We have some turbulence from Santa Ana winds," the pilot's voice said. "Remain in your seats with your seat belts on. We'll be through this before we land."

A flicker of light from the window caught Jake's eye. He rose to his knees, eyeing the ground below. Orange-red flames shot into the air from the blackness of the mountainside. Shaking his head in disgust, guessing its origin, a low-life, firebug seeking delight in the destruction of thousands of acres of forestland and homes. A single strike of a match, fueled by intense winds and parched brush, had quickly become a raging inferno.

A friendly voice came from within inches of his face. Jake turned to the pretty stewardess leaning across the seat. "May I have your tray?"

Nodding, he passed it to her and leaned back, letting his feet dangle, hoping to relax, knowing this would be his only time to rest for the next few days. What lay ahead required his cleverness and cunning, something no one expected from a Japanese dwarf. Discovering that the gold bars in Seaman's garden were a hoax had been a major setback. His suspects, Vince, Snookey, and Rizzo had been duped by a clever shell game played out over many years following World War Two. His clients, Taki and Grace Sasaki would be disappointed by his final report. The case, which had taken him from his home in Pomona to a rugged mining area in Western Pennsylvania, had been a waste of time, until now.

The lights along Sepulveda Boulevard sparkled as the DC 7 glided above low, flat rooftops, preparing to touchdown.

After deplaning, Jake hurried through the terminal tunnel, searching for a pay phone.

* * * *

Adam Semans pointed to the house, instructing the driver to slowly drive past it and pull to the curb. He counted out a hundred dollars, in fives and tens, for the driver and asked him to wait.

"The meter's running," the driver answered.

"Just be here when I get back," Semans said, closing the rear door. He looked at the house that sat on the corner, surrounded by trees and vacant land. Heavy latticework on both sides of its rounded front porch gave it the look of a park gazebo.

Several lights were on but quickly went off after he knocked. Looking into the house through the door's round

216

window, he knocked again, this time rapping his knuckles on the thin glass, shouting, "It's me, Captain Semans. I know you're there."

He gripped the door handle, shaking it several times. Moving to a nearby window, he tapped it with his fingertips. "I'll wait on the porch. I'm here to make you a business offer."

Chapter Forty-Eight

Olivia pulled on boots and hurriedly wrapped a yellow ribbon around her ponytail. Failing to look into the mirror, she rushed out the door of her fairgrounds one-room apartment early that morning.

Driving through the ivy covered, arched gate she took a deep breath, hoping to relax as she headed to her meeting in nearby Claremont. A melancholy, orange sun sat atop the low hillside rimming the Pomona Fairgrounds and nearly blinded her when she turned east onto Mission Avenue.

Tall, slender palms that lined the street swayed gently. Vicious Santa Ana's, which whipped through the region, had temporarily diminished. Left behind was a gentle breeze, which carried an acrid smell of smoke from nearby fires burning wildly in the local hillside. Light ash floated, like blackened snowflakes, dropping on the foothill communities, which stretched for forty miles between San Bernardino to downtown Los Angeles.

Uprooted trees lay on the roofs of cars blocking traffic along Foothill Boulevard, forcing Olivia to detour through neighborhoods of small wood frame bungalows. It was still early when she arrived at the Sunkist Packing House. Its saw-tooth roof and skylights stood out among the other low, flat buildings. Empty boxcars waited for immigrant workers to load them with cases of lemons and oranges for shipment to eastern cities. Olivia attempted to shake off the memories that forced their way into her mind each time she passed by.

She spotted the Yellow Cab idling near a long, two-story, rectangular building, where the citrus was sorted, washed, and packaged.

The cabby stuck an arm out, pointing to a long shed built of corrugated metal and wood slats.

Olivia stepped over wind-blown crates and debris, pushing open the rust-stained, metal door to step inside. Sensing his presence, she stopped.

"This should be familiar," he said.

"For you, maybe," she answered.

"Our families worked here."

"Sorting fruit, cleaning smudge pots sixteen hours a day...for what? The pennies they were paid?

"It was a living."

"Like hell it was. We lived in the Barrios."

"You can change all that," Jake said.

"Too late for that. Why did you want to see me?"

"I'm disappointed. I thought you would find the gold."

"You're sure it's here?"

"It never left," Jake said. "I was stupid to think so. It's somewhere close to him, where he can get his hands on it."

"I searched the place. There's nothing at his house."

"He'll tell us." Jake said.

Olivia backed away, waving her arms in front of her face. "I'm done. I'm no longer part of this."

Jake stepped closer, looking up to her. "I'm afraid you are, you're not getting out."

"I'm done. No half-pint midget is going to change that."

"Good. You finally got that out of your system," Jake said laughing. "You're right, I won't, but these will." He reached into the breast pocket of his sport coat.

Olivia, from reflex, thrust her hand into her purse, gripping a pistol, keeping it hidden in the handbag, aimed it at Jake's forehead. "I won't miss."

Pulling his hand away slowly, he stepped back. "I'm taking out some papers."

"Keep your hands down, I'll do it."

Jake pulled open the side of his coat. "The brown envelope, take it."

Olivia leaned down, jerking it from his pocket. Watching him carefully, she released her grip on the pistol and pulled her hand free.

"Go ahead, read them. They're carbon copies…receipts you signed when you accepted my payments. Did you forget?" Jake smiled, closing his jacket.

"I haven't done anything."

"True. If you had, I wouldn't be forced to do what I'm planning. You'll be considered an accomplice, and just as guilty."

"You can have the money back."

Jake shook his head, as a brown mouse scurried under crates of lemons. When he raised his head, his broad smile returned. "Too late, you're in this to the end. What I'm after makes that look like child's candy money."

Olivia thought for a moment, managing a wry smile. "You won't kill him?"

"Won't be necessary."

"Your telegram said I'd get half," Olivia said.

"There's enough for both of us."

"After this, I'm done." She turned her back to him, walking to the large washing and sorting area. Olivia dipped her hands into a long vat of blue-green water where several lemons floated, and washed her hands, looking at her own reflection. "You're just like the others."

Jake shook his head. "No. I'm worse…but I try not to think about that."

"What happened?"

"At first it was a job to find missing gold and return it to my clients. The longer I worked the case the more I realized the gold would belong to whoever had possession of it. It legally didn't belong to anybody but the government. So, one day I decided it would be mine."

"How are you gonna get it out of Uno?"

"I know what frightens him," Jake said, sliding the door open to leave.

220

Chapter Forty-Nine

That same morning, Uno stepped out on his front porch. The foothills to the east of his home were gray with smoke and the wind was gaining strength, blowing in his direction. It was something he and the millions of other Southern Californians endured each winter.

There was no sign of his unwelcome visitor, Adam Semans. Instead, a business card fluttered down from the top ledge above the door. After looking down on it for a moment, he saw it belonged to Semans. He stepped over it to retrieve his morning paper. There was nothing the man could say to him that he wanted to hear. Today, his off day, he planned to work alone in his barn, tending to his worms, catching up on the backlogged shipments to bait shops and farms he serviced.

Curiosity bested him. Putting down the newspaper, he returned to the porch for another look at the business card. This time, he picked it up. Turning it over there was a note written in a small, precise hand. Shaking his head, not bothering to read it, he returned to the kitchen, tossing it into the trashcan under the sink.

Perturbed, Uno finished washing his breakfast dish and fork, placing them in the drying rack. He left the cast iron skillet on the stove to cool. After wiping his hands, he glanced at the trashcan, and yanked the curtain closed.

Hoping to settle his nerves, he lit a cigarette and stepped outside. After a few puffs, he ground it against the heel of his boot and hurried to his morning tasks.

The barn's smooth, dirt floor was as he left it the previous evening. The silent alarm had sent a blinking red light to the house, warning him of last night's intruder. They had discovered his secret.

While pulling on worn, leather gloves, Uno walked to a worm box, which sat near a tall, doublewide door. Lifting the heavy wood lid, he noticed the top surface of black dirt

221

had been disturbed. Several of his red wigglers curled themselves around the outstretched fingers of a hand that reached up from the dirt and manure compost. "It's a pity you're vegetarians," Uno said. He poked his pitchfork into the dirt, striking Hector's body several times.

Satisfied, Uno opened the doors next to the open worm bin. Within minutes he returned driving a faded, red pickup, backing it next to the worm box that contained Hector's body. A white, block letter sign on the driver door read, Uncle Uno's Worms.

Once he nailed the lid firmly to the box; Uno loaded it into the truck bed using a portable engine hoist. He drove across an open field of knee-high, dry grass and bumped down a long, rutted slope into a dusty wash, which sometimes carried runoff rainwater from the nearby San Bernardino Mountains. He headed north, toward Mount Baldy, dodging rocks and boulders that over years had been carried down from the higher elevations by raging waters from rain and snow melt off. After several miles of climbing into the rugged foothills, he stopped, directly in the fire's path, near a large accumulation of brush and uprooted trees.

Jumping from the truck, he winced at the bitter smell. The fire intensified as the winds rose and moved quickly along the ridge of mountains running along the northern area of the inland valley cities. The parched brush, that overgrew the wash he had just driven through, would become a path for the wild fire to feed on if the wind shifted, driving the burn down into the heart of several neighborhoods. Once there, the nearly unstoppable, whipping gusts would throw flames, like giant ocean waves over streets and homes, jumping capriciously from one to the next, in a feeding frenzy.

Feeling a rush of heat from the distant fire, Uno pulled the worm box from the truck bed, dragging it over scrub

222

brush and rubble, into a dense pile of heavy dried-out vegetation.

With an auger, he bored several holes into the coffin-like box, and then funneled several gallons of gasoline into it to hasten the burn and keep coyotes away. To complete the task, he dragged tumbleweed and several large branches to conceal the box. Hunched low behind it, he was ready to strike a match and send it up in flames immediately. He shook his head, and put the matches back in his pocket. He'd allow the rapid moving fire line to do the job as well as causing less suspicion if someone watched.

Tossing the empty gas cans into the bed of the truck, he thought of the surprise visit by Captain Semans and the business card left at his door. His initial anger turned to curiosity.

Chapter Fifty

Olivia rode from the unoccupied building in a remote spot of the racetrack. The door and hinges were sturdy, guarded by a heavy, steel bar and padlock. The only key hung from her belt. A few sparse pieces of furniture would need to be added to make it ready. Satisfied, she rode her buckskin at a slow trot back to the fairground stables.

She shoved the keys into her jeans pocket while getting off the horse. Looking up, three people walked toward her. She waved, forcing a smile. "Anything on Hector?" she asked.

"We checked the bars and watched Uno's house most of the night," Doc said. "No sign of him."

"That tree did a number on the car. You're lucky not to be hurt," Olivia said, standing next to her horse. "I tried to pick you up. You weren't there."

After a short pause, Lenora answered, "We should have called. A cab drove by, so we took it."

"You didn't come back here," Olivia said.

"I've got friends in the area," Lenora answered quickly.

Following Olivia's quick nod, Lenora stepped forward, patting the horse on the rump, but looked directly at Olivia. "Good work out?"

"It was all right."

"What were you doing in Uno's house last night?" Lenora hit her with the question they came to ask.

Olivia remained silent, rubbing the horse's coat with her hand. "No one was supposed to know," she finally spoke.

"Know what?" Sam asked.

"It's not what you think. The people I exercise horses for, will fire me if they knew."

"We're here to find Hector, that's all," Lenora said. "No one will know."

"I work for Uno part time, taking care of his worms. Last night, I went there to get my pay check."

"You stayed a long time," Doc said.

"We went over some things." Olivia said, nodding. "He asked me to handle more of the work. So…it may have taken longer." Olivia turned her horse and walked to the barn. "If it's any business of yours, I've worked there six months. There was a lot to talk about."

The three followed slowly behind and stood in the wide door, watching her unsaddle the buckskin. Finally, Lenora stepped into the barn. "Can we talk about Hector? He is a friend of mine as well."

Olivia slung the saddle over the rack, turning her back to them. "This is private property, you should leave."

"This is Los Angeles County property, we'll stay," Lenora said.

Olivia stamped from the barn toward her apartment, muttering in Spanish.

Lenora shouted, "Do you always take a shower after getting paid?"

Doc smiled, wagging a finger at Lenora.

"Sam's right," she said. "We should have called the cops."

Walking from the stall, Lenora stopped and faced Sam and Doc. "That buckskin didn't have lather. She couldn't have ridden too far or too hard. She wasn't exercising that horse."

"What was she doing?" asked Doc.

Lenora looked to the ground, pointing to fresh hoof prints. "Let's take a walk while the winds not so strong. See where they go."

"We're looking for what?" Sam asked.

"I'm curious to see where she went if she wasn't working out the horse." Lenora walked hunched over, staring at scuff and scrape marks on the hard ground.

Moving farther away from the rows of stables the ground softened, making it easier to see the shoe prints.

"Looks like she was alone," Doc said.

"She took her time," Lenora said. "The horse was walking."

The trail led through the stables to an open area used for exercising and training horses. They easily followed the deep prints for several hundred yards, taking them far from the track and grandstand area. They stopped to rest, admiring the stunning, panoramic view of the mountain range north of the fair grounds complex.

"Smell the fire?" Sam asked.

"Long as it stays in the hills," Doc said.

Lenora shielded her face, looking at a distant plume of smoke. "All the same, I've seen the wind turn, just like that." She slapped her hands together, causing Sam and Doc to flinch. "These fires can move down through this whole area if the wind is right. Nothing's safe when it's this dry."

Stopping at a paved road, well behind the backstretch of the racetrack, they looked back, seeing the large overhanging roof of the grandstands. The hoof tracks disappeared, except for light spots of dirt on the heavily cracked black asphalt.

Doc sat on the edge of the elevated roadbed. His face was red and covered with sweat. "I say we go back."

Lenora walked ahead, limping slightly, her head thrust forward, like a hunting dog, examining the faded trail. She abruptly stopped and pointed to an open gate a few hundred yards down the straight, narrow road.

Marching toward it, sudden rising gusts of wind ruffled their clothes, nearly stopping them. All three raised their arms, shielding their faces against flying trash and debris. After the gusts passed, they were greeted by the same steady, blowing winds they'd endured for the past two

226

days. Sam was the first to see the cluster of small, round buildings standing alone, well past the gate.

"Looks like hat boxes," Lenora said.

"I'd like to see the hats," Sam said.

Doc shook his head. "To me, they look like shanties back home."

"There's nothing else out here," Lenora said, hobbling ahead. "Why not take a look."

Doc and Sam hurried behind, finally catching her. They leaned into the wind, in step, as if heading to Oz, following an unpainted, split rail fence.

Crossing into the field, through the gate, they spotted a single set of horse tracks leading in the direction of the round, hatbox buildings. Lenora took little time examining them. With a wave of her hand, she marched off passing overgrown, long stringy vines and fields of wild strawberries that had long ago overgrown their stone and wood plank boarders. Nearby, in contrast, was a stand of neatly trimmed and topped orange trees. With her back to them, she said, "The Japanese called them hobby gardens. They planted them when they were interned here."

Approaching the group of buildings the whiff of urine and manure overpowered the air's sooty smell. A bare patch of dead ground surrounded the ten equally spaced, sun bleached, adobe brick buildings. Narrow pipes poked through their flat metal roofs.

Leaving the others, Sam rattled one of their metal doors, it swung open, smashing against the wall. Several crows cried, springing from an abandoned starting gate, flying low over his head. Ducking, he stepped inside and closed his eyes, allowing them to adjust to the darkness.

Chapter Fifty-One

Uno flicked the business card between his fingers and tossed it on the table. His anger swelled with thoughts of revenge, now that Semans dared show up at his home. Last year's visit from the midget private eye had been the beginning. He'd expected the bogus gold bars to have been discovered much sooner.

Considering his options, Uno chose to deal with Semans, the devil he knew. His father's scheming business partner had plotted to take everything from them. Except for the gold, Semans took thousands of acres of farmland in thriving Orange County from his father. Uno laughed at the irony and heavy burden of owning the gold bars, they were worthless to him unsold.

He slowly read the number from the business card to the operator. Bile rose to his throat, he'd see what this devil, Semans, had to offer.

Uno pulled off his sweat-soaked clothes and showered quickly. His appointment with Captain Semans was in two hours.

* * * *

Little Tokyo occupied nearly a square mile on the east side of downtown Los Angeles, within the shadow of its stately City Hall. After a thirty-minute drive, Uno parked on the street, several blocks from The Far East Café, preferring to walk along Central Avenue. He chatted with the few remaining fruit and vegetable farmers working from backs of trucks and pushcarts, hoping for last minute shoppers. Owners of the small shops that lined the narrow street, lowered clunky steel gates, guarding their doors and windows. He hoped the short walk would relax him enough that he could maintain control over his emotions. Taking a deep breath, he inhaled the sweet aroma of freshly picked strawberries before turning the corner.

A large red, metal sign, CHOP SUEY, hung vertically from the face of a two-story brick building, guided his way to the familiar Far East Cafe. Sitting alone, he sipped green tea while puffing on a Lucky Strike. A few customers, their backs to him, hunched over a small bar. None bothered to look up when he walked by. Napkins and silverware were meticulously being arranged by a waiter. Another lit a small candle at each table. Uno glanced at the entry each time the door swung open. Above it, a large, arched window allowed in pale, dusty sunshine, it felt warm on his face. Bent and twisted stubs of cigarettes filled the glass ashtray near the teapot. Uno used the same hand for both tea glass and cigarette. The other gripped a small pistol in his jacket pocket. He shook another Lucky Strike from the pack, vowing to finish it and leave if Semans had not arrived.

"What do you recommend?" someone asked, putting a drink glass on the table.

Uno rose to his feet. His cigarette hung from his lips, he stood face to face with the man he detested. Semans raven black hair now grayed at the temples, emphasizing his stern composure.

"I was about to leave," Uno said.

"I've been watching you from the bar. You appear nervous."

"Yellowtail's good," Uno said, butting out another half-smoked cigarette. He squeezed the wooden handle of the pistol in his pocket, ignoring Semans extended hand.

Semans smiled, pulling out a chair. After adjusting the crease in his slacks, he leaned forward. "I'll get to the point. You need me as a partner."

Uno's chin lifted, hearing the bizarre words.

"You actually do, whether you care to admit it."

229

Uno quietly drew on the freshly lit cigarette. "How so?"

"The same reason your father did."

"Keep him out of this."

Semans smiled, rattling the ice in his glass. "You live like a church mouse. No money to speak of."

"You don't know anything about me."

"I know enough."

"What's the business proposition?"

"Money and power, I can help you get it."

"Keep talking."

"I can sell the gold, something you haven't been able to do. Am I correct?"

"You and the soldiers took what my father had." Uno tightened his grip on the handgun still in his pocket.

Semans held up an empty glass, waving it to an approaching waiter. As soon as he left, Semans leaned over the table. "You were clever. They dug up your phony gold bricks."

"Then the soldiers have stolen from you," Uno said.

"You knew eventually someone would figure it out." Semans nodded, smiling, holding his thumb and forefinger close together. "You were this close. Other people are looking for the gold. They'll find you. Let me help."

"What do you want out of this?" Uno asked.

Semans paused while the white jacketed waiter dropped a coaster and napkin on the black lacquered table before delivering a fresh gin and tonic.

"Want one?" Semans asked. "It'll make it easier."

Shaking his head, Uno waved off the waiter.

"Like I said, I want to be your partner." Semans moved closer, looking squarely at Uno. "I'll sell the gold, I have buyers."

"Why would you do this?"

Semans picked up his glass. "We split fifty-fifty."

230

Hearing this, Uno sat back. "If I did have it, that sounds steep."

"I'd be doing you a favor. You're living like a criminal, hiding illegal gold."

"The government might change the law."

"I hear different," Semans answered. "You can be wealthy now. Quit living like a hermit."

"You want half?"

"Right now, it's worthless to you," Semans said taking a quick drink. "Besides…when the government confiscates it…you get nothing but federal prison. It'll be worse than internment camp."

Uno stubbed out his cigarette. "I'll think about it."

"You have my number," Semans said as he slid a twenty on the table and walked from the Far East Cafe.

Uno released his hand from the gun's wood grip, feeling he could have turned it to sawdust. Pulling the trigger would have been easy; however, Semans would be useful. Relieved, he remained seated, watching Semans' tall shadow slide past the thin curtain covered window. Realizing only one cigarette remained in the nearly crumbled pack, he grabbed some change from the table and walked to the vending machine near the rear door of the restaurant.

After taking the fresh pack of Lucky Strikes from the tray, he noticed an empty drink glass and burning cigarette on a table in a back room.

Returning to his chair, he stopped. A diminutive shadow moved by the window Semans had just passed. The jerky, up and down gait was easy to recognize.

231

Chapter Fifty-Two

Sam's eyes gradually adjusted as he looked at the round, empty room. The darkness could not be touched, however, it pressed at him from all directions. Stunted weeds grew in cracks of the concrete floor, struggling to reach sparse light, which leaked through narrow slits near the roof. Nauseated by the clammy stale air, he stepped outside. As he did, he noticed remnants of small triangle shaped boot prints. On one knee he knelt to examine them.

Lenora arrived and stood over him. "I saw the same prints back at the stables. They're Olivia's. She spent some time here."

"Doing what?" Sam asked.

"Don't know," Lenora said. "Wish I did. She's up to something."

"The huts are empty. Why bother?" Sam asked.

"Not this one," Doc shouted and rattled two pad locks fastened to a heavy bar crossing the door. "Why lock it?" he asked while guiding his hand against the gritty, clay brick, walking around the structure.

"Amazing stuff," Sam said, hurrying to join him. "Adobe bricks . . . just clay, dirt, and water baked in the sun…been around for thousands of years. Hell, it's fireproof."

Doc slapped the wall with his palm, while glancing to the mountainside, watching several large plumes of smoke. "She might've been looking for a safe place."

Lenora leaned against the building, running her hand along her prosthetic foot. "I'm not sure I can walk much longer."

All three saw the vehicle in the distance. A trail of dust followed it as it sped from the stable area.

"May be trouble," Lenora said as she stepped away from the building, pointing at hoof prints that they had

232

overlooked. "These are fresh. They're from the buckskin Olivia rode."

Sam glanced over his shoulder, at the stables. "Whoever they are, they're coming this way fast."

Grimacing in pain, Lenora hobbled, following the tracks near the locked building. She stopped and called Sam and Doc. They stared at what looked like scuff marks on the compacted soil.

"Why would she do that?" Lenora asked, not looking up.

"Do what?" Doc said.

"She side-tracked around this hut a few times." Lenora pointed to the slight drag near the side of the hoof prints. "Those marks tell me the horse was walking sideways."

"Why?" Doc asked

"Inspecting it," Sam said, watching the Jeep approach.

Lenora rested her hand on Sam's tall shoulder. "Olivia's definitely up to something, maybe with Uno."

"Might be Hector," Sam said.

Lenora nodded. "She was jumpy back at the stable."

The tan, roofless Jeep stopped on the gravel road near the round huts. "Can I help you?" shouted the smallish driver.

They all walked toward him. Lenora waved, shouting, "Why yes."

"A cab's waiting for you back at the stalls," the driver yelled.

Lenora climbed into the front seat, propping her sore foot on the beat up dash. "How about a ride?"

Driving away, Sam asked about the cluster of huts. Without a warning, their escort slowed the Jeep, turning it off the road and drove up a small hill. Parking the jeep, he pointed at the Adobe buildings. "There're abandoned. The state tested drying animal waste for heating fuel."

"What happened?" Doc asked.

233

"They stopped. Said it cost too much," the driver hesitated, then went on. "That was before the war. When they started keeping the Japs here, they used 'em as prisons for Jap spies. You can see where their gardens use to be."

"Come again?" Doc said.

"The families lived in the horse stalls," the driver said. "But the spies were kept in those huts."

"How about now? What are they used for?" Sam asked.

"Nothing," the driver answered. "During the racing season we keep horse dung there."

Lenora took a big deep breath. "I've seen enough."

The driver nodded and pulled away.

They parked next to a waiting Yellow Cab. A hand poked through the partially open window, waving a folded paper. "The lady who works here told me to give you this."

Doc took the note while he gave a questioned look to Sam and Lenora. "It's from Jake. Says we're done and he is taking over. We're to go home. How's that? Not even a thank you."

"What about Hector?" Lenora asked. "Should I hire Jake to find him since you two are deserting him?"

Chapter Fifty-Three

The wrecked red and white Ford wagon no longer sat under the fallen Eucalyptus when Olivia arrived at Uno's home. Dry ash drifted in the air, dusting her shoulders. Now visible, raging fires burned along the ridge of mountains north of Pomona. Along a smaller ridge, to the south, a new fire flashed to life. She watched the flames jump distant treetops, crashing into several houses atop the heavily wooded hills overlooking Uno's home. She wondered how long it would be before the raging fire turned toward the fairgrounds.

She flinched when someone tapped her back.

"This is a perfect time. No one's going to notice anything. They're all watching the fires," Jake said.

She looked at him. "It's getting bad."

"Ready?"

"He's not gonna be hurt?"

"Not if he tells us."

"He'll go to the police eventually."

"Can't." Jake smiled, looking up to her. "Uno's already breaking the law. That's the beauty of this."

"Everything's ready at the fair grounds," Olivia said.

Jake held up a black hood. "Let's go. Give me a head start."

Uno worked near the barn, offloading a truckload of peat moss. As Olivia approached, she forced a smile and shouted, "Need some help, farmer?"

Uno turned, with the pitchfork in his hands, smiling.

Jake moved quietly between the trees and barn, any noise would be covered by the howling wind. The moment Uno turned, Jake ran the short distance from where he hid, attacking Uno with a short Billy club, knocking him to the ground with a hard blow to the back of his knees.

Despite the shock and pain, Uno attempted to stand.

With a quick motion, Jake pulled a small .38 from a belt holster, jamming the end of its barrel into the side of Uno's neck as he knelt. Giving Uno a hard shove, Jake forced his captive to fall to his face, bloodying his nose.

"You're my size now," Jake yelled into his ear, driving a knee between his shoulder blades. With his left hand, he pushed the hood at Uno. "Put this on. You're going home."

Olivia stood nearby while Jake forced him to pull the black hood over his head. When done, Jake slapped handcuffs on Uno's wrists.

"Get up!" Jake shouted.

Uno stumbled, falling to the ground. Lying there, he twisted his head to look in Olivia's direction. "You betrayed me, Judas. How much is your soul worth?"

She stepped back, knowing Uno would not ever divulge the secrets he kept. They would die with him.

Jake helped him to his feet and shoved him toward the rear bed of the enclosed truck, forcing him inside with the peat moss. He looked up at a masked Uno. "Save yourself some grief, where's the gold?"

Uno answered with a quick shake of his head.

Jake jumped and swung his nightstick, striking Uno's calf, sending him to the floor of the truck. "Last chance, where is it?"

No answer.

After slamming the rear doors shut, Jake slid the bolt through the latch. Immediately, Uno's muffled shouts began.

Jake pointed to the truck's cab, wanting Olivia to drive. "I'll follow. Meet you at the place."

Fearing being stopped for a traffic violation, Olivia drove the short distance cautiously. After arriving at the remote and seldom used entrance of the fairgrounds she hopped out, unlocked the steel pipe gate and swung it aside. She spotted Jake's car, waiting for her at the curb.

Inside the fairgrounds, she followed the rutted lane past several abandoned sheds and a bone yard of scrapped tractors and equipment. The remains of an old starting gate, stripped of its tires, rested at the far end. In the distant background the massive roof, which arched over the grandstands appeared in the hazy moonlight.

She stopped next to the round Adobe brick structure. Jake arrived and rushed to open the truck while she unlocked the hut's steel door. Everything was in place.

Still hooded and handcuffed, Uno continued to shout and kick at the sides of the truck as he was pulled from it. Peat Moss clung to his skin and clothes as he was led to the round hut. He shouted threats and cursed while Jake pulled him through the short doorway.

Uno stood rigid, as if at attention, inside the dark room.

Jake stuck the nightstick into his ribs. "There's a cot behind you. Sit down."

Uno remained standing, exaggerating his stance, thrusting his cuffed arms further back, sticking out his bare chest. Jake raised the Billy club, aiming it at his knee. Olivia moved next to Uno and placed both her hands on his arms, guiding him, until the backs of his legs touched the edge of the cot. He eased down, dropping into the canvas, remaining silent, except for his labored breathing, which echoed within the confined space.

"You'll find what you need," Jake said. "You'll feel at home."

"You're crazy!" Uno shouted.

"Tell me what I want to know."

"There's no gold, it's gone."

"Rice and tea is on the table," Jake said, kicking the leg of the cot. "I'll leave the key to the cuffs here. When you find it, unlock your hands"

"The army took it. I have some coins in a cigar box, take it."

"Use the bucket. Keep it clean, you'll be here a long time." Jake led Olivia out the door.

"Feed my worms!" Uno shouted.

Before Jake locked the heavy steel door, he dropped the handcuff key, then kicked it across the concrete and straw covered floor.

Chapter Fifty-Four

Sam, Doc and Lenora stepped from the cab and stood before Uno's gray rock house. In the dingy light, its twin, stepped gables loomed over them, daring them to trespass. Not far behind it, the foothills and wash were gray with smoke. Hesitantly, they walked up a narrow driveway, past several leafless trees to the back yard to make a surprise visit.

An austere silence covered the house and barn. Doors and windows open, everything appeared deserted. A pitchfork lay on the ground next to a bin of peat moss. Lenora marched into the barn, repeatedly shouting Hector's name, pausing frequently, expecting an answer. After walking through the barn she hurried to the house's back door. Not bothering to knock, she pulled open the screen door and entered, shouting his name louder. Doc followed.

Sam's eye caught something near the large bin of moss. Uno's shirt, the one he had worn yesterday, hung flapping in the wind on an unpainted fence post. Lifting it off the nail, he noticed an unopened pack of Lucky Strikes in the breast pocket. A few feet away, the pitchfork lay. Picking it up, Sam shook off loose peat moss, then holding it in front of him like a bayonet, stalked into the dark barn.

Inside, he cautiously walked between the same rows of worm boxes as he had the other day. This time Uno didn't stand watch. Everything appeared the same as the previous night, except, at the far end, there was an empty spot, next to a set of sagging double doors. A horizontal two by four lay inside a couple of metal slots, bracing the doors shut. After dragging both doors open, the sparse light was enough to show him what remained of the missing box, an outline of four heavy legs that had pushed several inches into the soft ground.

Sam's footsteps nearly disturbed narrow wheel marks that surrounded the vacant space. Standing where the cumbersome worm box had once been, he questioned why it had been moved and to where. Sam shook his head, stepping out the double doors to escape the pungent smell. Next to the doors, he spotted the heavy-duty hoist pushed against the barns outside wall. It was the same type he had used to pull the engine block from his truck. It would easily lift the worm box.

Sam leaned back, propping his boot heel against the barn's cinder block wall. He stared at the tire trail in the dirt road that led to a dry wash of tumbleweed, granite boulders and long dead, sun-bleached tree stumps.

Resting against the building, Sam thought of the past week. He suspected Uno and Olivia were, somehow, a part of what had happened to Hector. The same hunch told him they moved the box, but not why? There was more. What drew them together? They were part of the reason he and Doc were in Los Angeles, and why Doc's home had been burned? Jake's sudden and unexpected arrival from Pennsylvania led him to think Snookey and Vince were no longer part of his hunt. The gold Jake looked for was here, close by, Sam sensed it. Hector had become a casualty, as had so many others, including him and Doc. He was ready to add Uno's name to the long list.

Hearing Lenora shout for him, Sam stepped from behind the barn. She and Doc stood facing one another on the back porch when he arrived.

Lenora turned to look at Sam her cheeks were flush red. "Adam Semans was here."

"At least his business card," Doc said. His eyes widened under his white lashes.

"Semans from home?" asked Sam.

"The same." Doc held up a business card. "This was on the kitchen table."

"It couldn't be a coincidence," Lenora said. "Semans wrote a note, offering Uno a business deal."

"I got a strange feeling inside the barn," Sam said.

240

"About Hector?" Lenora asked.

Sam shook his head. "Uno, there's something going on. I need to look around."

"We better find answers in a hurry," Lenora said, glancing to the burning foothills.

"How do we talk to Semans?" asked Doc.

"He's got to be close by," Lenora said, stepping inside the house. "I'll make a call to the phone number on the card."

Minutes later she returned smiling. "Hotel Mayfair, it's here in town."

"Let's have a talk with him," said Doc. "Our cab's still here."

"I'll stay and look around," Sam said.

Doc swallowed hard. "Be careful."

Lenora waved through the back window, as the cab pulled away from the house.

Sam felt the eerie silence as he stood surrounded by the towering Eucalyptus trees which walled Uno's property. Uneasy, he rushed toward the barn, feeling the smoke from the fire penetrate his lungs, tightening in his chest.

Walking along a line of trees, he came to an abrupt stop. With both hands shading his eyes, he stared up into the tree in disbelief. For the first time in a long time, he laughed out loud.

In front of him stood a mature, eighty foot Eucalyptus growing through the center of an abandoned windmill. At the base of the steel frame, its twisted and bent legs splayed outward, long ago yanked from the earth, suspended in air. Looking higher, the still intact wood blades and tail vane perched within the tree's boughs. He laughed again, this time at himself, for failing to notice what had been hidden in plain view in Uno's back yard.

After a last look, Sam half-grinned giving the comical tree a nod, then hurried to re-inspect the area where he had

241

found Uno's shirt. The faded, blue work shirt that had been hanging on a post, when he had first arrived, was now twisted and blown into a corner against a work shed. Bending to retrieve it, Sam felt the ache in his back. The pack of cigarettes fell from the breast pocket. He remembered Uno was a chain smoker and wouldn't have left them.

The pitchfork, he had earlier found haphazardly thrown to the ground still concerned him. Doors and windows had been left open, not matching Sam's read of Uno's behavior, neat and orderly. He nearly lost his balance, when a wind gust swirled peat moss and loose debris into his face, stinging him. Not bothered, his attention went to the sky immediately overhead. It had begun as a low, grinding rumble to the east and rose to a crescendo passing over him.

Low flying B-17's dropped water and fire retardant, like bombs, over the inferno that continued to consume heavy forest, brush and grassland. Flakes of black ash mixed with hot glowing embers dusted nearby dry fields, igniting small fires. Sam ran to tramp one out near the moss. After it had been smothered, he took a closer look at where he'd first found the pitchfork.

He slapped the side of his leg and threw his head back, looking into the hazy sky. There was more he had missed. The ground markings were nothing more than slight scuffs on hard, compacted soil. Struggling against the wind, Sam stood over the faint pattern, attempting to imagine what, if anything had occurred. The faint, rough image of snow angels came to mind. Unlike them, what he looked at was formless, but he was sure there was a struggle that took place. Something large had brushed the soil, leaving subtle traces. Squatting closer, he saw dark brown splatter and quickly got to his feet, knowing it was blood.

242

Close by, additional footprints surrounded the struggle. One set stood out, prints shaped like long, pointed triangles they'd found near the remote buildings at the fairgrounds.

For a moment, the relentless wind became still and silent. Sam held his breath, his eyes fixed on the distant flames that no longer leapt wildly, appearing briefly tamed. He felt himself relax after enduring several days of the nerve-racking wind.

His peace didn't last long.

The new shifting wind hit like the driven head of a sledgehammer. Invisible blows came with no warning battering him. Flames shifted, burning to the south, consuming brush and timber, like an enraged dragon, swooping towards the valley, searching for prey.

Warm blasts of fire-heated air hit Sam as he stared at the growing inferno, which raced down the long slopes of the foothills. He faced a dilemma, wanting to search the nearby wash or to travel back to the fairgrounds and inspect the Adobe huts, hoping to find Hector. Both stood in the path of the fast moving firestorm. He'd have to choose.

Nothing was certain, only the need to act quickly. He ran to the back porch of Uno's house where his transportation waited.

Chapter Fifty-Five

Uno sat in his dungeon, shirtless, rubbing his bruised calf. Small dots of light entered from narrow openings in the brick wall, high, out of his reach. Open handcuffs lay near his feet. Bending for them brought sharp pain to his ribs, reminding him of the clubbing from Jake. For the first time, fear sneaked into his mind as an unwelcome guest and refused to leave.

In a rage, he stood and screamed, throwing the cuffs into the darkness, they clanked off something metal and hollow, knocking it to the concrete floor. It rolled on the ground for a second or two, gradually rocking to a stop. Curious, despite the ache in his beaten calves, Uno shuffled across the room. His foot nudged something, moving it slightly. Reaching down, his fingertips felt the cold, round coils of a hot plate. He patted his pants pocket, finding the Zippo lighter he had forgotten. He flicked it open sending up a small, weak flame.

Next to the hot plate, lay what he had knocked to the floor. Immediately recognizing it, he slumped to his knees to examine it, recalling how his mother tied it to her waist the day she was taken away. Her soft voice had trembled, telling the soldiers her family were American citizens. They answered her, shouting, dirty Jap as she walked, terrified, to the Jeep. Feeling the coolness of the metal in his hands and against his face, he placed the copper teapot on the hot plate.

"Where am I?" he screamed.

Outside, a murder of crows cawed, returning his plea.

Uno wrapped his arms across his bare chest, suddenly feeling the damp chill, wanting a cigarette.

There was something else oddly familiar about the confined space and sickly odor. He pressed his back against the grimy brick wall, straining, gathering his vision, letting his eyes dilate, forcing them to see his shadowy prison. A single stool was pushed under a table near where he had found his mothers cherished teakettle. Walking across the room, he grabbed a wool blanket that had covered a large chair. It was as if it had materialized from his nightmare. The heavy, straight back, wood chair with rotting leather straps had been used to torture Japanese-American detainees suspected of spying.

Jimmy Koba, his father, died in it.

The weight of Uno's memories overcame him, like the crushing collapse of a mineshaft. Despite the heavy blanket wrapped over his shoulders, the menacing chair forced him to shudder uncontrollably.

The clink of a latch startled him.

The sudden burst of light forced him to flinch and shield his eyes with his forearm. The hut's door swung open. Something was tossed to the floor and the door slammed shut.

"Army rations and water," a voice shouted from outside.

Clutching his blanket, Uno walked to the burlap sack near the door.

"What do you want?" He shouted.

"Eat and stay healthy. I want you to live a long time."

Uno leaned his hands against the steel door, peeking through a narrow gap between the doorframe and brick. He looked at the top of Jake's head. "My friends will find me. Then I'll find you."

"Tell me where it's hid."

Silence.

Jake kicked the door and walked away, toward a small grove of orange trees. Uno watched the miniature private eye. Something outside looked familiar.

He remained motionless, finally understanding. His hand clutched the burlap sack at his side until his knuckles turned white. With his free hand, he beat the door until blood ran between his fingers.

245

He knew his prison.

The horrifying memory returned. Uno heard his childhood cries fade and then become distant screams of pain coming from the hut he watched while tilling soil in the strawberry field. Living in the Pomona fairgrounds prison camp, it had taken him several days to discover the isolated location of his father who had been accused of spying and plotting a Japanese invasion of California. Toiling in a newly planted garden allowed him to observe the remote hut that held him.

By chance, he discovered the location. A military guard had sent him to pick oranges from a nearby grove. This soldier stood sentry at the hut he suspected held his father. On arriving, with the fruit, the hut's door banged open as two soldiers stepped out, giving him a glimpse of his father, sitting like a creature in a cave, strapped to a chair.

Beginning that day, he kept a daily vigil at the hut, each time delivering freshly picked oranges to the guard. On one of those visits, he witnessed his father's tortured body, still wearing his army uniform and ribbons, carried from the squat hut by two unknown MP's and thrown into the back of a canvas-covered truck. The guard, he knew, carefully laid a green blanket over the body. On that day, he learned the guard had been giving his father the oranges. The previous night, Uno watched several MP's enter the round cell, and afterwards, he heard his father's thick-voiced scream for the last time. The official report stated he had killed himself, biting off his own tongue.

Uno felt blood run down his knuckles and fingers, when he picked up the stool to smash it against the high backed chair. Before he did, he paused, listening to the animal-like winds wailing outside. A bead of sweat ran down his face, thinking of the previous night. The howling wind covered his approach, when he had snuck behind the barn's intruder. They both had come close to a sudden death. The gold bricks remained secure. A slight click of the trigger would be the thief's sole warning, the land mine, hidden under them would detonate, blasting chards of gold into their flesh. The mines location was his secret. Diffusing was not possible.

Uno saw the daylight fading through narrow openings near the hut's roof. Wanting to see the orchard again, he kicked aside the sack of army rations and looked through the tiny gap above the door. After returning home from internment, he secretly began entering the fairgrounds, faithfully caring for the abandoned trees.

The evening sun was at the top of the grove of trees when Uno looked out. The sky darkened to a hazy, orange tinge, filled with smoke and a heavy smell of soot. For a time, he stood at the door, both hands rested against the steel frame, squinting into the crevice. Outside a hawk soared, free in the sky, hunting fleeing prey. Echoes of coyotes wailing in the surrounding hillsides added to his desolation. His thought of Adam Semans and yesterday's offer. Could he be responsible?

Ramming his hands into the door several times was all that he could do. Some dust fell from above the steel doorframe. After examining the mortar between the large heavy bricks, Uno grabbed the copper teakettle and started to scrape at the softer joints between the bricks using the long spout. Its curved tip fit perfectly between the bricks, grinding out material, giving him hope of an escape.

Chapter Fifty-Six

Sam rolled up the cuff of his overhauls, and rode from Uno's property on a red and white Shelby bicycle. Taking a last glance back at the fast moving fire, he saw it moving directly towards the house and barn.

As he passed the Eucalyptus tree, which had grown, inside the windmill, he realized, he again missed what had been hidden in plain sight. He turned the bike around, peddling as quickly as possible back to the barn. Inside, he switched on the overhead lights, and searched the dirt-filled boxes. With one hand propping open the lid, he used the other to rake deep into the moist soil, feeling for Uno's hidden gold. While he dug, his mind remained on the blaze. After hearing a helicopter circling overhead, he stopped to look outside. The oncoming fire had reached the nearby wash and moved toward Uno's house. Sam looked back into the barn, and reluctantly abandoned his hunt.

* * * *

Sam peddled the bike west on Mission Avenue at a slow and steady pace, his mind on the gold bars and not the rush hour traffic. Several cars swerved at the last minute, avoiding a head on collision on the narrow street.

After several miles, exhaustion forced him to stop for rest and directions at one of the few stores that remained open. Before Sam entered the butcher shop, a stout Polish man wearing a blood stained, white apron and carrying a cleaver, stepped from the door. He shook his baldhead, looking past Sam to the north. He spoke, but not to Sam. "Fires headed to the horse track." He spit a brown wad of chewing tobacco on the sidewalk, then looked at Sam. "You come for meat?"

Shaking his head, Sam pointed to the track and asked, "What's the best way to get there?"

"In a fire truck," he said, looking at the bike Sam held at his side.

Sam grinned, backing away from the butcher. He peddled away not bothering to wave. Behind him, he heard the butcher shout. "Turn right on White Avenue. Ray's Liquor is on the corner."

Heavy smoke hung, trapped in the valley. Visibility became poor as Sam headed west into a setting, dull orange sun. Each crank of the petals brought numbing pain to his thighs and calves. Street signs pointed south towards "Downtown Pomona." Sam thought of Doc and Lenora who had gone into town to locate Captain Semans. He considered ditching his plan and giving up. The fires were spreading into the area quickly. After a few deep breaths, he forced himself to go on. The smell of fire grew stronger. He had to reach the remote hut.

The sprawling Los Angeles County Fairgrounds sat north of downtown, close to the foothills, near the growing inferno. The street he rode was flat, running parallel to the line of mountains, which bordered Pomona. Sam paced himself, peddling occasionally and coasting when he could to conserve his dwindling energy. Ahead, he spotted the large sign on the roof of a two-story building, Ray's Liquor. Breathing heavily he slowed, asking himself if he should continue.

He shook his head, still not convinced, but turned on White Avenue into a heavy north wind carrying smoke and ash.

He had entered a combat zone. The raging blaze was at the doorstep of Pomona. Echoes of wailing sirens and blaring horns bounced off the nearby mountains, magnifying the intensity. The ride was torturous. Muscles in his legs, arms, and shoulders ached as though they had been ripped and torn by a lashing. With each strained breath, his lungs grew raw, inhaling heavy smoke-filled air.

Sam arrived at the racetrack grandstands, awestruck by the scene. Furniture, luggage and pillowcases stuffed with clothes covered manicured lawns of hillside homes that surrounded the fairgrounds. Frightened husbands and wives took only possessions they could carry or load into their cars. Many stood in the congested narrow streets, frozen, defeated, their arms hung at their sides, staring into the blazing foothills where bulldozers cleared brush from the fire's path.

A few stalwart homeowners stationed themselves, armed with water hoses, on roofs, to fight off the inferno. Several had dug trenches, and planned to remain, guarding their homes against eventual looters.

Police cars crawled through jammed neighborhood streets, their roof speakers blasted warnings of arrest to those who stayed. White helmeted volunteers wearing Civil Defense arm bands, blocked streets, turning away carloads of Lookey-loos who descended on the area.

Cars sped across lawns and sidewalks, fleeing the area. Sam abandoned the bike and traveled through the chaos on foot. The racetrack's familiar overhanging grandstand became his reference point for locating the cluster of huts he searched for. Daylight faded rapidly with the increasing smoke and soot hanging in the air. Breathing became more difficult the closer he moved into the foothills. He reached into his back pocket and pulled out a red bandanna. After folding it into a triangle, he tied it over his nose and mouth.

Approaching Arrow Highway, Sam saw the weaving pickup truck jump the sidewalk's curb, and slam into the rear of a parked city bus. Wood chicken pens flew from the truck's bed, crashing open, sending dozens of frightened poultry into the busy street. The truck's driver and several bystanders chased the fanatical birds. While they did, Sam turned the corner to Arrow Highway, slipping past a police barricade, and began to look for the rear entrance gate to the fairgrounds.

Constant streams of emergency vehicles and horse trailers sped past. Sam held his hand to the side of his face, feeling the warmth of the fire. In the hillside, he heard and saw the rage of red flames leaping skyward, driven by powerful Santa Ana winds roaring toward him. Dry timber cracked and sizzled, exploding in the inferno.

The air attack on the firestorm stopped with nightfall. Courageous ground fire fighters, using picks and shovels, continued the hopeless battle.

Sam had no idea who he'd find in the hut, Uno or Hector, maybe an empty building. Despite his growing doubt, he pressed on.

Each step was a struggle, not sure if he could go on. Sam walked into the street, looking for help, waving unsuccessfully to a speeding police car. A sedan, with a mattress tied to its roof swerved and narrowly missed him. Returning to the sidewalk, he saw the lights of hillside homes flash out. The fire had reached the power lines, which ran along the base of the foothills.

In the fading daylight, Sam propped his hand against the fairground's rusty chain link fence. It looked several miles long, disappearing into a grayish veil.

After a second failed attempt to flag down a police car, he realized there would be no help. Moving along the fence another hundred yards, he came to a section heavily overgrown with ivy.

He stumbled from exhaustion, nearly missing what he looked for, the steel gate was set back from the street, closed and locked over a cattle guard. The faint, familiar outline of an abandoned starting stall sat, not far, inside the opening. It was no time to celebrate, but he felt like it. He found the gate he looked for and quickly ducked under the single bar that blocked the entrance.

Close by, he recognized the rickety fence he had followed the previous day with Lenora and Doc. Most of its rails had been knocked from their posts and lay scattered

251

like a game of pick-up-sticks. They became his escort, leading him to the round huts.

Darkness came fast. Flames in the hillside glowed bright, seeming to float in air, defined against the blackness of the mountains, taking shapes of jagged spikes flung from earth, others leapt like solar flairs. Sam walked close to what remained of the rotted wood fence, unsure of his footing; he took short strides and stopped frequently, attempting to recall the location of the huts.

Flames, as if hurled by a demon, swept at Sam. Fires appeared quickly, ignited by blowing embers of wood and bark, burned heavy brush along the fence and dry, grassy field. He needed to find the shelter of the Adobe huts to survive the racing fire that surrounded him.

A sudden slash of white light cut through the dingy, gray smoke and firelight. It lasted a few seconds, like a tiny star, just long enough for Sam to get a partial fix on its location. It led him to the group of huts. However, he was unsure of the lights origin. As the flames got close, he hurried to the hut where he had previously found the locked door and hoof prints. Approaching it, he shouted over the roar of the fire, "Anybody here?"

At first, he only heard deep and hollow sounds of metal scraping.

Moving closer to the locked door, conserving the little energy he had left, Sam bent close to it and knocked.

"I'm in here," came from the hut.

Chapter Fifty-Seven

Jake leaned against the open door of Olivia's fairgrounds apartment watching the blaze shift downward from the foothills. "Before I give up, I have to do this."

She looked up from packing her suitcase, angry that he stood watch over her. "So far you're batting zero. It can't get worse."

"The gold's there. It's been there the whole time."

"In the worm boxes?"

"At least in one of 'em."

Olivia paused to look at Jake. "I worked there…Why didn't I find it?"

"You weren't expecting to. Hell, Uno fooled the army with gold-painted lead bricks."

"It's over now," Olivia said, pressing her clothes flat inside her suitcase.

"Before we leave, I got to know."

"Do what you want. This 'we', is getting out."

"You're making a mistake."

"The mistake I made was letting you talk me into this."

Jake left the doorway and walked next to her bed. He pushed the suitcase closed with the handle of the sledgehammer he carried. "I don't recall you resisting. I still have those receipts you signed."

Her somber brown eyes remained on the hammer. "I need the money. Whatever you're thinking, better be fast."

"Ten minutes, that's all." Jake looked at the large hammer. "This is all we need. It's so obvious, don't know how I missed it."

Olivia swung her suitcase off the bed, pushing past Jake. "I wanna be in Laguna Beach before this place gets scorched."

Jake nodded.

The horse trailer was hitched to her black Hudson, and waited in the empty lot near the vacant stalls. The buckskin was loaded, his black tail hung over the rear gate, swishing as he stomped and snorted. Olivia shoved the beat up suitcase next to her saddle and re-arranged her few belongings in the cars large trunk.

Jake slid in beside Olivia. "This time tomorrow, we're gonna be rich."

"Better be," she said. "I'm not gonna have anything to come home to."

* * * *

"This place gives me the willies," Olivia said pulling into Uno's driveway. Waves of blowing smoke crossed the wide expanse of field, nearly choking them. Jake leaned to one side, pulling out two white handkerchiefs and folded them into triangles.

"Put this on," he said.

Olivia tied it over her mouth and nose after setting the parking brake. Jake hurried to the barn, dragging the steel sledge.

Small fires burned in the surrounding grass fields. In the hillside above them the fire raged, splitting off, running into the deep wash near Uno's home. Cracking sounds, like Fourth of July firecrackers, snapped from hungry flames, battled for dry parched fuel, turned south and took aim at Pomona.

With the sledge hoisted over his head, he looked to Olivia. "Should 'a thought of this sooner." He swung it like a baseball bat into the heavy leg of the worm box.

Olivia leaned one arm against a post. "This is your plan! Ever hear of a metal detector?" Throwing her arms in the air, she walked out.

Jake continued his assault on the box. After several hit and miss blows the thick leg collapsed. Its corner crashed to the floor, splitting open. Moist dirt and worms spilled out covering Jake's feet. Sweating and breathing heavy, he shouted to Olivia. "The gold bricks are gonna be in one of these. You know I'm right."

254

Olivia stood in the door. "You're sure about that?"

"Gotta be. Where else?"

Olivia grabbed the sledge. "Take a rest Babe Ruth."

She busted a box open, then another, each time stopping to sift through dirt and crawling worms. Finding nothing, she leaned the sledge and herself against an unopened box. "Too slow." Olivia pointed to the pitchfork leaning against the wall. "Pull the lids and poke it into the dirt."

For the next twenty minutes, she smashed boxes while Jake pushed away the heavy lids and poked the long tines of the pitchfork into the dirt. Only a few boxes remained. Olivia looked them over for a moment, finally pointing the sledge toward a vacant spot close to the rear sagging double doors.

"One's missing," Jake said.

"Shit, what if he moved it?" Olivia said.

"Where?" Jake asked. "Where do you hide a couple hundred thousand dollars of gold?"

"Jake...I don't know. You have all the answers." Olivia slammed the sledgehammer into the leg of the box she stood next to. The leg buckled and collapsed, splitting open with a sharp crack. Soggy, black soil spilled to the ground. Jake rammed the pitchfork into the dirt. It traveled a few inches and stopped. After jabbing it again, he dropped the tool. "There's something here."

Olivia fell to her knees, still keeping her gaze on Jake. With her fingers moving slowly at first, she scraped away the top layer of dirt and worms. The bars of gold sat three high, wedged at the bottom of the wood box.

A rush of guilt stirred in Jake. He betrayed his clients and himself, he'd free fallen to the level of Snookey. Next to him Olivia leaped into the air screaming, her arms wrapped around his neck, hugging him.

"Uno fooled people before," Jake said. "We need to be sure."

Kneeling again, they ran their fingers and palms over the buried treasure.

Olivia got to her feet and grabbed the sledge, knocking out the three other legs, leaving the wood box flat on the floor. Once the sides were pulled free, more dirt fell away, exposing additional gold bricks. Using the pitchfork, Jake cleared the remaining spongy dirt. Taking one of the gold bars, he pulled out a pocketknife and scrapped deep along its side.

Olivia put her hand on his arm. "What are you doing?"

"I traveled across the country and watched two burial vaults get dug up and a man get shot over the counterfeit gold inside."

"Well...is it?" Olivia asked.

Jake repeated the cutting on several more and nodded. "It's real."

"Fire's getting close, let's get out of here," Olivia said.

Jake pressed his palm against the side of his sport coat.

Olivia moved closer to the pitchfork. In a quick move, she grabbed it and leveled the sharp tines close to Jake's neck. A few pressed into the collar of his shirt.

"Take the gun out of your pocket," she shouted, continuing to hold the pitchfork at his throat.

Jake froze. For a moment, he remained quiet, taking a deep breath. "Jumpy, are we?" A smile broke out on his heavy face.

"Give me the gun. Then I won't be."

Exposing his belt holster, he pulled the semi-automatic out, ejecting the round in the chamber and pulled the clip, handing them both to her. "Neither one of us should get greedy, there's plenty for both of us."

"Just making sure it stays that way."

"Where do we put it?" Jake asked while he stepped outside to check on the fire.

"I'll put the horse in the field. We'll use the horse trailer, there's room."

"Good. Bring the trailer to the door. We'll load it."

While Olivia checked on her nervous horse, Jake found a broom and swept off the neatly stacked pile of gold bars. He retrieved a wheelbarrow from an outside shed. Hearing the car, he stood at the double doors directing Olivia as she backed the empty horse trailer into the barn. Jake signaled her to stop, leaving the trailer a few feet inside the barn. They'd wheelbarrow the remaining twenty feet.

As Jake lowered the trailer's ramp, Olivia rushed back to the stack of gold bricks and began pulling them one by one from the pile, loading the wheelbarrow. Olivia heard the soft click of the detonator. The gold bar she held in her hand no longer rested on top of the mine's trigger.

It detonated.

The blast rose through the gold bricks, instantly disintegrating the soft gold, creating thousands of gold nuggets and splinters, launching them like a shotgun blast. The concussion leveled two walls of the cinder block building.

At the same moment the firestorm roared down the wash, like a rampaging river. Curling flames enveloped the barn and small sheds near Uno's house. Flames were drawn into the air vents of the houses eaves, spreading the blaze into the attic, igniting the house.

Chapter Fifty-Eight

Flames slashed at Sam, standing in front of the Adobe hut's steel door. He was trapped, unable to reach the safety of other huts. The hairs on his arms were singed, and for the first time he was scared. Red-hot embers, blowing ahead of the firestorm, ignited dry grass near him, bursting the field into flames.

Trying to stay clam, Sam pressed the side of his face against the door, shouting over the wind. "Who are you?"

The response came at once. "Uno, I'm Uno. I can see you."

"You okay?"

"Get me out of here."

"Hector with you?"

"Just me. Get me out." The door rattled against Uno's pounding.

"It's locked. You're safe in there. I'm trapped. The fires everywhere, I need in."

Neither spoke, then Uno shouted, "I've been scraping out mortar."

Sam pushed closer to the door, as fires snapped at his back. "What can I do?"

"Pull on the top hinge. I'm gonna hit the wall."

Sam gripped the bulky hinge and metal frame of the door. "I'm pulling. Hit it," Sam shouted.

The hut was his only hope against the approaching wall of fire. His exposed arms reddened and blistered from the heat waves that blasted him.

The flame heated Sam's back while he strained, gripping the door and hinge. "It's moving, keep hitting," he shouted.

Sam's hold slipped, he fell backward to the ground. Uno failed to stop, continuing to bang at the stubborn brick. The bulky, fourteen by ten inch block of Adobe slid a tiny bit from its slot. "Couple more good shots," Sam yelled, pulling himself to his feet.

The wall shuddered and the brick came loose, it hung, swinging, still attached to the hinge, leaving a hole in the wall.

The door remained shut.

"Pull on the bottom one," Uno shouted.

Sam pressed both feet against the wall and held the large, rusty hinge with his fingers. The wall vibrated, while Uno pounded against the heavy block. Particles of brick and mortar flew into Sam's face, at the same time glowing, hot cinders blew against his un-protected back. He refused to let go and reach back to slap out the smoldering flames, which seared small holes through his cotton shirt.

"It's coming loose, couple more hits," Uno shouted.

Sam's fingers were raw from the corroded, sharp corners of the hinge. The brick and hinge grudgingly slid toward him and fell from the opening.

Hollow eyes appeared in the rectangular slot to meet Sam.

"Help me with the door," came from inside.

Sam jumped to his feet, grabbing the edge of the steel door, as it broke free. They swung it open, using the lock and hasp as a hinge.

"Get in!" Uno yelled.

Sam threw himself inside, crashing into Uno as he pulled the door shut.

"Get to the middle," Sam said.

Both sat quietly on the ground. Finally, Uno spoke, his voice a whisper. "Welcome to the gateway to hell."

With the little strength Sam had left, he forced a slight laugh and wrapped his throbbing arms around his legs. After a short period of silence, Sam tapped the side of Uno's leg. "We'll be okay. Adobe brick can handle this."

"What's it like out there?" Uno asked.

"Hysteria, people are packing and getting out."

259

Uno's voice was somber. "The day before the Army came to take us, my mother insisted we polish the floors and wash the windows."

"Nothing wrong with being clean," Sam said.

"By the time we finished the whole house was clean inside and out."

"Bet it looked good."

"House was nearly empty. We gave away most of our furniture."

"Had to be tough."

"Yeah."

Flames roared, crashing against the aged Adobe structure, draping it in fire. Smoke pushed down from vents near the steel roof, filling the round room. Sam pulled Uno close to the floor, finding breathable air.

"You came looking for Hector," Uno said.

"Both of you," Sam said.

"I knew you were looking for him when you came back to the house."

They remained quiet. The only sound was the burning and cracking of the fire that surrounded them.

"Getting hot in here," Sam said, fanning himself.

"It was self-defense."

"What was?"

"When I hit him." Uno took a deep breath. "I did it in self-defense . . . how the shovel got in my hand, I don't know."

"You're talking about Hector?"

"I didn't know his name. He broke in my barn."

"What happened?"

"I panicked," Uno said. "When he fell, his head hit the corner of the box."

"He's dead?" Sam asked.

Uno could only nod as he stared at the ground between his feet.

"His body, where is..."

260

Uno cut him off. "I didn't want it found."

"Where is it?"

"Burned up in the fire."

"Why not call the police?"

"The war's over, but they still don't trust us."

In moments, the roaring sound of the fire that had surrounded them diminished. They eased the steel door open a few inches using the wood stool. The fire had passed.

The overgrown, tall, dry grass that overran the area had been consumed by the rampaging inferno.

Uno and Sam staggered from the building that had saved their lives. Dingy light from fires and a muted moon gave visibility. Both went in different directions, stomping through charred, black stubble, which smelled like a filled ashtray.

Sam slowed his pace, finally stopping to look back at Uno. "Thanks for what you did back there."

Uno grunted, waving a hand over his head, not turning to look back. He shuffled to the blackened skeletons of what remained of the orange grove. Stopping beneath a charred limb, he stood nearly motionless, his hands deep in his pockets.

Far off sirens and a blur of flashing, red and blue lights sped seemingly at random around them on the city streets.

"Who put you in there?" Sam asked, nodding to the huts.

"Come on...you don't know?" Uno said, turning toward him.

"I wouldn't ask if I did."

"Trees are gone!" Uno fell into a brief silence. He reached up, breaking off a branch and tossed it at nothing. "I trusted her."

Sam stood quietly, at a distance.

Chafing his hands compulsively, Uno fixed his blood shot eyes on the stripped stubble of the burnt orchard. He turned toward Sam. "Something in me always wanted this place to go up in smoke."

Sam nodded, keeping his distance. "The horse stables are gone."

"Nothing but bad memories here. Maybe the dreams will stop."

"Who locked you in there?" Sam asked again.

"The midget private eye."

"Jake?" Sam said, jolting upright.

Uno nodded, not meeting Sam's eyes. "Jake was supposed to find the gold for my family. Instead he wanted it for himself."

"Anybody with him?"

"I trusted her...The Mexican girl, Olivia."

"You tell them where the gold is?"

"I told them I didn't have it."

"But you do?"

"I do," Uno said, letting out a deep breath. He turned back to face the carnage of the fires in the close-by hillsides. "Maybe those people could use it?"

"Let's get out of here." Sam said.

They passed close to the hut as they left. Uno held up the palm of his hand and stepped inside. He reappeared carrying a copper teapot.

"Did the fire reach my home?" Uno asked, looking up at Sam. "There's one more thing I need to do before anyone gets hurt."

Chapter Fifty-Nine

The following morning, Sam and Uno sat in the rear seat of the San Bernardino County Sheriff's cruiser as it swerved past sawhorse barricades, heading to Uno's home. After arriving, Sam was surprised and relieved to find Doc and Lenora standing with several fire fighters. The air still hung heavy with the smell of smoke and cinder.

Uno ran toward the ruins of his house, stopping at its smoke blackened rock walls. Two firemen, their faces streaked in black soot, stood over the smoking rubble, dousing charred wood beams with a spray of water.

"What was in the barn?" An officer, whose face had a crooked twist to it, asked walking toward him.

Staring in bewilderment, Uno forced himself to answer. "I raised worms."

"That a fact?"

"It was a business."

"Anything else?"

"Why?" Uno asked. "What's wrong?"

"There was an explosion."

"From what?"

"We were hoping you'd tell us."

Uno looked at the barn, then at the sheriff in front of him. "Did the fire miss it?" Uno asked.

"The blast probably blew out the fire and kept the barn from burning."

"Anybody gone in there?" Uno asked.

The sheriff sniffed, "When we got here, we chased off twenty or so of your neighbors."

"From where?" Uno asked.

"It looked like some were in the barn." The sheriff waved his arm over the area. "Others were out here in the yard. They looked like chickens, the way they poked around. They were picking up something. I didn't see what."

Uno remained quiet as he paced the area.

"What do you suppose they were doing?" the sheriff asked.

"Don't know," Uno answered, then shrugged.

"Wanna take a look inside? Maybe you can identify them?"

Uno took several steps back, reacting to the sudden question.

The sheriff's lopsided grin twisted even more as he motioned Uno toward the barn. On cue, another grim faced officer stepped forward, handing them rain parkas.

Uno, puzzled by the parka, stepped through a hole left by the blast.

The windows had been blown out. On two sides, cinder block laid scattered from collapsed walls. The interior of the remaining walls and roof were plastered with spongy soil, dripping to the floor in uneven cadence. Jagged, splintered wood poked from overturned boxes. Worms and dirt covered the floor.

Uno's weary, blackened eyes drifted to where he had hidden the gold. "The fire missed my barn?" he asked, forcing his attention back to the sheriff. "Like I said outside, firemen think it suffocated, no air to feed on. The sheriff slapped his hands together over his head. "Just like that, the blast sucked the oxygen out of here, snuffing out the fire."

The sheriff's grin disappeared. He stood face to face with Uno. "The timing had to be perfect, like someone set it off remotely while they watched."

"You think I did this?" Uno asked, running his hands through the soil of a tipped box. "I lost my home and business. Why would I do this?"

"That's not all," the officer said pointing to the far side of the barn.

Uno moved cautiously, climbing over shattered and toppled boxes.

264

"Do you know them?" The sheriff yanked away a wrinkled canvas, revealing a body. Without speaking, he casually moved across the room, unveiling a second body. His eyes held on Uno, probing.

Uno stopped abruptly, seeing Jake's and Olivia's bodies sprawled and twisted in the rubble. Dirt and debris covered parts of their faces and torsos. Jagged bone and muscle hung from where Olivia's arms had once been. A few strands of flesh remained on her once beautiful face. The only things recognizable were her boots.

"She must have been closest to the explosion," the sheriff said, laying the canvas to the side.

Uno turned his back.

The quiet lasted for only a moment. "Do you see anything strange?" the sheriff asked.

Uno shook his head.

"Take a look. It's got us puzzled."

Uno turned, looking at Jake's small frame inside the bent and twisted metal of the trailer. Propped up like a ventriloquist's puppet, his face and clothing peppered with blood.

"Do you own a horse?" the sheriff asked.

"No. Why?"

"How about a horse trailer?"

Uno shook his head.

"You know why a car and horse trailer is in your barn?" the sheriff asked.

"That's Olivia's. She must have been evacuating," Uno answered.

"They live here?"

"No. She worked for me sometimes."

"What were they doing here?"

"Don't know."

"Guess." The sheriff tilted his head at Uno. "She worked for you. Did you ask her to do something?"

265

Uno shrugged his eyes frozen on the jackknifed horse trailer still attached to the car's hitch.

With the palm of his hand, the sheriff nudged Uno's shoulder. "I asked you a question."

"Maybe she forgot something. I don't know for sure." Uno struggled for words. Mud dripped on his arm.

The sheriff moved closer to Jake's body and waved Uno to him. "I don't know what to make of this. At first it looked like a shotgun blast," he said, pulling part of Jake's torn shirt away from his chest.

Uno's knee pressed against Jake's shoulder, bending to examine the wounds. The scent of gunpowder and Old Spice forced Uno to lurch back.

The sheriff opened a Case pocketknife, poking the blade onto a wound on Jake's shoulder. With little effort, he pried out a small jagged piece of metal and held it at arms distance.

"What do you think it is?"

"Don't know."

"Take a guess."

"Piece of wood."

"Gold," the officer said. He tossed it to Uno.

"Gold?" Uno said.

"Yep, I have enough in my teeth to know what it looks like." He raised a lip, exposing a gold tooth.

Uno noticed several more crude slices on Jake's body where gold had been removed. He looked up at the sheriff, not saying anything.

"Must have been the scavengers we ran off," the sheriff said, tilting the bill of his cap. "Both bodies have the same gold fragments. They didn't walk in here with them, did they?" The sheriff paused, taking a deep breath. His crooked smile returned. "That's what your neighbors were doing? Weren't they? They came here after the explosion. They saw what happened and found a gold mine scattered over your yard."

266

The sheriff used his knife to dislodge a large nugget from one of the walls. He held it close to Uno's face. "The bomb squad is gonna tell us what happened here. Why don't you save us some time?"

"Don't say another word," Sam shouted.

Chapter Sixty

Two days later:

The landing gear of the DC 3 locked in place. Lenora lounged in a leather sofa near the bar, her removed prosthetic foot laid next to her.

Sam and Doc looked out the plane's small windows. "Lot of fire damage down there," Doc said.

"Everything's black," Sam said after he lowered his oxygen mask.

"It always comes back," Lenora leaned to take a look. "After the rains this spring you'll see how green it is."

"We're coming back?" Sam asked.

"You bet we will," Lenora said. "That's when Uno's trial is. I got the feeling you two became buddies."

"I wouldn't go that far," Sam said.

"What made you do it?" Lenora asked. "You were nearly killed."

"Guilt," Sam said. "After Jake had us spy on him and what he and Olivia did."

Lenora smiled. "You took a big chance, Sam Simon."

"I wasn't sure who I went after," Sam said. "I hoped it would be Hector." After a pause, he went on. "To tell the truth, if I knew it was Uno, I would not have gone."

Shaking his head, Doc said, "Jake fed us a line and we took the bait. We should not have drug Hector into it."

"We came out here and stuck our noses into Uno's life. He had lived through so much," Sam said.

Doc slid next to Lenora, handing her a drink. "Hector was trying to help us, it should have never happened."

"Uno thought he was a burglar," Sam said. "It was a bad idea."

Lenora slugged down her drink. "The lawyer thinks the worst he'll get is six months for illegal disposal of a body. The land mines another story."

"The gold?" Sam asked.

268

Lenora winked at the both of them. "A friend of mine in the sheriff's department thinks because there is so little of it left and the circumstances, they'll let it go."

Doc toasted his glass of bourbon. "Hell, I think everybody in Pomona got a handful. God knows they needed it."

"Semans might complain," Sam said, returning the toast.

Lenora leaned back, massaging the stump above her missing foot. "I'll shove this up Semans tail end if he makes trouble."

Sam's laugh was quickly aborted by the pain in his back, arms and legs. He jumped to his feet, gritting his teeth.

"Medicines worn off," Doc said. First-degree burns are no worse than sunburn. I'm more concerned with the heat inhalation. You'll be on oxygen for another week."

Sam slid the oxygen mask to his forehead. "We still have Woody's frozen body in your car."

Lenora grinned. "I reported that last week. It's been taken care of."

"The first body we found belonged to Herkey Dixon," Sam said.

"That's how all this started," Doc said.

"Herkey was in the army with Vince, Snookey and Rizzo." Sam said. "Snookey killed him too soon. He was eliminating partners and should have waited until he dug up the vaults. He never suspected Herkey and Semans double-crossing him and moving the gold."

"Herkey was supposed to bury the gold under the Quonset hut at the airport," Doc said. "Instead he buries it in Semans Japanese garden."

"All the while the real gold's buried in a box of worms," Sam said.

"Looks to me, the right people got the gold," Lenora said.

The planes cabin door opened. Lenora smiled to the young co-pilot. He helped her up and assisted her as she hopped to a private suite in the tail of the plane.

She poked her head from the room, smiling. "These long trips are so boring without entertainment."

* * * The End * * *

14485009R00144

Made in the USA
Charleston, SC
14 September 2012